Charlie and Me

STUART MILLARD

Also available by the same author

Frantic Planet: Volume I

Frantic Planet: Volume II

Dirt Baby and Other Small Mercies

The Beach Diaries 2011

The Beach Diaries 2012

Smoke & Mirrors and Steven Seagal: The Burning Pants of Popular Culture

So Excited, So Scared: The Saved by the Bell Retrospective

For more information, visit

www.franticplanet.com

or Twitter @ franticplanet

ISBN: 9781549808128

This is a work of fiction.

1 ALL ROADS

Had you asked how I saw myself spending the new year, I could have given you a list of possibilities. Enduring one of my dad's lectures; getting ready to shiver through another night at the raceway; or feeding myself into the mouth of a hungry gator, singing Hosanna as the teeth closed over my face. Each of these were more likely than where I actually found myself, some twenty-odd days into '71. Earlier that week, when I'd been pushing a mop through the aisles, and directing creaky-fingered elderly shoppers to the jars of gherkins and past-their-date holiday snacks, I never imagined myself on a cross country Greyhound, breathing in that stink of sawdust piled on old vomit. But there I was. I was already farther from home than I'd managed in the previous eighteen years, yet still not halfway to where I was headed.

Even in that weird sleep place where you're vaguely aware of the sounds of the waking world, I was thinking on the craziness of it all, like I'd open my eyes to find myself slumped in an armchair back home, but a judder snapped me awake, thunking my head against the window, where the world outside was still moving past. My new year's resolutions had been to knock out a hundred push-ups every morning and get myself a girl. Come summertime, I'd be kicking sand in Charles Atlas's face, with a slender arm threaded through my own, which would be bulging and veiny. As it was, January 1st saw me pushing out an earnest but feeble seventeen, topped off by a couple of weedy half-pushes that even I couldn't bring myself to count. My shoulders ached so bad the next morning, I figured I'd get back to it in a couple of days. A couple turned into three or four, into a week, into "hell, the year's as good as over anyhow." Figured I'd just eat better; go for runs; give it a proper bash in another 51 weeks.

That was me in a nutshell. Next year. Later. Someday. I wasn't really a live-for-the-moment, see where life takes you kinda guy. Much of a thrill as it was to give the driver my ticket and hear the door close behind me, I knew it was all just a temporary rebellion; a freak-out that'd get brought up at family gatherings by laughing uncles as that week Thomas ran away, and I'd blush, but not too hard, because it was so long ago, and we all do dumb shit when we're young. Soon enough, I'd be feeling foolish, and happy to be back, although definitely grounded. But I didn't feel that way yet, still roleplaying as the kind of wild and interesting guy who acted on the fly, jumping out of planes and kissing strangers. "There he goes. That boy's got some tales, I tell ya..."

If I could nod off again for a few minutes, maybe I'd feel less of a phony when I woke. Open your eyes as someone else; the sort of person who just does stuff like this, just because.

They say he's gonna walk. That's why I'm gonna be there. If he doesn't, it won't make for such a bitchin' story, but it'll be a story all the same. Anyway, that's what they say, but then they say a lot of things about him; call him a lot of names. Killer. Christ. Psychopath. Hippie. Brainwasher. Guru. Murderer. Misunderstood. Someone with so many labels has to at least be interesting. It's something to tell the grandkids for sure, like the way momma talks about seeing Bill Haley. Not that there were any crawlers on the way. You're listening to a guy who lay clinging to the bottom of the drapes, faking a bout of vertigo, to get out of going to senior prom by himself. Tab Hunter I wasn't. Maybe She was on the bus, waiting to be found. *Then* you've got a tale worth telling.

"Pop-Pop, tell us again about how you met Grandma!"

"Well," I'd say, ruffling the scamp's hair, "I was headed to see this naughty rascal by the name of Charles Manson, and across the way, a captivating young beauty caught my eye..." Uh huh. I pulled myself closer to the window, hugging my backpack to my chest. Thin, gangly trees passed like indignant flamingos at a bad safari park, flickering the sun across my face in filmic strips, and with the comforting, rhythmic rocking of wheels on tarmac, I tumbled into nap time.

Sometime later, I lurched awake, with an icicle of drool slavering from my chin. Worst of all, I had an awful feeling I'd made a noise. One time in church, this guy didn't get out of his seat for *Bringing in the Sheaves*, head rolled back, and mouth cranked like he was catching flies. Then, during a quiet reading, surrounded by bowed heads, he spazzed awake in the pew with a rousing cry of "Ahab!" Any gigglers got shushed, and I don't think he ever knew,

3

not for sure. It doesn't leave an after-taste, like a fart, so he probably told himself it was as much a part of the dream as the rolling fields and cats with human fingers. He still shows up every Sunday, to behind-the-back nudges that "Ahab's here..." That lingering fear of doing an Ahab would haunt me to the end of the journey. I guess it didn't really matter what a bunch of strangers thought. That's what I'd tell myself.

"Weather's started to turn." I jolted a little at the first human voice I'd heard in a dozen hours. Maybe it was still part of the dream. "Hey," said a ragged man in the seat across the aisle.

"Oh, hi," I replied, with a chilly smile I hoped would convey my desire to be left alone.

"Smoke?" he asked.

"Oh no, I'm good, thanks."

"No, I mean, do you got a smoke?"

"Oh. No, I don't, sorry."

"Huh." He turned to face front, poking a dirty pinkie in his mouth and nibbling at the nail. I didn't want to stare, but it was hard to look away from such a striking figure. His tatty, dark green jacket was ripped at the elbow, his jeans were faded and frayed, and the thick leather boots on his feet were scuffed like he'd done a lot of walking. He looked to be mid-twenties, but the rough beard and darting eyes had the air of someone who'd lived more than they should have. "Well that's cool," he said, spinning back around to face me, "just another bad habit I should quit anyhow." I nodded, smiling and glancing back out of the window. "So what's your deal?"

"My deal?" I replied

"Yeah. All jittery, ain't more than, what, seventeen? You was curled up there like a toddler."

"Were you watching me sleep?"

"Yeah," he replied, matter of factly. "Oh, nuthin' creepo, just like to be aware of my surroundings, you know?"

"Sure..."

"Something I picked up in the army..."

"Oh," I said, "were you in..."

"Nam?" He said, before nodding like there was nothing more to be said, like any questions I could ask would only bring horrible answers. "Out five months now." I made a noise of affirmation. They say they either come back crazy, or dead, or so crazy they wished they was dead. Couple of neighbors' kids got sent out there, and neither of 'em came back. Not even the one who lived. I tried talking to him once, but it was like waking someone to ask what they wanted for breakfast, not realizing they'd snuck out the window and left you chatting to a stack of pillows. I saw that same look in the fella on the bus, something broken and distant. Feeling bad, I changed the subject.

"You'll probably laugh," I said. He stared at me like he'd forgotten what that word even meant. "My deal. You asked what my deal was..."

"Oh, yeah."

"Yeah, so I'm actually... and I bet this sounds pretty dumb, but I'm headed to California for the verdict."

"The verdict?"

"Manson. Charles Manson and them girls." The stranger slung an arm over the seat in front and shot me a quizzical grin. He wasn't expecting that. "Just figured it'd be interesting, is all."

"That's it? Because he's interesting? There's no..." He flinched in his seat, swishing at a fly that I didn't see before continuing. "There's no other reason? Been travelling a long way? And all because you find a man *interesting*? Ain't doing it to piss off the folks?"

"Well, maybe a little. They're a bit... uptight, my dad especially. He's real big into Jesus and all – not that I don't consider myself a good Christian, it's just..."

"Too much, right?" he replied. "Sometimes it's all just too much."

"Yeah." It *was* too much, a lot of the time. Just because a man follows Christ, he can't be expected to live to those same standards. "That was the thing that pushed me over the edge," I said, "made me go from thinking 'that'd be a gas' to actually throwing stuff in a bag and buying a ticket. When the reporter on the tee-vee said that he'd addressed himself as "Charles Manson aka Jesus Christ," and the top of my dad's head just about whistled like the factory in *The Flintstones*, I knew what I had to do." The stranger looked at me, wide-eyed, mouth curling at the corners. Against my better judgement, I heard myself asking, "So what's your deal?"

"No place to go."

"So, what, you just travel around? You must be headed somewhere?"

"Always headed somewhere. Headed nowhere. Headed down the wrong path, looking for the right one.

See, when I came back, everything was different. Or maybe I was. Didn't feel like home. You can't go back into all that everyday shit; buying gas and chatting with the mailman. You don't live in that world no more. Like popping your cherry, man. You can't un-live the things you done..." That final word trailed off and hung in the air like a distant alleyway scream, and we sat in silence for a while.

The bus pulled up at a red light, and I gazed across at a diner on the other side of the street. It looked so inviting, with booths, and warmth, and a toilet you could pee in without pushing against the walls for balance. As the light changed and we began moving away, there was a loud bang outside. The stranger jerked in his seat, smashing his elbow as he recoiled. Clutching his arm around himself, he was breathing hard.

"Just a car door," I said, "it's cool. What's your name, buddy?"

"You got a smoke?" he replied, anxiously patting down his clothing and rummaging through pockets he did and didn't have.

"I don't, sorry. What's your name?"

"Clark. Just Clark."

"Thomas," I said, offering my hand across the aisle. He took it with his, which was trembling and clad in a ratty woollen glove with no fingers. I fixed him with my firmest, friendliest glare and suggested he try to get some sleep.

"What, like you?" he replied, "I dunno how you can do that."

"I'm just exhausted is all. There's no air on these

things, wears me out. If you're tired enough, you can sleep anywhere."

"Don't be so sure."

"No, really. One summer, working on my cousin's farm, I was so exhausted, I fell asleep in a turnip patch, and the goats ate the shoes right off my feet. I just lay there snoring. Had to walk back barefoot. Yeah, goats will eat anything..."

"If exhaustion stopped you from dreaming, I'd be runnin' my ass to collapse every damned day."

"Oh. It's cool," I said, "I won't ask." I didn't have to.

"Some things, when they happen, you know they're going to be here forever." On the word *here*, he prodded a finger into the center of his forehead.

"*Ah, hell,*" I thought.

"Close your eyes, and you'll see it, every time. It's like God's done a painting on the inside of your skull, so's you'll never forget what you done." He shut his eyes for a moment, and something about it reminded me of when you hold your hand over a lighter. Opening them with a sharp intake of breath, he continued. "It's like the Sixteen Chapel in here. Don't make no matter now tired you are, if that's what you see in the dark, you'll find no rest. Hump turnips for a month, it don't matter."

"I can't imagine," I replied, figuring I'd let the Sixteen Chapel thing slide.

"No you can't. No you can't. And you should thank God every day for that."

"Yeah," I said, "thank God for flat feet too, right?"

He didn't laugh. Instead, he stepped across the aisle and pulled himself into the seat next to mine. He smelled like a burning locker-room, and I squished myself up against the side.

"See, we were on manoeuvres..." he said. I scalded myself for ignoring the film they'd shown us in middle school about talking to strangers. It was fine. I'd make like I was listening, but think about something else. About baseball, or *The Mod Squad*, or– "...doing a sweep of this village. It's all routine, as routine as it got out there anyway, and uh... I'm sorry, 'we,' it's me and my squad, right?"

"Got it," I said, nodding.

"Me and my buddies. Brothers, really. Not real brothers you understand, but better, tighter. You got any brothers?"

"Only child."

"I had one, before I went out there. Then I had five. Five brothers. Now, I'm an only child, just like you. Fuckin' orphan. Orphan of the war, man, good as. My parents didn't raise this," he said, pointing at his eyes, widening them for emphasis, and laughing a laugh that was halfway to a wail of anguish, "that's what my dad said, 'we didn't raise this... didn't raise *that*...' Anyway, Remmy looked out for me, right from the get-go..."

"Remmy?"

"Yeah, one of my brothers, Remmy. He, uh..." He trailed off, picking up a few seconds later. "Remmy looked out for me, right from the get-go. We went through basic together. He was older than me. Not by much, year or two, but when you're young, that's a big deal. First real action we saw, first time I even heard gunfire, I'm not ashamed to say, I pissed in my pants. Honest to God, peed on myself. Remmy, he didn't laugh or nuthin', just kept me calm, kept me focussed. Weren't even anything to be scared of when you look back; gunshots, that's all, but that was the first time it all became real to me. Up till then, it felt like a game, but those pops and bangs – that's death, son, and it's all around you. Remmy kept me from panicking; from running off into the jungle to get my chin blown off. He got me through it. Got me through other tough times, and me him; a lot of hairy situations. We always had each other's backs. Remmy, Lieutenant Black, Big Mike, Larry the Jew, and Sergeant Moses. We were a fuckin' tight unit. You got a best friend?"

"Yeah," I said, quickly adding "Not really."

"I had five. I was blessed. Big Mike, man, he's so funny. Was. I mean, he'd do all these voices and shit, real fast, all these characters. '*Bonjour, I am Frenchie Le Frog*!' shit like that. There was this one character he'd do called Mrs. Easylay; put two grenades down his shirt like tits, walk around all sexy, talking about how he fucks this and that. He was like Jerry Lewis or something, just pulling us out of the misery for a moment. And those moments were enough to keep you sane. That kinda bonding, man, there's nothing that can explain it. You have to live it. I can't tell it with words." As he started telling his story, Clark had been gently rocking back and forth in his seat. By this point the rocking had become more pronounced, like he was physically picking up steam; the pounding drums in a serial matinee getting faster and faster, louder and harder, all speeding towards a terrible conclusion.

"So anyways, we're out in the wilds somewhere. Hell, it's all the wilds. Huts and swamps, fuckin' bamboo. We walk on this village – little shanty lookin' place just outside of Lam Dong. And right away it feels wrong, just *off* somehow. And the place is completely empty, not a soul.

That's not unusual, I mean, often-times people just pack their shit and get, but like I say, it didn't feel right. Real quick, you just get this instinct. Comes over you, just a *sense*. Like how a dog knows when its master's coming home. So we're scoping it out and taking it real easy, 'cuz you always gotta be on the lookout. Sometimes they booby trap shit. Could be mines, or maybe you see a pile of leaves twitching and some little gook pops out with a rifle. They're so fuckin' sneaky. Remmy's on point, and he suddenly stops, so we all stop. Then he throws up, right there, just pukes all over his boots. Before anyone can speak, we all see what he's looking at, and why it's so quiet. See it, smell it…" Clark brought a shaking hand up to his face and rubbed it across his jaw. The sound of weathered thumb on stubble was like a childhood monster scratching at the bedroom door.

"Behind this hut there's this big… pile." With his arms, he indicated something large; eyebrows up in his scalp and half-shrugging at my lack of recognition. "It's people, man, *people*. Bodies. A whole village, stacked up high and wide like dirty laundry. Probably fifty corpses. At first you don't know what it is, like the brain takes a while to put it all together, then you see something familiar. A finger, a face; little hand." My mouth opened to speak, but hung silently. "Men, women, old people, little kids. Even goddamned babies."

"Jesus," I said, "Who would do that? Was it us?"

"Us? Who even is us? Man, us and them; once you look back on that shit, sides ain't so clear. Anyway, your senses get kinda dull out there. Numb. Things that would've sent the old you to the spaz farm in a diaper don't mean shit now, but this – hell, everyone's someone's family, you know? Someone's dead old naked momma dumped on someone's dead brother. No humanity. Like fish at the market. Little babies just…" He stopped, mid-word, eyes staring off over the edge of the world. "I'm sorry," he said, his hard voice faltering. "Do you know how fuckin' weird it is to hear myself saying all this out loud? I've never talked about that day before, not to a civ. You go home and it's just... I guess there's something to be said for the comfort of strangers." He blinked out a tear onto his cheek, where he just let it be. "I never could talk to my parents about this shit. How could they ever get it, you know? It's like, I wanted to, but at the same time, why would you want your mom to know what kind of a world she really lives in?"

"It's fine," I said, relieved the worst part was over. "Let it all out, buddy. I'm not going anywhere." And I couldn't if I tried.

"Course, we'd all seen bodies before, but there was something so goddamn inhuman about it all, nobody knew what to say, so we just stand there. Then, from behind, there's this noise. I'm at the back, so I spin around, and I'm looking at this kid. No more than five years old. I see her face through the iron sight, just terrified, man. She's bawling, so afraid, and I know, I know that her family is on that pile somewhere. The lucky ones anyway. Momma and sisters, well. She must'a hid, somehow. I tell her it's okay, but she don't understand me, and I'm gesturing to her like *c'mere*. I didn't wanna run toward and spook her, 'cuz you might end up chasing into a minefield, get you both killed. The guys are calling my name, but everything's so far away. Not for real, just in my mind, you know? They're a thousand miles away, 'cuz I'm focussed in on this kid. Like, if I can save this one kid, it'd atone for all the fucked up shit, and if I have to turn around and look back at those bodies, at least I'm doing it with her safe in my arms, you know? Just one soul in that godforsaken, soulless mess. One tiny match, burning in the darkness. I lay my rifle down real slow, at my feet, and show her my empty hands, like 'it's okay,' and she starts tottering towards me, stumbling through the grass. Then I hear Remmy – always was the smartest one. He's screaming at me, screaming something, but I just want to grab the kid. Then there's another sound. *Chu-chunk*. A rifle being cocked. I remember turning around and seeing Remmy, and he's got his gun pointed right at me, and I'm so confused that I almost want to laugh, like why would he shoot me? We're bros, dude, come on! But it's not me, it's her. I see his lips, and I swear, his voice and everything is all slowed down, like a record at the wrong speed, and he's saying "*moooooove*!" I spin back around to the kid, just as that tiny little foot hits the wire."

"Wire?"

"Yeah," he said softly, "booby trap. That's the split second everything changes. There's this bang like you've never heard, and a white flash. Like the sun fell outta the sky. *Boom!*" He smacked his fist into his palm, causing me to flinch. "The force of the explosion knocks me into the dirt so hard I don't even realise I'm on fire. As I'm face down in the mud, in that silence you get after something like that; a silence so loud; all around me, I can hear stuff hitting the ground. I lay there for a little while, probably only seconds, just listening to that sound. It was comforting. You know when you can't sleep and you hear the rain against your window? I liked it, and I wanted to stay there. And that's a thing that fuckin' haunts me. That peace I found as I lay there. Before I realize. It's only the screams of the kid that shake me out of it. As I pull myself up, she falls into my arms. She's all burned, like a melted doll. Flesh falling off her bones like wax. Kid takes one last breath; big, full breath that arches her back and pushes out her arms like wings. And then, just dies. Looking right at me the whole time, staring into me as the lights go out of her eyes."

"My God..."

"Pile was rigged. They'd packed TNT under the corpses – in the corpses – set up a wire. Kid was bait. I couldn't have set it off better if I'd yanked on it myself. I was the only survivor. Only living person for miles. Only reason it went off. Remmy always said I'd get us all killed someday. Some of the oil drums caught, and that's what hit me and the kid. We're all just meat, man. You see some beautiful girl, like, sometimes you see a girl so pretty you think it wouldn't be right to even talk to her; to dirty her with your dick; a girl like that, or a movie star or some millionaire business guy; cut us up and we all the same inside. Your beauty queen, they ain't no different from what you're digging into with grandma's silverware when you're done saying grace. None of us are."

"Yeah," I said, so faintly that it barely existed as a sound.

"Funniest thing," he said, with a wagging finger that suggested a knock-knock punchline, "all around me, were these pieces of people. Arms, legs, livers, you name it, scattered across the whole village. Hundred metre circle of offal, with me in the bullseye, still smoking. No more than a couple'a inches away from me, I shit you not, right there in the mud, right at my feet, was Remmy's hand. I recognised it right off – high school football ring, he was always showing it off. It was like even in death, he was trying to comfort me. Or bust my balls. I picked it up, and I just held it; held it like you'd hold the hand of your date. I mean, it was only a hand, but goddamn if I didn't wanna be alone right then. I sat there holding onto it. Just holding it and talking to him. And I didn't feel so alone. My memory kinda craps out, but I remember walking around looking for bits of my buddies, sifting through skin and fingers, and mush. Found a fuckin' tooth embedded in the wall of a hooch. A whole boot with half of a foot inside it.

Somebody's dick. I think I thought if I could put 'em back together we could all go home. Fuckin' jigsaw. All the while I'm still holding onto Remmy's hand, holding on tight, just talkin'. Another squad finds me eventually; next day so they said. They had to knock me out with a rifle-butt to prise his fingers away from mine. Don't remember much after that. I was on psych for a while, then they sent me home. Discharged on mental grounds, like it was something wrong with *me,* like I'd done something wrong. Anyway, now I'm here."

Clark was calmer, even subdued. The rocking had stopped, and he was slumped into a normal seated position, arms no longer hugging at his body, shoulders slack and relaxed. He closed his eyes and rubbed a hand across them. On one finger was a high school football ring. It was large and ill-fitting. He met my eye and I glanced away, and as he continued, he unconsciously twisted at the ring. "So, there's that."

"Maybe now you've told that story it might help you," I said. It was one of those things people say just to fill the silence.

"Help me?"

"Help you let go? Move on?"

"Yeah," he sighed, "move on..." Clark turned away from me, pulling down the collar of his jacket, yanking the shirt away from his body and leaning down so I could look underneath his clothes. The skin on the left side of his neck was thick and twisted, scorched into shapes like the topographical maps on classroom walls; rivers and tributaries of scarred, burned flesh that were as much a part of his body now as all the bits he had when he first came into the world. He unpopped a button on the sleeve of his jacket, rolling it up the wrist and holding the arm in front of my face.

"Gosh," I said, as I looked at the thick scarring that extended from his neck and shoulder, all the way down to the top of his forearm. He nodded, rolling the sleeve back down, and pulling the collar up above his chin, as though sheltering from the cold.

"So I figured if anyone can help, if anyone can give the answers that I ain't heard yet about why things go down how they do, maybe it's that guy. Like you said, Charles Manson aka Jesus Christ. I know it's all probably horseshit, but can't hurt to go see."

"Wait," I said, "what?"

"Maybe he's more than just... meat. Fuck, I'd like to think there's someone out there that knows what they're doing, or we're all just flies or worms. No destiny, no purpose..."

"Why didn't you say?"

"Say what?"

"That we're going to the same place. We're both going to see Manson, right?" He responded with a "Yeah" and a half-smile, like he still hadn't made the connection. We sat for a while, in silence, before he moved back across the aisle 'cuz he wanted to stretch his legs. That was the last thing we said to each other. It felt like there was nothing left to be said. He'd let it all out, and now he'd have to toss me aside, like blowing all your devils into a balloon and watching it float away. As we got closer to Cali, both of us managed a little sleep. I don't know what Clark was seeing, but my mind was entangled in sweating, in-and-out dreams of war and death, and napalm raining from the skies. As I huddled against the window, eyes pinched, I swore I heard a whimpering; the sound of a sleep even more disturbed, but I didn't know if it was part of his nightmare or mine. After the vivid image of a baby on a bonfire, I decided to stay awake until we got there. At mid-morning, the bus pulled in at the final destination.

I tilted a friendly nod to Clark as I peeled myself out of my seat and made my way down the aisle. When I got off the steps, into the sharp morning air, he was right behind me. There was a buzz outside, and everybody seemed to be talking, either to each other, or to themselves, while some watched a commotion across the street, where two shouting men were pulled apart by a news vendor.

"The big city," I thought to myself, as the men stomped their separate ways, the older of the pair hurling his hat through the air as he marched down the street. A middle-aged man spat the word *bastard* as he bristled past, while a pair of zipperheads leaning on a wall excitedly chattered between themselves.

"Hey," said Clark, to gaggle of men and women on the sidewalk, "what's going on?" A fifty-something man in a white trilby inhaled so violently on a cigarette, we were almost sucked into his mouth.

"It's madness is what it is!"

"What?"

"That bastard got off! They let him off, can you believe that? The justice system is a joke! Goddamn pinko faggots running our courts! Put a father on the jury, a husband, you'd have a different result. I'd have pulled the lever myself, and don't tell me I wouldn't! And now that killer is walking the streets, walking *our* streets. Charles Manson, innocent man! As innocent as you or I! It defies belief..." Clark put his arm around my shoulder, and started leading me away, the raging of Mr. Trilby echoing behind us. "Makes me fearful for my daughter..."

"Well," said Clark, "what's one more nutball walking around, anyway?"

"Yeah, I guess so," I replied, adding, "hey, I have a question."

"Go." It wasn't an easy thing to ask, but I couldn't go on not knowing. It'd needle away at me until I went cuckoo crazy, and that trip, all the miles I'd travelled, everything I was about to do, that was more than enough crazy to be getting on with. Steeling myself, I just came right out with it.

"Listen... you know when you were watching me sleep? I didn't happen to make a funny noise when I woke up, did I?"

2 THE LOOK

Early that afternoon, news spread that Manson had left the courtroom and given his speech to the waiting press. The whole, weedy reasoning for me being out there was to catch that moment, but I'd missed it. I'd missed it like I always miss everything. So now I had to just turn around and go back home? Then we heard what he'd said out there. It was just a sentence or two, about how truth had finally defeated the system, and something about being crucified, but that they'd rolled away the rock, and now everyone had seen his resurrection. Then someone asked what he was gonna do now; where he was gonna go? He'd said but two words before drifting off back into the world – Spellman Ranch.

A guy on the street who'd watched the coverage was relaying it to a pair of teenage girls. His voice was too loud, and he flailed his arms as he spoke, putting on accents and pulling faces. Me and Clark listened from a distance; me, amused, and Clark, fixing in with a squinting intensity

"If you could have seen him," said the man, "I don't

know how I could describe to you, that *presence*, it just... transcends words." I nudged Clark, a 'get a load of this joker,' but his attention was rapt. "All these big-shot reporters, calling him Mr. Manson, like they had to acknowledge he wasn't below them. They couldn't paint him as a lowlife or sicko any longer, it was *Mister* Manson. And when they asked him what was next, he had a real twinkle in his eye, ya know? *Spellman Ranch*. Like it was an invitation! Who am I to be turning down an invitation from *Mister* Charlie Manson?" The guy seemed a little cracked, but there was a comical logic to what he was saying. I imagined myself stealing that line when I got back. "*Who was I to be turning down...*"

"Where is that?" I asked, surprising myself, but having booked all that way, I wanted to push on a little bit more, and it made my belly tingle to wonder just how far I'd go. Clark moved towards a group of people gathered around a tourist map behind a sheet of glass. It was one of those 'You Are Here' deals with a giant red arrow skewering the ground where we stood. A tangle of arms and hands fingered across the map, clad in colorful rings and home-made twine bracelets. There was a kid about my age, with hair down to his shoulders, with a girl whose head was buzzed like a freshly recruited marine.

"I think it's here," he said. "See this road, Spellman Drive..."

"It just trails off though, it's just green."

"Maybe it's not on the map..." They wheeled away and into the street, leaving me, Clark, and a shabby-looking woman in her thirties glaring at the map like horse at a songbook, not sure if we even cared. The guy who'd seen Manson on the news was telling his story again, though most just walked on by. I wondered if he'd stand there for a while, repeating to strangers his line about the personal invitation, before going home and quietly getting on with the rest of his life.

"I don't know what I'm looking for," I said, with a sigh, seeing nothing on that sun-faded board but journey's end. Then, a voice from behind.

"Hey!" It was the long-hair, gesturing at us from the middle of the street. "It's 'bout five miles walk from here." He was stood near an elderly local with glasses almost as big as his face. As we walked over, long-hair said "...to see Manson. Charlie Manson..." and the geezer made that old people noise, like "ehhh!" and swished his hand through the air. He watched long-hair and his girl skip away like they were on their way to the carnival, with me and Clark following behind. I caught the old man's eye as I passed, and felt a prod of shame, suddenly embarrassed. His withering gaze cut through me like a grandpa who'd caught me with a nudie centerfold, emptying my sausage into the bathroom sink. But on we went, Clark and me, striding to catch the couple in front, who were hand in hand, arms swinging with each step.

The chick looked over with a smile, her eyes flashing a look of "isn't this *exciting*?" They were large and green, with lashes like a Venus flytrap, and I responded with as confident a grin as I could. I couldn't expose myself as a square, even though I was mentally preparing a list of excuses in case they started passing out LSD. I'd probably tell them I had epilepsy. Clark made a strange, low rumbling noise to get their attention.

"So... are you two together?" he asked.

"Nah, we just met, like, twenty minutes ago. Are you two together?"

"Nah," I said, "we just met." Look at me, bantering with exotic strangers. *Girls.*

"Right on," she said. I tried thinking of something else to say, but nothing came. But even that quiet space felt good. The friendly chick with the sunflower lashes wasn't wearing a bra, and every step sent them bouncing against the inside of her shirt. It was a long trek through streets, beaten paths and off-map trails, but it didn't matter. It's lame, but walking through the hills of California with a group of strangers felt like I'd wandered off the map for the first time into adult life. No parents, no teachers, no small-town bullshit baggage, where everyone knows the last five generations of your family tree, and all the retarded things you did as a kid. Just me, doing stuff, because I felt like it.

When somebody did speak, it was about what we might find up there. The girl said she always knew Manson would get off, because nobody that beautiful could be capable of such wicked things. It had to have been a plot, she said, by The Man, to keep the kids down, to keep everyone afraid of being themselves, make them conform and behave and spend money on *stuff* and *things* that were bad for the soul. As she talked, my eyes, as though on magnets, would find their way down to those energetic cans. Out of shame, and not wanting to ditch old labels just to gain the nickname Tommy Tit-Stare, I dropped a step behind. I started thinking about X-Ray Spex in the backs of old comics, and the nightmare I'd had as a kid, where I'd ordered a pair out of an imaginary comic book called *Willy Honks and the Win Twins.* Thick black frames with a red and white spiral over the lenses, I snuck them into fifth grade homeroom so I could check out Mrs. Page's panties. When I put them on, I could see right through to her bones. I turned away in fear, and at my classmates' desks were skeletons; hollow, black-eyed skulls like on pirate flags or bottles of poison, with clattering, gumless teeth. I ran screaming into the street outside, trying to rip the glasses from my face, but they'd become a part of me, and all that came away was my flesh. All around, everyone was bones, even dogs on leashes and a baby in a stroller; all pointing with skeletal fingers, at what a dirty little pervert I was. When I woke, I still felt the sense of shame, and I tore every single one of those ads from my comics, shredding them into tiny scraps.

The dim afternoon sun hung above us as we walked. The friendly girl and the long-haired guy sang Beatles songs, loudly and proudly, tune giving way to volume. Me and Clark stayed quiet. My old man wasn't so keen on music. One time Diana Ross came on TV, and he started yelling about the Whore of Babylon. A third voice joined in the "*na, na-na, na-na-na naaa*" from *Hey Jude* from behind my shoulder, and I realized we'd picked up others along the way. Our group had grown to seven; two more girls and another guy. Behind were other packets of walkers, some alone, others hand in hand and excitedly chattering, like scattered worker bees flying home to the queen. The two new chicks were barefoot, while the guy had a pair of sunglasses and nothing but a leather vest up top, with a duffel bag slung over a shoulder. We walked out another couple of miles, attracting glares and nudged whispers from townsfolk along the way, which put me a little on edge. I'd heard stories about longhairs being pulled from their cars and beaten by cops, but there was a giddy thrill in being called "pothead" and "cult member" by a man pumping gas. The barefoot girls just giggled, cooing with girlish waves and mocking shakes of the butt, and a "you want some of this, Daddy?" in baby-voices, like they get it every day. Funny. All it took for them to see the polite neighborhood boy as a pothead cultist was the direction he was walking.

Eventually, we found ourselves out of the suburbs and into the tall, frayed grasses and weather-beaten tracks that weren't on any map. It didn't feel like we could get lost, as there were were people everywhere, all headed the same way; moths all flitting toward the same raging fire. None of the folks looked like they belonged anywhere else.

"It's somewhere round here," said Longhair, "we'll just follow those cats." He threw a thumb at the grassy slope ahead, and the figures pushing along the same path. That's when it started to feel crazy. I'd got on a bus, met a guy, and started walking, and now we were here. I wasn't sure I wanted to come, but I'd said I did anyway. Maybe we'd all done the same. How many people have to believe in a lie before it becomes the truth?

Clark saw it before I did.

"Jeez, where are we, Woodstock?"

"More like the Twilight Zone." There it was, the ranch that suddenly found itself the hippest destination for flower children everywhere with one simple mention by the most reviled man in America. A handful of scary-looking biker types stood by the gate, arms folded, while in front of the entrance were a hundred-fifty people, maybe more, dancing, singing, hugging, laughing, smoking. We just stood, taking it all in.

A guy with waist-length plaits wore a long jacket made entirely of flowers, and wandered though the crowds with the slow, measured gait of someone who'd deemed themselves to be important.

A circle of people knelt on the ground, hands clasped together and heads bowed as though in prayer.

Two girls, each riding on the shoulders of their boyfriends, cast the long shadows of giants in the afternoon sun.

A juggler, all wiry, veiny arms and a wolfman beard, performed intricate tricks with four plastic balls. Nobody was watching, but he didn't care.

A tiny baby wrapped in a colorful blanket slept through the madness, while a child cackled with laughter as its hippie parent swung it around by the ankles.

Soon we were among them, in the crowd, with everyone just waiting for something to happen; waiting for him. The others from my group had vanished, leaving just Clark at my side. They'd dissolved into the hordes of bare feet and unbrushed hair, and I couldn't have picked them out again if I'd tried. Hippies – they all look the same.

There were reporters parked up on the grass, with television crews whose cameras were under siege by kids shoving each other, shouting "*Hi, mom!*" and flipping the bird, or aggressively making out and whooping with defiance. Amid the identikit heads, the press were the freaks, marked out from the crowd by straight shoulders and sensible shoes. In that jumble of energy and hair – and a guy using his penis as the brush to paint a rainbow – my focus was drawn to the news man, gripping a microphone like a safety blanket, with the horrified look of a scientist who'd discovered the disease that would wipe out humanity. The crew observed from a safe distance, as they may have done on wildlife shoots, knowing the animals writhing in front of the lens could pounce at any moment, hurling pawfuls of feces and slipping through the sunroof to hump their legs until they snapped.

I began to notice others detached from the maelstrom, sat by themselves, shoulders hunched and eyes to the ground as dancing feet patted the grass around them. As Clark and I walked towards the entrance, a freaky guy jogging through the crowds crashed into my chest, and we momentarily snared in each other's gaze. His watermelon pupils ricocheted between pinball bumpers, and he didn't say a word, but did this odd movement with his hands in front of my face that made me recoil, before wheeling away and back into the crowd, dancing to a music only he could hear.

I dropped my bag onto the grass and sat down, with Clark vacantly standing nearby. He was a thousand miles away and back in his bad place.

"You're quiet," I said, "everything okay?"

"Yeah," he replied, immediately becoming more animated and leaping onto the ground in a seated position, "just a lot to take in." He wasn't wrong. They didn't have girls like that back home – they didn't have anything like that back home. A pair of sandled feet planted next to me and I followed them up, up the long legs and bare belly, all the way to the smile of the beautiful girl with curly blond hair who was shielding her eyes from the sun.

"This seat taken?" she said. I shrugged and shook my head and she sat herself down. I knew she was just using us to keep the sun out of her eyes, but I didn't care. "I'm Jack."

"Tom," I replied.

"Really?" she said, through an exhalation of laughter, as though my very name was so square she couldn't contain herself. At least I wasn't a girl with a boy's name.

"Clark," I said, indicating him with a thumb. Though he was only two feet away, she waved, one of those waves where the fingers ripple one after the other, and drew back on the remains of the joint she'd been smoking.

"This is something, huh?" she said. I just nodded. "Everyone here, all brought together. Different ages, genders, sexualities. That's what he does, he unifies."

"Who," I said, "Manson?" She threw a look to say "*Of course.*"

"He's amazing, just *amazing*, don't you think? He's gonna come out soon, that's what everyone's been saying. I was just watching that gate, see if I could see anything. Wanted to be the first one he saw, like a baby bird. That was my plan. Imprinting! But there's so many cats here. I wasn't expecting it, which was kinda dumb on my part, wouldn't you say?" She talked so fast, I had to watch her mouth as she was speaking. "I wrote him when he was inside, you know. Every day. Sent some of 'em, too. Told him all my secrets, like a priest; all the bad things I done just cleansed away. He's so sexy. I'd let him do whatever he wanted. Just use me, ya know? God..." She inhaled deeply, drawing the smoke inside herself and letting it linger, before casually exhaling through the side of her mouth in a well practised, perfectly formed plume. I turned away from the sickly-smelling cloud, making like I was looking at something over my shoulder. She held out her hand, the marijuana joint resting between two fingers.

"Uh, no, I'm good," I said, my cheeks audibly sizzling. Before I could add "actually, I'm an epileptic," Jack's restless mouth cut me off.

"So, where ya from?"

"Idaho."

"Oh, that's cool."

"You?"

"Just around. Here and there. Here, right now. I just spent six months in a commune in Frisco, just living. That's where you find your family. Family's always where you are, not where you come from. You got family?"

"Yeah," I said, thinking that it was an odd question. Who doesn't have a family? "Back home."

"Ah," she said, wagging a finger, "well, stick around for a while and we'll see. 'Back home.' Naw, I got outta there, it got a little heavy. One bad apple rots the whole bowl, ya know? I remembered this guy who'd passed through who used to talk about this old motherfucker he knew, one of the pioneers. Supposedly he lives somewhere out in the desert in a hollowed-out whale dick. No possessions, no ties, just living off the land inside this giant pecker. I was like, fuck it, I'm gonna go and find this cat, but then I was like, Charlie, man! Why wouldn't I go be with him? Three days later, he's out. If that's not a sign, I don't know what is, right? So I made my way down, and here I am."

"You move around a lot, huh?" I said.

"Me? Ha! I'm a novice, got a lot to learn. Charlie? He's like the ultimate nomad, even when they stick him in jail, he's totally *free*." On 'free' she stretched out her arms like she was flying, drawing out the word so that if you wrote it down, all the E's would fall off the edge of the page. "They're the prisoners, he's... you can't contain that. How can you put walls around a man's soul?"

Before I could bark another monosyllabic response, a hand reached down and snatched her up and away. It was attached to the arm of a laughing man, hand in hand with a chain of other girls. Jack shrieked with laughter as they dragged her off. I was kinda relieved. I didn't know what I was doing. She was pleasant and all, but you're always waiting for the moment you realize they're not laughing with you, any they go hang with the cooler kids instead. Everything had begun to feel pretty foolish. It was fun to be somewhere; all the sights, people; but everyone else seemed so moved, pulled by some cosmic yearning I didn't feel. In the middle of this party, there sat a big phony.

Suddenly, there was a yell from the crowd. The yell grew into a series of screams and frantic hollers. The aimless dancing and chitter-chatter stopped, and the scattered individuals began booking it as one, fast and reckless; like they were running from something dangerous. Me and Clark pulled ourselves to our feet, and our bodies were swept up into the tidal wave, everyone jostling and shoving, pushing past, pushing through. I made a break for it too, and didn't know why.

Trapped inside the mass of bodies, the ground rumbled with pounding feet; limbs thundering the dirt like a pack of mad buffalo. Most running simply because others were running. Not from something; *to*. Him. Finally, we all came to a bruising kind of stop. I was pinched between shoulders on either side and surrounded by the warmth and odour of people. Crammed together, we bucked and tottered like an ocean, with hands shoving and necks craning up towards the gate. The piercing shrieks made me think of newsreels where girls fainted at the feet of John Lennon. There were cries of "Charlie!" and "Yeah!" but I was too far back and too short, and couldn't see. Clark was next to me, one of his boots crushing my toes, and above the whooping I bellowed into his ear.

"Where is he? Is he there?"

"He's small, man," said Clark. "Fuckin' five-two, I read."

"Can you see him?"

"I think so. I see somethin'."

"What?"

"Top of a man's head." The screams and claps became louder and more sustained, a rhythmic, off-kilter thump that I could feel in my chest, in-between heart beats. I don't know why, but I found my own palms smacking together, and even though I was pretty sure he was a murderer, above the ruckus, I could pick out a "Wooo! Char-lee!" coming from the vicinity of my own face. Not for the last time, I was caught up in something I felt, but didn't understand. Then, at once, everything stopped. The screaming and applause vanished into absolute silence like all the sound got sucked out of the world. Later I figured he must've waved us all to hush down, but my first thought was that our parents had shown up, and everyone stopped acting all crazy and put on some damn shoes. But it was just him. And he was enough. The atmosphere in that silence was almost crackling. If someone had dropped a match into the crowd, the resulting explosion would have blown a new Grand Canyon in the center of California. Then, he spoke.

"It's a little strange to be back out here with the air and the trees and the people. They had me in that little room, couldn't even feel the sun on my skin or the wind on my cheek. If y'all are waiting on some big sermon, waiting to hear me say what I wouldn't say to those pigs, with their microphones..." His speech patterns were strange and colorful, like an eccentric teacher.

"What are you doing here?" he said. There was a murmur in the crowd, with those of us squashed at the back shuffled and shunting to see who he was addressing, hoping to catch Manson looking right into their eyes, waiting on his answer. A girl at the front of the crowd responded too quietly for me to hear.

"This little girl says she's lost and looking for something," said Manson, "looking for home." Cries went up, shouts of "*Me too!*" and "*Yeah!*" Many were openly weeping, their bodies swaying, hands clasped with those beside them. "You are home, darlin'. Home is where the love is. There's enough love here for everyone; the forgotten, the lost, the abused..."

"We love you too, Charlie!"

"Charlie!"

"I love you!" Cries went out from all around; anything to be recognized by him, to be singled out, to be embraced like the girl had. The crowd started to jostle again, and the air got pushed out of my chest. I felt myself crushing against the person in front, and squashed by whoever was behind. In an instant, the sense of peace and wonder had gone, leaving panic in its place. Elbows dug into my ribs, hands on my back, penned in by hot flesh and hard bone. A weight on my neck tried to bully me downwards, and the sky above was dark with arms and twisted faces of those who'd tried climbing up and out. Something warm and damp squished against my nose, and I think it was a foot. That's when the terror set in. I had to fight to fill my lungs; each breath a one-inch shoving match with another body who wanted that precious space for itself; a dance floor riot where staying upright was a struggle. If my feet went from under me, I knew I was done for. The frenzied love-mob would trample the blood and guts right out of my screaming mouth, like a tube of toothpaste. Christ knows how a shell-shocked sumbitch like Clark was coping. As one of my legs buckled, I felt myself heading down. I never thought this was how I'd go out. Then, a voice yelled out, cutting through the madness.

"Whoa!" It was Manson. "You're fighting for space you already have. Stop. Breathe." And so we did. I heaved myself upright and steady, scoffing down mouthfuls of air. Calm had descended again, just like that. "Just settle easy, we don't want no-one gettin' hurt." At my side, Clark was still holding it together, staring over at Charlie. And then, from my new position I saw him, for the first time. A glimpse, really, as he flitted across the gap between two heads. I'd never seen anyone famous before, and a small and unexpected jolt of excitement shot through my body.

"Now, there's room enough for everyone, inside these gates." A huge cheer erupted. "But listen... listen!" Silence again, giddy, ready-to-pop silence. "You wanna put down here, be wise and be aware – in here ain't like out there. There ain't no rules... 'cept one." A hush dropped over the throng; anticipation, fear. What if he wouldn't let us in? What if he'd only allow chicks? Or only men? Nobody under eighteen? Over twenty-one? The TV said he didn't like coloreds, but what about blondes or Republicans or Jews?

"*Brand New*. Everyone who comes in here is Brand New. You leave all that baggage, all that old you, dependent you, closed you – leave it all outside. In here, once you step through these gates and over this line, this is the place to be reborn. Everyone. Even me. If you didn't need to be Brand New, what're you doing here?" In the quiet, a voice to the front of me muttered "Fuckin' a," while his girlfriend sobbed.

"Oh, and if there's any press out there, any snakes, well..." Manson paused, chuckling through the syllables, as eyeballs turned toward the boob-tubers filming his every word, "come if you like, but know that you ain't welcome, not if you're not willing to be Brand New. Be press out there, not in here. You come in here, looking for something, looking for profit and not hope, to exploit and not to love, well, I'll sniff ya out, expose that snake in the nest. No man lets a reptile around his family; no man could let that stand. Could you? You gotta protect what you love, and believe me, Charlie got a nose for snakes. Now, let's all be Brand New."

There were a couple seconds of silence, this tiny moment where we all bathed in that stillness. Maybe people were saying a final goodbye to their old selves. Then, a huge cheer; a single voice from a hundred mouths, as though Manson had finished off with a bow. But they told me that's not what happened. They say he just turned and walked through those gates, becoming Brand New, with everyone following behind. And how they did follow.

I stood watching as everybody brushed past, sprinting, jogging and skipping through the gates to their supposed rebirth. Manson stood on the other side of the entrance, greeting each like St. Peter, enveloped by his fans. He hadn't sounded too bad. Certainly not like a killer. But what would a killer sound like? But I wasn't weeping with emotion either. He was just a man. Confident, charismatic, a good talker, but just a man. My plan had been to see him leave the courthouse, but I'd screwed that up. I'd screwed it up, and somehow been a part of something bigger; film crews, near-death experience and all. But I'd seen enough. I was still just a big phony.

"You heard what he said," said Clark, "Brand New."

He was so excited, like he just knew he could wash everything away if he walked through the gates; paint a happy portrait over all the images that kept him screaming in his bed every night. "You comin'?"

"I..." Clark shrugged and followed the others towards the gate. Ah, heck, I thought, it's a long trek to a motel anyways. "Hold up!"

I'd bed down for the night, keep an eye on Clark, see that he was okay. Just for a day, maybe two, see what the place was about. There were no chains or locks, and everyone was free to come and go as they pleased. This time next week I'd be back with my family, and I'd have an awesome story. Way better than five minutes stood outside a courthouse. Maybe I'd even tell people how I'd been a member of the Manson Family. Just for a day, but it still counts. The image of my old man's face on hearing that was enough to make me go in.

Clark was ten steps ahead of me and already inside, with this look like he magically expected to be a different person, with his scars flattened baby-smooth. Above the entrance hung a large white wooden sign, with streaky red paint unevenly fingered into big, bright letters. It read *Eden Ranch*, and gently swung creaking above my head as I crossed the threshold and went inside. Brand New?

3 HIPPIE HIPPIE SHAKE

Somehow, one night became three. Four days after following Clark inside, I was still at Eden Ranch, where a ton of different people had walked through those gates, in both directions. Some stuck around, while others left after half a day, their cameras filled with snaps of tourist poses next to gen-yoo-wine hippies. Yesterday, the longhair Beatles-singing guy left. He didn't make a thing of it, just quietly strolled back into the real world. Funny, someone like that taking off and me still there. Maybe he was as much of a phony as I was – maybe they all were, they just took the trouble to grow out their hair first. My mind was made to call it a week's vacation and head back home in a couple of days, but another 48 hours in that place felt like a push. My Grateful Dead shirt was starting to get pretty ripe, and I'd probably have to burn my underwear when I got home.

Should have guessed a hippie commune wouldn't be the most organized of places. I figure if you're inviting a hundred people to stay, you'd have tents or bunks, but on the first night – or first day, as the partying went long past sunrise – I sacked out under the clouds in a patch of dirt, shivering inside my spare sweater. It's every man for himself, and though there's a childlike thrill of no authority figures, as an adult, you're aware that, while there might be nobody in charge, there's nobody in charge. Not that there wasn't a hierarchy, though a chump like me wasn't even within fingertips of the bottom rung.

Eden Ranch, as it'd been renamed, was no longer a working ranch, and according to talk, was formerly the property of an elderly couple, until the deeds found their way over to Charlie. Sat on four acres of land, the old buzzards had been living up in the big house up back that overlooked the camp, while everything fell into rust and rot. There were no cattle or horses, just the occasional piece of rock-hard poop that you had to dive clear of, when some pothead flung it through the air like a Frisbee.

There were various barns, stables and outbuildings, all of which had fallen into disrepair, but were something for excited hippies to poke about in. About fifty yards inside the gate was a huge campfire that burned around the clock, fed with broken beams from the stables, or fallen branches from the nearby woods. The fire was the focal point for camp – at least, the lowly serfs who hadn't been personally hand-picked to go and play at the feet of the king – billowing a thin plume of wispy grey smoke into the sky over the city like a finger beckoning the kids inside. At least it was warm. I'd even managed to sleep beside it for a little while on the second night, curled up like a bagel, until some drunk faggot started bashing on a battered guitar while a pair of girls swayed in front of the flames like those chicks at the start of the James Bond flicks.

Seems like every night there were a hundred things going on just to stop you from getting any sleep. Maybe sleep was for squares too. The third night I went into one of the stables, figuring I could bed down in the straw and be half-comfortable. Inside, five people were having sex in a big pile. I scooted back out and lay alone in the dirt, my mind filled with all sweaty tushes and peckers and pussies going every which way, and feeling ashamed just for having seen it.

During the days I mostly kept to myself. Other than hanging with Clark, I stayed away from the crowds. It was their home, not mine, and I didn't feel so Brand New. Such solitude was familiar to me. But it was hard to be a loner at Eden. You couldn't help getting pulled into conversations with the sorta people you'd never usually meet; folks who were more open, less judging than those on the outside, and eye contact or a smile would rarely get returned with those sneery looks you remembered from high school. People like that didn't stick around. You could chat to a stranger and not be afraid you were part of a dare, being giggled at from safe distance behind painted nails. Everyone at Eden wanted to buy into the freedom, the openness, the oneness, even if they had to fake it, even if everyone was faking it. That was all that kept me from walking straight out the exit the second I saw my first smelly longhair taking a hearty piss while eating a sandwich with his free hand. If I'd ended up like those kids who spent their lunch breaks trudging out lap after lonely lap around the playground, I'd have been back on that bus long ago.

One afternoon I got talking to a mousy girl who was really into dreams. She told me how she kept a detailed journal of everything she saw while sleeping, and asked if my dreams had gotten stranger since I'd arrived. She talked about about lucid dreaming and the ancient dreamscapes that link our unconscious minds, and said the word *dream* so many times it started to sound like a foreign language, before reading aloud to me from the chicken-scratch pages of her sleep diary. Church-faced soldiers, mice the size of horses, a tit on a bike; when she got to the part about her vagina singing the song that healed the planet, I excused myself to take some long, solitary laps around the stables, like the lunchbreak hikers.

But it was still hard to be alone, hard not to get a "Hey!" or a smile. Strangers, but all with the bond of choosing to be there; all guests at the same party, all friends of the host they'd never met. One kid stepped alongside and joined me, chatting about nothing in particular, as we took a couple of lazy circuits around the barns. Seemed like he wasn't sure what he was doing either. I haven't seen him since. It was kind of a bummer that with all funky people willing to shoot the shit, there was no point learning names, not if you're passing through. Maybe that was an excuse to be unsociable, something I'd probably regret when I was back among the drones.

Inevitably, I'd find myself orbiting back to Clark, who I barely knew at all, but who had a comforting familiarity about him, like that guy you meet a half-hour before everyone else on the first day at a new job. It was good to see his twitchy face, particularly at meal times – if you could call it that – where we ate a pap of beans or eggs slapped onto paper plates while sat around the fire.

There was another reason too. With Clark at my side, it was easier to say no to the various drugs that were constantly passing around. I'm sure he'd done his fair share, and I saw him puffing on a doobie a couple of times, but it made me less of a stand-out square to be waving away a tab of acid if he was shaking his head too. I don't know that he needed my company like I did his. He was happy to mingle, and the pacifist types seemed to view him as a perfect example of what war does to a man. Hell, he'd probably end up as camp mascot; Charlie's living specimen of The Man's evil handiwork.

Not that Manson had been around. Everyone hoped he'd walk among us, working the floor as the gracious host, but I hadn't seen him since the first night. Maybe he was settling back into life on the outside. He'd been staying in the house, which most gazed at with reverence, always with half an eye on the distant front door hoping to see someone emerge. Occasionally they would, but just a biker or shaven-headed female, who'd walk down into camp and make small talk with a chick or three before leading them up to the house, hand-picked and disappearing inside. When someone did wander down, the atmosphere changed, with everyone on their best behavior; heads high, shoulders straight. Even those cats who acted like they were too hip to care about anything would be twisting their heels into the ground like blushing débutantes. With us roughing it down in camp, and him staying hidden away in the house, everything felt on hold; a strange limbo, until the day he was ready to be with his people. Then, and only then, they could finally begin their new lives.

He'd been busy pow-wowing a record deal, that's what they said, as one of many avenues to take his ideas worldwide. Even though the public thought he was a killer, they still listened, but as a celebrity, they'd *really* listen. Supposedly he'd got word out that he'd sell a tell-all to the highest bidder. It'd be his propaganda, they said, but the press would print it anyway, and anyone who was meant to get it would get it. Folk were convinced he was gonna be bigger than the Beatles. I heard one girl say he had "...a voice as beautiful as his soul." If you believed what they wrote about the trial, he must sound like a coyote being fucked by a firecracker.

But business deals with record executives meant the snakes had to come into his world, and take that long, long walk up to the house, briefcases clutched to their chests, running the gauntlet of catcalls, which became a fun game to pass the time. Everyone would run to join in the fun, hooting, teasing, and taunting, with hisses and yells of "Snake!" and "Pig!" while they got redder in the face, suddenly so aware, under scrutiny, of the mechanics of their own bodies, that they almost forget how to walk. This morning, a guy from a record label took that walk, and was circled by one of the dune buggies the higher-ups get around in, until he was lost inside a cloud of dust. As the buggy sped off, the poor bastard coughed his way up the hill, accompanied most of the way by a guy who'd pulled out his pecker, his arms raised in victory, as he thwacked it back and forth between his thighs.

Snake baiting aside, the free-wheeling novelty was wearing thin. Without direction, without routine, it's the summer vacation and you've run out of stuff to do. Everyone hates their job, but a couple weeks on the unemployment line will get boring real fast. There's nothing duller than total freedom. Maybe that's why God livens things up with disasters; tsunamis and mudslides to keep things interesting. When I got back I'd play up the excitement – I'd have to. There'd been a couple of minor arguments, but nobody'd been murdered by the Hippie Death Cult. I had seen a flick-knife, but it was used to peel an apple. I'd probably change the apple to a stoner's face and get a half-decent story out of it. Despite how it was probably being told on the outside, the people at Eden weren't a cult, much less a psychopathic one. It was all just a house party that had gone on for too long, with the owner not kicking anyone out yet. With no alarms or bedtimes, no TV or radio, or clocking in and out, and no place to be, everything blurred into one perpetual dawn. I figure you hang around too long, pretty soon, the passing of a week or a year would begin to feel much the same.

And then I saw her.

I saw her, and the hours and the days and the parade of blank faces all slammed to a halt. It was as though someone lit a match inside my chest, which spread outward down my limbs and up into my skull, out into my toes and fingertips, which went so numb I found myself pushing them together to feel the tingles. I sensed a danger; that to look at her was to fall down into something I'd never be able to climb out of. But I couldn't help it. I was staring at the sun, and laughing as I went blind. I watched as she walked through the entrance; huge brown eyes sweeping slowly over the camp. My heart pumped in thick, broken-hydrant squirts as she surveyed the brave new, Brand New world, feeling like I'd burst into flames if she looked in my direction. Her long, wavy blond hair was swept from the right, up and across the other side of her head, in a kind of beautiful chaos. A slim waist swooped out into a pair of Coke bottle hips that made you want to put your hands either side and feel the bones against the inside of your palms. I wanted to approach; to offer a handshake, a name, a "Welcome to Eden, welcome to the Brand New you" that the regular greeters would dispense to new arrivals, but she was already in the welcoming embrace of a trio of girls, pulled into the group with hellos and hugs and led away. Away into camp. Away from me. Since arriving, it often seemed like I fell in love with a new girl every fifteen minutes. I told myself this too would pass, but it felt different. Everything did. Maybe that's what people talked about. Some things can't ever be unseen.

Throughout the rest of the day, I'd occasionally see New Girl around, and find myself snatching a glance. I don't know if I did or didn't want her to catch me, and come over to say hi. I just knew that the camp seemed better with her in it, like any funny joke or piece of wisdom I might've said could find some value by falling on her ears. The reverse was that, should she disappear, like most quickly did, the camp might feel worthless. There's this saying I never understood until now, about a tree falling in the forest. Suddenly, I got that. I didn't want to fall without her being there to see it.

Late that afternoon, two girls from the house returned from a trip to the outside world, swinging a big burlap sack between them. I was sat with Clark, rubbing the belly of a shabby dog we'd named Mr. Barky. At the sight of a donut being pulled from the sack and tossed onto the ground, Barky took off in a sprint, with the rest of camp quickly following right behind. The girls began to fling brightly-colored donuts into the crowd, two or three at a time, raining down on us like beads at Mardi Gras, to the whoops and cheers of those who'd had their fill of campfire rations. A donut bounced into the dirt at my feet; snatched by a guy who stuffed it straight into his mouth and leapt victoriously into the air.

"Over here!" I yelled, and a brunette with hair that looked like she'd cut it herself flung one like she was pitching a fastball straight at my face. I snatched it out of the air with both hands, and almost choked myself shovelling it past my teeth in a way that would have enraged my parents. It was dry as hell. I didn't care. I hadn't seen sugar in a week. "What did you get?" I said, in indecipherable cake-vowels. Clark held up two pink O's, with a third stretching out his cheeks like a plastic carnival clown. With a hard, satisfying swallow, he spoke.

"I pushed a guy."

"Who bought these?" I said, to a longhair, striding past with harlot's lipstick smeared in chocolate. "Charlie?"

"*Bought?*" he replied, screwing up his face. "Dumpster, dude. Back of the bakery." The thud of another into the dust then sent him diving to the floor for a second helping.

"We're cheering being hobos now?" I said. Clark just shrugged.

"Food's food. I've eaten worse, believe me."

"Like what?" He paused, no doubt running through a long, disgusting list of Vietnamese street-puppies, crickets, and charbroiled human flesh before replying –

"Rattlesnake. They peel off the skin and fry it alive in this jungle moonshine shit. It don't taste too bad, but you have to watch it dancing around first, peeled. Fuckin' chef always thinks it's funny. They put music on, "Hey, lookit that little fella go!" Honestly, most meat just tastes like meat, anyhow. There's no sense of being able to taste the crocodile's actual ass, or whatever."

"I'm just saying, this is the freedom everyone's aspiring to? Kick against the rules, sure, but there's a homeless guy in my town who lives like this. He ain't Brand New; his wife died in a car wreck, and it broke his brain." At that moment, though the crowd, I saw her again. Upper lip curled into a smile, exposing a row of brilliant white teeth. I imagined myself kissing them, wondering if they'd feel like porcelain on my lips. "Did you see the new girl that came in today?" I asked. "The blonde?" Talking about her made it feel more real, making a silly thought solid, as though I could tease the universe into making something happen.

"What girl?"

"Doesn't matter," I said. And it didn't. Couple of days, I'd never see her again. I watched as she broke a donut in two, eating one after the other, in a way that somehow seemed too elegant for this place, and I wondered what it would be like to be one of those guys who can just saunter over and introduce themselves. The football captain leaning on the locker. Maybe in the morning, I told myself; maybe I'd walk over and say hi; knowing that I wouldn't. *It's not you*, said the voice in my head. *You don't do things like that. You can't do things like that.* Another voice replied – *Brand New*.

A couple of hours later, and the sun was sloping off over the edge of the world. The period between dusk and dawn was always the most active, as most had spent their days sleeping off the excesses of the night before. A gangly hippie did cartwheel circuits of the fire, while his buddy gave chase on foot, pulling a girl behind him on a broken wooden sled. Charlie was referred to as a teacher, but if that was true, the class had been left unsupervised. That was about to change – everything was.

Just beyond the entrance, I became aware of a commotion. A few of us heard it, and turned as one towards the gate, shielding our eyes from the orange glare peering through the trees. A large crowd was entering camp, twenty or thirty strong. Right away, something was off. They were striding with intent, and even at a distance, you could tell by their threads, they weren't the usual Eden clientèle; dress shoes, slacks, the first necktie to pass the threshold. When they got close enough to see their faces – men and women – they were old, too. There had been older people in camp; burnouts, widows, old hippies who'd never found somewhere to settle; but these newcomers weren't like that. They were, as they'd say at Eden, normies, and as always, the sight of a normie had the zoo behavior kicking right in. Once you get a whiff of squares, the game is on.

I jogging across to the gates, throwing myself into the jeers and sarcastic applause that was flung from Charlie's Camp Eden. The group of adults stared us down, unamused and unflinching. A middle-aged man with circular sweat patches under his arms was the first to speak.

"Where is he?"

"Here he is," replied one of our girls, lifting her top and jiggling her dime-nippled breasts. "...*and* his best friend!" Cheers erupted on our side. The olds responded with looks of disdain, the tuts and head-shaking of a fart being shooed from a library. I heard myself shout "Nice patches, sweaty," and though the laughter that followed was from weed-heads who'd giggle at a cloud, it felt good. I wondered where the beautiful girl was, and if she'd found it funny too. A bedraggled guy with dark rings under his eyes who'd once told me his name was Bilbo pushed to the front and approached the group. There was a huge doob pinched in his lips, which he took between his fingers and offered to the sweaty man. Sweatstains slapped it out of Bilbo's hand with a hard thwack, turning the playful lip into harder shouts of "Hey!" and "Fuckin' pig!" Someone on our side shoved someone on their side. His buddies held him back, pulling him away and into the crowd, but the atmosphere had been changed. There was a sharper edge now, as though everyone in camp had recognized them for what they were; foreign invaders. It felt like something terrible was about to happen.

"Fuck you!" cried Us.

"Give me back my daughter!" Them. The two groups stood like opposing armies, one side waiting to charge. Shirts peeled off; arms outstretched in macho posturing. "Fuck you, old man!" My mind flashed to news footage of violent street clashes; tear gas and riot shields, flowers in gun barrels, and soft young faces bouncing off the sidewalk. A hippie stepped out into the no-man's land between the two masses, his sinewy arms out by his sides, veins taut and full.

"Come on and come on then, motherfuckers!"

The adults didn't break, staring back with steely eyes, any fear hardened by something I thought I saw bubbling beneath the surface; revulsion or just "no more." One had his hands balled into fists, his pink neck thick with tension. I couldn't take my eyes off him, waiting for the moment he'd lose it and come out swinging. My pulse was banging against my temple, as bodies jostled with an energy that felt like someone squeezing on a balloon. One punch would put a match to the fuse and send us all sky high. I knew the old man's glare was something to be heeded. After days of idleness in the so-called dangerous cult, I finally felt afraid. I finally felt alive.

In the frozen breath before the Big Bang, every head turned to the guttural buzzing sound that cut through the rabble. A dune buggy was tearing down the path from the main house, with a lone figure astride. Three more followed behind, each with two riders; an Old West posse in leather and dirty cotton. The tattered figure leading the pack was lean and poised, body bucking with the bronco motion of the buggy, and long hair billowing. Charles Manson skidded the vehicle to a showy stop three feet from the protesters and dismounted. They regarded the unarmed, smiling Manson like you would an unfamiliar dog, who might nuzzle affectionately at your feet or make a mess of your throat with his fangs. Maybe it was seeing him framed against normals rather than his own kind, but rarely did you appreciate just how small Charles Manson was. He wasn't stumpy like a midget, but perfectly proportioned, with reed-thin limbs and the girlish frame of a little sister. Next to a full-grown man, he stood shoulder-height, and yet somehow seemed bigger than everyone. All that fear and hatred and respect and rage; the eyes of the world that one hot summer; all because of that little man. You could see in the faces of the invaders they knew they were facing down an icon. Everyone with that teeth-grinding anticipation, dying to hear the first thing that'd come out of his mouth.

"Hayjakoo-bu-bu-bu-deebajocadja!" said Manson, flailing his arms, and twirling in a strangely graceful, utterly bizarre free-form dance. "Jacoomacacha-hu-hu-goomooma-ga-ga!"

Team Eden met the gibberish with laughter and fist-pumping cheers. "That's our Charlie," you could hear them thinking, "freaking out the normals," but as a normal myself, I too was freaked. Manson's back-up hung ten paces behind, with an amused nonchalance. The man himself had a glint in his eye that was pure mischief.

"You're not going to intimidate us, *Manson*," said the sweaty man, "and nobody's impressed by that little show. It's not difficult to be weird." Manson turned, eyebrows up in his scalp, with a look that said '*get a load of this guy*,' and I caught myself laughing.

"Well, what can I help you with?" said Manson. "You're up here on my land with my people, can I take that as your proclamation that you'd like to join us?"

"Yeah, join us!" came a shout.

"Otherwise, I'm gonna have to assume – 'cuz of that ugly, jealous world out there; that tiny little world you all come from – I'm gonna have to assume you're here to upset my family." He gestured towards us – all of us – and a glow of pride flushed my skin, followed by a smaller, duller ripple of shame. "Did you come up here to hurt my family?"

"What do you know about family?" came a voice that was cracking with emotion. A heavy man with a large, red face stepped out of the pack toward Manson. He was clearly nervous, but his speech was carried through on a greater wave of anger. "I came for my daughter," said fatty, "my *real* family, not that you'd understand, common criminal…"

"Now I *know* you're lying," replied Manson. "We're all Brand New in here. We got no parents. No bosses. No wives or husbands, professors or pastors. Just got each other."

"Cheryl, honey…" The fat man had spotted somebody in the crowd, a shy looking girl arm in arm with a chick on either side. He took a few steps towards his daughter, causing Manson's lieutenants to prick into alertness. Manson waved them back with a gesture. "Oh, thank God, you're alright. Just come on home now. Come on." Fatty outstretched a hand towards her. "Come on, sweety. Let's just go home and forget all about this." Clark craned his head around me to get a better look, nobody sure how it would play out.

Giving the dad the skunk-eye, one of the girls holding Cheryl's hands whispered softly into her ear, and then, in that mocking babygirl voice I'd heard by the gas station, Cheryl spoke.

"Or you could let my friends suck your prick. Would you like that, daddy?" Uproar. Cheryl beamed with wicked delight, while the sound of her father's cracking heart was drowned out by raucous cheers. A guy in a leather vest lifted Cheryl by the waist, high into the air, spinning her in celebration, and when the conquering heroine came back to Earth, she was swallowed up, enclosed in the safety of fifty half-dressed bodies; cornered animals who'd do anything to protect their own. Names began to call out, desperate parents, guardians and concerned citizens trying to reclaim their lost.

"Michael?"

"Gracie? I see you there..."

"Jessica? Jessica Strope? Has anybody seen my daughter? Please... she's blond, green eyes, sixteen years old... Jessica, are you here?" Those whose parents stood across from us were embarrassed or amused, but they'd been buoyed by Cheryl's resistance and the strength of her stand, and huddled among the arms of new friends. Who could show weakness now? Who could take that shameful walk past Charlie, who'd fought for their freedom and called them Family; the walk that'd say *I reject you*? Instead, the kids of Eden began calling out in response. There were shouts of "Roy!" and "Spartacus!" and "Mickey Mouse!"

"Hairy Asshole? Has anyone seen my Hairy Asshole?" I wondered how I'd have reacted had I caught my mom's voice on the breeze. Would I have slunk out the gate and back into the world, or stood among the longhairs and the dope-heads, chest puffed in false bravado? If the beautiful girl's parents were there, aiming to snatch her from us, would she stand firm too? Amid the chaos, Manson stood, taking it all in, the gentle draft in the nexus of the storm, those eyes of his betraying nothing of what went on behind.

"Well you see," said Charlie, his soft voice cutting underneath the din and signalling by its presence alone that all be quiet, "there's no locks here; no chains. Everyone's free to come and go as they please. If the Cheryls and the Gracies and the Jessica Stropes want to be with you, then be with you they shall. And if they want to be here, the Cheryls, the Gracies..." As he recited their names, Charlie pointed at each, a light prance in his step, their faces ablaze with the thrill of recognition. With an arm playfully draped around a tiny little thing in oversized pants – "the Mickey Mouses... then here is where they'll be. I can no more tell them where to be or who to be than you can. Who are any of us to be controlling somebody else?"

"Control people? That's what you do, goddamn cult leader, with your brainwashing and your mind control..."

"Cult?" said Charlie, chuckling like it was the most ridiculous thing he'd ever heard. "Brother, if you wanna be nice, you're welcome to stay. Plenty of love to go round..." Cheryl's father had heard enough. Incensed, he lunged towards Manson, who calmly sidestepped.

"Murderer!" he shouted. "Sick murderer!" The rest of their crowd began shouting too, words like *killer* and *beast.*

"See, here it is, that outside world; those outside *them* thoughts, coming in *here*," said Charlie, "you're the ones trying to murder these kids! Murdering thoughts and ideas, beautiful souls strangled at birth. You come into our home, shouting your threats and your insults, thinking you'll drag them back into a 'home' they don't wanna be in; a prison. You know, you can lock that little girl in a room, but you can never lock away her spirit. You can't put a manacle on hope. What are you all so afraid of? Maybe that I'll hear about the nasty things *you* did; the things that brought these children to me?"

"Screw you, Manson!" came the cry, this time a female voice. A mother, pushed to the brink. Both sides began to advance, shoving, heaving packs of people, preparing for that rush into battle, sword on sword, fist on face.

"You know what," said Charlie, "it's time to leave." I watched intently, fingernails digging into my palms, wondering if the Manson character from the news reports would show up, to whip a switch-blade from his boot and stick someone in the ribs.

"Yeah, fuck off!"

"Fuckin' cocksuckers!" I turned to Clark, in case the warlike atmosphere had triggered a flashback of torching a Viet Cong orphanage, but all I saw was a blackened log from the fire, sailing through the air. It arced across the cooling sky, over Charlie's head, and landing with a heavy clunk on the forehead of the sweaty man. That sound was the starting pistol that set everything going to shit.

From the first roar that went up as Sweaty hit the floor, Eden Ranch hit a mad scramble to grab anything they could. Charlie just watched, arms folded and grinning, as a rain of logs, rocks, dirt, shoes, and whatever came to hand rained on the adults, soundtracked by a thunderous deluge of "Fuck off!" and "Piggy!" Covering their heads, the intruders turned tail and retreated to the exit. We gave chase, palming Red Indian whoops at their fat little frightened legs scrambling for safety, and I felt a rush of energy like nothing I'd experienced. My blood felt hot and fast under my skin. By the time they'd scuttled back into their world, the first victory song was already chiming. I stood beneath the wooden sign with a small log in hand,

and I slung it sideways through the air as hard as I could. My bulging eyes followed its spinning trajectory, through and down to its eventual end; square in the back of a man in a suit who sacked to the floor. As he hit the dirt, I felt an arm around my shoulder; Bilbo. Together we watched another old guy heaving his friend back up to his feet.

"We'll be back" he said, from a safe distance. "This ain't over, Manson."

"Go on, fuck off, drags," shouted Bilbo, "fuck off back to your rules, freedom-rapers!" He slapped my back, and I suddenly realized that Manson was standing right next to us, so close I could have heard him breathing if not for the sounds of high-fives and celebration shaking the camp. I don't know if it was fear, or celebrity, or the adrenaline rush of what just happened, but I felt my body lightly tremble, as Charlie stared down that path like he could somehow meet their gaze half a mile away. Then he turned, strolling back to the buggy and casually starting it up.

"Good arm, man," said Bilbo, before wandering off. I couldn't believe what I'd seen. All those people; the type of people you spend your life being told are in charge; the ones you have to listen to; the ones with all the power. It wasn't true. One little guy, barely raising his voice, he took all that power like it was nothing.

That night was spent with Eden Ranch partying like never before – with purpose. Beer, weed and pussy flowed like the last days of Rome. I chatted with some guy for a good ten minutes before I realized a girl was jerking him off inside his jeans, and even Clark disappeared with a couple of skirts to get his donger wet. I figured I should finally let my hair down, and guzzled a beer as I danced with a couple of chicks in front of the fire. But even after everything that happened, Charlie still didn't come down. Some of his girls did though, strolling from the big house to join us.

One of them walked right over, like she'd singled me out, zeroing in like a jungle beast chasing down its prey. With wild hair and wicked eyes, she handed me a joint. I puffed on it for the first time, spluttering a sweet tasting cloud at the girl from the house on the hill, who giggled like you would at a kitten surprised by its own tail.

She told me her name was Jem, "...like diamonds," although she used to be called something else, and that she was from Texas. She took my hand and lead me out behind one of the barns, where she pulled aside her shorts and fucked me in the dirt. Like everything that had happened there, it was strange and dreamlike, as though viewed from a great distance. Though I thought I should be feeling something, there was nothing much beyond finally getting it over with, and "that felt nice on my dick." After she emptied me out, like she was icing a birthday cake, we lay there on the grass for a little while.

"I broke you in, boy," she said, "like a horse," in that jokey, nothing-matters way all the girls spoke, before slapping my butt and walking off into the night. Everything at Eden was so goddamn casual and carefree, it was hard to be stressed. When I finally crashed around daybreak, I wondered how many other guys Jem had laid with that night, but didn't care. I'd been thinking about that other girl anyhow. Asleep under the stars, with dreams of giant burning sunflowers marching on Washington, my only worry was how dull the rest of my life was gonna feel.

A couple of hours later, I was wrenched out of my

sleep by shouts. I could barely remember where I was, as I peeled open dusty eyes that creaked as they swivelled in their sockets. On all sides, there was harried movement and raised voices; some in anger, others distress. In the confusion, my focus fell on the sight of an older man lightly grappling with a half-dressed girl who was seated on the ground. His hands were clasped around her arm, and he was trying to pull her to her feet, but she sandbagged him, her butt dragging along the dirt. That was the story all across camp, with shoving and pulling and screaming between old and young. Instinctively I looked for Clark, like the primal instinct of a lost child to call for its mother.

Over by the entrance, the returning protesters were piling through the gate in far greater number, this time bringing placards and banners, and television news crews. Parked just outside was a WKLA van with a satellite dish on the roof, and at least three LA County squad cars. I hung back and watched the chaos from a distance, half expecting to be tackled from behind by my own father. For the most part, the mob marched together as a single unit, while the parents who could no longer control themselves scuffled with their wayward children, tugging or pleading or giving chase. A hand-painted banner held high above the heads of the protesters, read "MURDERER!" in dripping letters that looked as though they'd been slashed into the flesh of the card. Another read "CHILD-STEALER." A TV cameraman focussed on the sign, before swinging back around toward the action of the ranch.

This wasn't like yesterday. In numbers, or perhaps with the film crews at their backs, they'd found bravery; reclaimed that power. They knew the watching audience would be on their side. My heart sank heavy, knowing this signalled the end. Truthfully, it was a miracle things lasted as long as they had, and the much-delayed decision to go back home had finally been made for me. I pulled my jacket over my head like a courthouse-steps babyfucker, and looked for the clearest path to safely scoot out without being seen. The disguise wasn't to save myself from the lecture of a father whose buddies had seen me "scrapping with the police on that tee-vee," but the thought of how disappointed my new friends would be when they saw me taking a powder. "Well, shit," they'd say, "Tom was just a phony. We wasn't one of us at all..." But the protesters seemed to outnumber us, blocking off the exit, with cameras pointed directly into the fray, and there was no way through.

A bracing chant of "*Mur-der-er! Mur-der-er!*" began to fill the air, like the choking stench of a beautiful field being razed to ash. The early morning raid had caught us unawares, putting everything off rhythm, unlike the tight single unit of the previous day.

A small slip of a girl faced down the advancing pack, bravely and firmly standing her ground.

"*Mur-der-er! Mur-der-er! Mur-der-er!*"

"Don't you talk about him that way!" she yelled.

"He's just a man," came the reply, "less than that. He's scum!"

"*Mur-der-er! Mur-der-er! Mur-der-er!*"

Of all the ways for everything to come unravelled, this was the most crushing, having the grown-ups sweep in to put an end to our foolishness, like they told us they would, our whole lives. Babyish ideas of freedom and harmony, in a land with no rules, and of hot girls I'd never see again.

"*Mur-der-er! Mur-der-er! Mur-der-er!*"

A raggedy shoe spun into the crowd, but was slapped away. An impotent protest, captured for posterity by television cameras, to be broadcast as a warning against daring to dream. Stray outside the path and you'll be slapped down too.

"*Mur-der-er! Mur-der-er! Mur-der-er!*"

Bilbo sprung towards one of the adults, socking him in the jaw with a wild swinging punch. They rolled clumsily together in the dust like a long-brewing Thanksgiving fight between father and son. Still they came, moving forwards, backing us away towards the house.

"*Mur-der-er! Mur-der-er! Mur-der-er! Mur-der-er!*"

"Stop!"

Everything went quiet and still, like he'd knocked the record off the needle. On top of the huge boulder, looking down on the rest of camp, stood Charles Manson, a fire in his eyes that could have scorched the world. His outline was bathed in the light of the morning sun, and I was terribly afraid of the words that were about to come out of his mouth, and the havoc they'd bring.

"I told you," said Charlie, enunciating each syllable with stark emphasis. "It's all about love, all of it, *everything*. And you try to poison that. Is this how you people behave? Look at yourselves. You're beasts. This isn't love, it's—"

It was a rock. Small, heavy, hard.

The only thing that could have stopped him from speaking had been thrown by the Sweaty Man, striking Charlie clean in the forehead. The collective gasp was so great, I swear the sky moved a little closer. Charlie didn't drop, didn't fall. He stood, hunched, on top of the rock, and wiped his forehead with a hand that was steady as can be.

"You see what these pigs do?" said Charlie, suddenly showing his temper for the first time. I could feel myself shaking. My legs began to wobble beneath me.

"*Don't faint,*" I thought, "*please, not here...*" I forced some deep breaths down my tightening throat, but the world felt loose and my head span dizzily.

"Who are you to tell these children anything?" Every eye upon him, every lens flickering, Charlie held aloft a hand that was smeared with his own blood. "*Look at what they did!*"

My legs shook violently. I was passing out.

No, not dizzy, not *me* – it was... it was the ground. The ground was shaking; *swaying*. Everybody started to scream. Then they started to fall. The Earth below let out a deep rumble, as though so pained by what she saw, she could take no more. All around was pandemonium; the end of the world. Bodies fell into bodies; wails of fear; the crash of uprooting trees. I threw myself to the floor and lay on my chest, where the planet grumbled beneath me – Mother Earth's death rattle. As I lay sprawled, I was hypnotised by the barn behind where I'd had my first poke of snatch, which gently wobbled to and fro, like it was made of paper.

As quickly as it started, it was over.

In the stillness of the afterglow, nobody moved. Some lay crouched and cowering, too afraid to open their eyes to the blackened wasteland they feared would be waiting. Charlie, atop the rock, was still standing, and looking out over the field of the fallen. From the city below, the far-off shrieks of sirens mewed their way up into the hills, smoke billowing high from the buildings and streets that had shunned our kind and now laid cracked and burning. The first to make a move was a protester, who heaved himself to his feet and sprinted out of the camp like the Devil was at his back. Others followed, with panic-painted faces, leaving their signs where they fell and scrambling back to their world so frantically, they tripped over their own feet.

I watched from my place on the floor, with no sounds but the whimpers and huffs of frightened men and women fleeing for their lives, dragging heavy cameras, dragging each other, desperate to get away from Charles Manson before he called the seas across the land to drown us all. Two didn't run. A professional-looking guy in a suit and a middle-aged woman. They rose, as we now did, casting their gaze toward Charlie with fearful reverence.

"Charlie shook the Earth!" came a shout. As one, we walked towards the rock and gathered below, surrounding our bloodied leader, hands outstretched, just wanting to touch, to connect with the man whose rage and love had shaken the planet from its axis. Charlie dove into our arms. He was caught and embraced, and tossed high into the air with a cheer they'd have heard from their crumbling buildings. We surfed him around the camp on our hands; Poseidon riding on the waves of his own creation, to the sounds of ecstatic weeping. With King Charlie held aloft, another chant broke out.

"*Char-lie! Char-lie! Char-lie!*" This was backed by a second mantra, threading through and under and in the first like a melody.

"*Love! Love! Love! Love! Love!*"

4 MAUNDAY WEDNESDAY

They called it the San Fernando Earthquake, but most people here say they know different. Eight days ago, Charles Manson raised his hand in anger and the ground shook beneath our feet. I wouldn't go so far as to say it made a believer out of me, but nor did I feel like I could leave just yet. So there I was, still eating dumpster food and wearing communal pants.

The feeling in the wake of the incident was that we were completely untouchable, having witnessed the dawning of humanity's second age. Many walked aimlessly in a teary daze, speaking of Christ's return, saying how this must be what it was like in Jerusalem. The barefoot rapture of that day was rocked by a series of aftershocks, each met with jubilation, and everyone looking towards Charlie, his arms raised skyward like the rain-maker who'd healed the crops. People would drop to their knees, literally bowing before him, but he'd always shake his head and lift them right back up.

"No human should kneel before another," he'd said. I watched one girl fall to the floor and kiss Charlie's feet. He responded by giggling playfully and kissing hers in return.

Some of the aftershocks were so big, it felt like the end times, as though this would be the one to crack the Earth in two, and we'd all tumble down and never hit bottom. Nobody seemed to care. Not even me. If the end did come, we'd embrace it with open arms. It was exhilarating to feel a part of something, even if that was the end, and whatever new beginnings were to follow. That kind of far-out shit suddenly seemed possible. Everything was strange now; different; like all the rules and laws, and the way things were supposed to be had been wiped away. I wasn't speaking in tongues or having old scars healed by Charlie's breath, but I'd felt *something*. I didn't know what, only that I was glad to be on the right side. Like someone said, if there's a guy who can grab the world by the lapels and show it who's boss, you wanna be right there with them. And we weren't the only ones who saw it that way. The protesters' raid on camp had made news all across the world, and in the days that followed, a steady stream of new members flowed through the gates. They were so stirred by those images in their living rooms, of shaking earth, and of the righteous and the respected turning heel and running from the so-called criminal, that their old lives had lost all meaning the second the cameras fell to the floor. Sixty-five people died that day, out in their world, but hundreds, maybe thousands more, across the planet, were reborn. They'd start on the path to living for the very first time, beginning the instant they stepped over the threshold at Eden Ranch and became Brand New. But all those people and all that exposure brought with it something else – paranoia.

With so many new faces, Charlie and his generals

started tightening shit up. It was weird to see hippies getting organized, but with the whole world seeing what he was capable of, he knew there'd be narcs and undercover journos looking to walk among us and bring us down or sell us out. First order of business was for all to hand over their personal possessions; ID, money, clothing; nothing, said Charlie, could belong to any one person. Ownership of *stuff* and *things* was a piggy conceit. What little cash I had, along with my rucksack and its contents, was swiped by a biker with a handlebar moustache and tattoo of Snow White sucking her own tits. Clark was less willing to part with his things, gripping onto his wallet like a dog with a boot. When they'd tried to take the ring on his finger, he started spazzing so bad, they let him keep it.

The biggest barn was designated as the communal wardrobe, and whenever you needed a fresh change of threads, you just picked something off the pile. What's yours is ours. Some girls took laundry duty using big tin baths outside the house, but nobody had spare, so you went to the barn or you went naked. I rode it out as long as I could, but all the sitting around in dirt, plus that time I'd been surprised by a strong wind when taking a leak, had left my jeans pretty filthy. Inside was a mountain of faded tie dye and ripped-up denim, with the shirtless and pantless rooting around like rag-pickers at the city dump. Empty outfits hung on the roof beams; the ghosts of the people who'd walked through the gates and no longer existed; shedded skins from the creatures who'd crawled out of the filth of man and evolved a pair of legs to walk wherever they pleased. A shirt that'd been bought for a job interview; shoes that had walked to see grandma; pants that'd sat at family dinners – everyone's and no-one's. The person that used to fit inside had been broken into pieces and mixed in a giant stew with all the bits of everyone else, and whatever combination you picked out, you'd be wearing the mix and match uniform of the outcast. I yanked out a black sweater with a tatty hole that exposed my shoulder like a teasing cheesecake pin-up. As I pulled it over my head, I thought about a show I'd seen on the Nazi death camps, and an enormous trunk filled with thousands of pairs of glasses.

I'd now been there so long that names and faces were finally starting to click. A new guy hiked up from the city a few days back. He was wide-eyed as he strode across the lawn, hands on his hips and breathing hard, and collapsed into the dirt with a sigh, like it was a comfortable settee after a hard day. After quaffing back a plate of beans so fast he almost choked, Jedro Haze – "Not my real name, just something people will remember..." – told me how he'd moved out to Hollywood in search of fortune and glory, but got knocked back for every audition, casting and showcase he could bullshit his way into, and found himself waiting tables.

"I swear to Christ," said Jedro Haze, in a thick Southern accent that was comical when you thought about it in the pictures, "I could have bussed shit back home. Diners and factories filled with people from high school. Assholes who never aimed higher than three kids and a job you take to the grave. How could I fuckin' go back and tell them about my 'great adventures' scraping by like they do? I made such a big noise about coming out here to be a star. It was my destiny, man! 'Fuck y'all, I'm not going out like that!' Then I'm selling my guitar to pay the rent in some shitty-ass apartment where I can't sleep 'cuz I can hear the bugs fuckin' in the walls, and I'm like, this is what Lady Fate had in mind? This was the cosmic pull towards Hollywood I felt my entire fuckin' life? Star on the Walk and a slot on *Sullivan*? City of dreams? Then I see this guy with his bloody hand, and I'm like, goddamn, man, maybe that's why I came out here in the first place! Why else would I have stuck that shit out? I was taking an order, right? Some wiseass all Billy Big-Dick in front of his girl, calling me 'boy'. Then the fuckin' diner starts shaking. Cups and plates rattling, tip jar rolling off the counter, smashing on the floor, coins at my feet. Billy Big-Dick diving under a table and screamin' louder than his girl. If that ain't a fuckin' sign.."

"You ever been on TV?" said Clark.

"Nah. Parked Warren Beatty's car once. It smelt like lavender. He gave me a buck. Oh – I was almost in The Monkees."

"Oh yeah?"

"Yeah. Just got out here a few years too late, is all. If I'd been around in '66, I'd have nailed that shit. Bad timing."

"Well, shit," said Clark, "you been around the other day, you could've finally got yourself on the boob tube."

"Hey, yeah," I said, "did you see us?" I was teasing, but for all I knew, I had my own reputation back home.

"I waved to my mom and everything!" said Clark. "Did they show my teen idol features? Look at this profile." He turned, jutting out his chin and running a finger down the length of his face. He could be fun when he was relaxed. Though, when the cameras had come, he'd suffered a major freak attack, hidden his face in his hands and run for cover.

"Whatever," said Jedro, "least I ain't in a fuckin' factory..." He trailed off as his eyes followed the peachy-round asses of a pair of passing girls, "Jesus Christ, that's what I'm talking about." He looked at us as if to get our permission to ditch.

"Oh, please," I gave a 'new guy' roll of the eyes towards Clark, as Jedro Haze took off with a wink and a finger-gun, finally living the dream.

"Another one," said Clark.

"Another what?"

"Another of those folks looking for something. A home, or a family, something to fill that empty space, or... fuck, I dunno, a little peace. Fresh start, like me. Like all of us."

"Maybe that's my problem. I ain't looking for anything."

"Just 'cuz you ain't looking, don't mean you can't find it."

"Oh hey," I said, "there's my shirt!"

"Changing the subject, Mr. 'I'm going home tomorrow and tomorrow and tomorrow'?"

"No, dude, it's my Dead t-shirt." Torn in the back where I'd snagged it off a nail, it hung off the tiny frame of the girl who wore it like an XXL slung over a fence-post on a hot afternoon.

"Hey," I shouted, "Dead-Shirt!" She stopped as I jogged over, full of cockiness, full of Brand New. "Looks a little big for you." Her turning round was all it took for the New Tom swagger to scarper and leave me with my jittery anxieties. It was the blonde girl. My heart did a beat so hard I'm surprised we didn't both fall over.

"Oh, was this yours?" she said, half-wary like I was

gonna wrestle her to the ground and take it back.

"It was, I mean... nobody owns anything, right? That's what Charlie said..." The Girl nodded, sneaking a nervous glance to the side. "I was just kidding, anyway. I don't even like the music, really, I just thought the skeletons were cool."

"They are!" She flashed a smile; a big, bright, sunrise on the morning after the apocalypse, everything's okay grin, an igniting spark that lit her eyes, and then the whole world. "Imagine if you had x-ray eyes..."

"Huh?"

"That's what we'd all look like," she tugged the shirt out towards me, stretching the design, "just bones, running around. And wherever you went, there'd be dogs chasing you." I laughed, but wondered if eyes that beautiful could see right into my soul and know all my dirty secrets; X-Ray Spex and the time I shat myself on a Ferris Wheel, everything laid out for those coffee browns of hers, like a hidden jerk-mag falling out of a textbook.

"So yeah... I don't want it back, it was just... I dunno, like seeing an old friend or something," I said.

"That's cool. An old friend with a new friend inside. Judy," she said, extending a hand.

"Tom," I replied, clasping her warm little hand inside mine. We stood for a moment, locked in a politeness that was strangely rare at Eden Ranch. The last girl who'd introduced herself to me did so by dry humping my back and blowing pot-smoke into my mouth. In those seconds with Judy, I was aware of nothing else – the crackle of the fire, the laughter of a guy on LSD scorching his balls with a lighter – it all just scooted off into the distance.

"Better go," said Judy, gently sliding her fingers free, "I've been helping out with the babies."

"Babies?"

"Yeah, Charlie says children should be raised by everybody. Parents just make them into another version of themselves, you know? Like a ventriloquist dummy. They feed them milk, but they feed them how to think too, right? It's not cool, that's what Charlie says. He says it's unhealthy for them to get attached to just one person. Children need love and learning from everyone. Imagine this whole place, everyone here, loving those kids like they were their own. I wish I could've grown up with that much love, even a little piece..."

"So you've been up in the house? You've talked to him?"

"Oh *yeah*," she replied, her voice coated with passion, and eyes more alive than ever. "God, you haven't met him yet? You so should. I mean, why are we here, right?" I nodded out a *yeah*, but knew it didn't work the same for guys as it did for beautiful girls. A lot of bods had gone up to that house, but none were packing penises and bad posture. "I really gotta go though. See you around?"

"Yeah, for sure," I said. "Well, I have to get back soon, back home I mean, but I might catch you before I go." Her face dropped, just a little, but enough to leave me both elated and crushed. Then I heard myself tell her "you never know though, right?"

"Right!" she said, smiling, "anyways..." She threw up a nonchalant wave, beamed that smile for the last time and pirouetted on her heel, a gawky little spin, graceful clumsiness. I watched the entire walk back to the house; wayward steps cutting a lazy zig-zag; long, blond ringlets falling over a t-shirt that was way too big. I stood with her parting gift, a warm, radiating feeling in my belly like I'd quenched a hunger but at the same time was starving for more. My daze was interrupted by the yell of Clark's voice.

"Took you long enough, you dick..."

That night, I sat looking at the stars and playing the conversation over in my head so many times, it was like a shitty drama club remake of a movie none of the cast had seen. For a while I watched Clark sleep. Occasionally, you'd get the feeling he'd actually become that new person, but most times, all you could see was the shambles from the bus. He'd be fine, and then something would throw him off. There was no rhyme or reason to it. A new face or a turn of phrase, or a loud noise would trigger the projector inside his head, and you could feel the anxiety rushing in like when you open a hot oven. At times he'd have to go off to be by himself, while other days you could tell he'd rather die than be alone, and he'd overcompensate by being loud and social, shouting down the voices in his head with the din of drunken laughter. He was asleep on the ground beside me, flat on his back and taking slow, peaceful breaths. I needed to clear my head with a stroll, so left him to it. From behind, I heard Clark gasp himself awake.

It was some time later when I had my first proper taste of Charlie Manson – my first real chance to hear the words that'd been deemed so dangerous the outside world didn't want us to listen. Those who'd never seen for themselves were convinced that he'd turn us into killers; the false prophet of madness, murder and hate. The only acts of violence I'd witnessed so far at Eden had come from the hands of the protesters who came to 'save' us.

"Just like the good old days."

That was the first thing he said. Something your dad might say, kids home from college for the weekend. And that's how it felt, like daddy had finally come home, sat at the head of the table for family mealtime.

The whole camp was there that night, in a semi-circle around the fire, buzzing but trying not to show it. Charlie sat at the center, but there was no throne, no air of superiority. He was just there, eating the same mushy food from the same little wooden bowl, cross-legged on the bare, February grass. Seeing everybody together for the first time really made you appreciate all the different walks of life who'd found connection there, all together for the same reason. One man – the man who'd shook the world – had the folks outside so afraid, and yet everyone in there with him felt safe, many for the first time in their lives. My soul was full, surrounded by kin with whom I broke bread, not because we shared the same blood, or arbitrarily found ourselves in the same canteen, but because we'd all chosen to be there, together.

My meal waited uneaten in my lap, with the unspoken agreement that nobody started until everyone was ready. When Charlie wasn't around, it was every man for himself, but we were on our best behavior tonight. As the food was dished out, Freck, a small red-headed girl, and one of Charlie's lieutenants, surveyed the crowd like a prairie dog peering out of its hole, neck taut and extended, head moving from left to right, right to left, seeking out those who dared to disrespect our home.

"Alright," said Charlie, "let's eat!" His cheeky grin would've changed the minds of the news if they could have seen it, and as he took his first mouthful, we all dug in.

Besides the sounds of smiles and yummy noises, we ate in silence. We knew why we were there; not to talk, but to listen.

"If people out there are afraid of us, don't you think they have reason to be? They're afraid of what we can achieve, of all that we can do *together*. They're all singular beings, these little cockroaches, scurrying around..." Charlie waggled his fingers on his head like antenna, "...all scampering in different directions, this way and that. But us, we're a united entity, all these minds and bodies and souls, running in a pack, like animals. Animals are so much smarter than man – why'd you think they survived so long?" Every head in that place was nodding, every eye fixed on Charlie, who stood in front of the flames, playing out scenes and ideas with his body, painting a mural on the air with words.

"You ain't running in a pack with those people out there, those so called families you came from... that's like tying yourself to a crazy horse, man. Sure, you're going somewhere, but that horse is dragging you through the dirt, taking you where he wants to go, and sooner or later, ain't nothin' for a crazy horse to do but run in circles till he falls down dead. There's no direction out there, there's nothing but fear. Everyone's afraid, *all the time*. Afraid of dying, afraid of living. There ain't no fear, man. I got no fear. I'll teach you all to stop living in that fear. There's only one thing those pigs truly need to be afraid of, and that's me. *Us*. If they try and stop what we're doing here, they'll really know fear..."

My whole body was restless and full of energy, like it was fighting the urge to rise from the floor and yell '*a-fucking-men!*' I wondered if those sat beside could hear the blood rushing through my veins; my brain crackling beneath my skull. On every face, I saw the same thing, eyes opening for the first time, overwhelmed by what they saw.

"Rules, and laws," said Charlie, the words leaving his mouth with disgust, as though spitting out the last globs of a heavy vomit, "to keep each other down, keep themselves down. Everyone's so busy stepping on the next guy's throat, they don't notice the hands around their own..." Charlie petered out and sat back down, calmly going back to his food. There was a hush, as everyone watched and waited. In the silence, a girl with a boy's haircut turned and mumbled something to the chick sitting next to her. Like a rattlesnake, Charlie lashed out with a backhand that struck her across the face.

The crack of flesh on flesh scattered my tranquillity like pigeons in the park. Charlie's face was a blank mask of calm, but I didn't know if the ground was gonna shake, or if birds would drop dead from the trees. Beside me, I could feel Clark's body tightening with anxiety. The girl with the shitty hair clasped her cheek in her palm, with this goofy love-lorn look on her face like she'd just been clit-flicked by The Almighty. Still chewing a mouthful of food, Charlie brushed a hand lovingly across her cheek, which was flushed a wounded pink. Somehow, it felt like we were intruding on a private moment, so I looked away, at the faces around the fire. What I mostly saw were peaceful smiles, like that of Judy's, while others stared at that girl like a hundred-foot tall green-eyed monster.

"That was *good* eatin'," said Charlie, flipping the empty bowl off the back of his hand and spinning it onto the grass. He draped his arms around the shoulders of two girls sat either side; pretty things. Charlie moved his hands towards the backs of their heads, gently guiding them forwards. They reacted to his touch as though it were something more than simple skin on skin. Charlie's hands, like a puppeteer, had the girls scoot across the grass on their knees and towards each other, until their faces were almost touching, before finally, their lips were softly mashing together. The girls giggled nervously, but soon began to kiss each other deeply. Charlie lifted his fingers free and stood clear, lightly swooshing his arms through the air as though conducting an orchestra. As they kissed, hands finding their way to faces and bodies, fingers caressing cheeks and the inside of thighs, we cooed with Fourth of July glee.

"Look at these sweethearts, ain't they beautiful?"

"You got that right, Charlie." "Woo!" "Hell, yeah!"

"Don't matter to me if you're a girl with big blue eyes and curves like Mansfield, or some dude with a pot-belly, you're all beautiful. *We* are all beautiful. Ain't no image in here you got to live up to, nothing I'm asking you to be except yourself. Keep open-minds, treat each other as equals, and we'll all be free. Only way to let this family down is by spreading that 'outside' fear, by keeping those minds closed and chained. Just be you. Just be free. You do that for me, and I'll never, never look at you and say 'you are a disappointment.' I promise you that."

At that moment, Charlie's eyes met mine, and I felt, like you always did when he spoke, that he was addressing me, and me alone.

"...nobody here cares about grades, or..." His lips were moving, but all I could hear was my father's voice, telling me I'd never be half the man he was.

"...all take care of each other..." He stood in the glow of the fire, sparks and floating embers flickering like comets pulled into the orbit of the great creator, the universe bending towards His word. His body shimmered behind the rising heat haze, as though he was a projected figment of our collective imaginations; a shared hallucination of those who'd waited their whole lives for unquestioning love and acceptance.

"We gonna get a performance now, huh?" said Clark. Charlie was on a buggy and halfway back to the house.

"Huh?"

"He's gonna play for us. You alright, man?"

"Nah, fine," I replied, "just thinking."

"Aw, you don't wanna do that. That's some dangerous shit. Hey, see when he clocked that chick? The fuck was that about?" I didn't answer. That was so long ago, and I didn't want to pollute my mind with its image. A chubby girl called Janey or Jonie, or something like that, pushed herself between us.

"He did it out of love, like everything else. That's all Charlie knows. Love, love, love!" Jonie-Janey twirled away into the crowds, lightly brushing her fingertips across everyone she passed, as though imparting luck or good wishes.

"Mm-hmm," said Clark, "this morning she told me Charlie breathed on a dead bird and it flew away. God, just think of all you could do."

"How do you mean?"

"Look around you, man. How many people here; hundred-fifty, two hundred?"

"Maybe, yeah."

"All these hot hippie chicks, bikers, regular guys like you and me, everyone hanging on his every word. Can you honestly say you'd be able to keep your feet on the ground, a hundred-fifty people..."

"And more every day." I nodded up towards the gate, where two girls, sixteen, seventeen, were arm in arm and practically skipping inside.

"See," said Clark, "he's recruiting. His own personal army. Think of all you could do with that." As if agreeing, the camp broke into spontaneous applause, and the sea of bodies parted to reveal Charlie, guitar in hand. Everyone flung themselves forwards to get the best seat by the fire, as Charlie clambered up onto the rock he'd been stood on when he got cracked in the head.

He sat with his legs dangling over the edge, looking down on us all, and idly plucking random, single notes with his fingers.

"Ol' Charlie's been busy. Shakin' hands, makin' deals. All those suits and ties you seen... a necessary evil, gonna take us where we need to go, put us where the whole world's gonna hear what we have to say. I'm laying down an album real soon..." The usual explosion of noise. Charlie didn't look up from his guitar, twanging and tightening the strings until we were done pumping our fists. "We're going out on the road. Gonna spread the word right across this nation. You think the Beatles and the Stones are big? Those cats out there ain't seen a thing." He strummed out a melody, his bare, dirty heels rhythmically kicking against the rock.

"She got a broken heart and a broken back..."

His voice was gentle and melodic, something you could barely imagine coming from that bedraggled little figure. It sang of ego and deception, of metaphors and allusions that were beyond my feeble understanding, and of love, always of love.

"...we got the love that'll open their eyes..."

That chorus, man, it found its way from Charlie's mouth into ours, back and forth and swirling round camp, pulling everyone to their feet. *"...we got the love that'll open their eyes..."*

I saw a toy once, on the desk of a friend's dad; little silver balls hanging in a row, and once you start it off, it keeps itself going forever. That's how it was, this one line, stronger and louder, swirling in unison. I felt it vibrating in my chest, *"...we got the love that'll open their eyes..."* Without thinking, a large circle formed around the rock, hand in hand, no man, woman or child left behind, everybody beautiful, everybody free, so natural, like how it must've been at the moment of creation, with Charlie at the center, the center of a world of his making, singing and swaying with a single voice.

"...we got the love that'll open their eyes..."

A salty taste slid into my mouth as I looked at all the circling faces, each so different, so unconnected – hippies, drop-outs, burnouts, the lost, the afraid, and a guy like me – but in the moment, each part of the same being, cogs in some vast machine, heads on a beautiful and ferocious monster, rising out of the ocean. Jedro Haze, frustrated failed superstar; Michael, forty-something father who'd left his family to come follow Charlie; Shanna, who'd spent her first days sobbing with homesickness; and Judy, beautiful Judy. The most exquisite creature I'd ever, the fire reflected in her eyes, so alive and vibrant. At that moment, with Charlie's words – all our words – on her lips, our gaze locked.

"...we got the love that'll open their eyes..."

Looking right at me, right into me, Judy smiled. In the midst of everything, in the spiritual fucking upheaval, from across the circle she gave an impish wink, an "I feel this too, and isn't it wonderful?" Just for me. I'd never been so connected, so wonderfully, utterly connected; to people, to the world around me. My spirit was so full I felt myself creaking at the seams. Not taking my eyes from hers, or she from mine, the world filled with song, I smiled back. It was a smile of release; of letting go. It was a smile that said, *"I'm home."*

5 THE LOTUS BIRTH

"Guess who?" I didn't have to. I knew those hands better than I knew my own. Soft, warm fingers, nails painted with tiny flowers and yellow smiley faces, or whatever took her mood at the time. Hands that had tossed balled-up grass into my mouth as I chilled, thrown peace signs and devil-horns and mischievous middle fingers, and tightly held onto mine as we sprinted away laughing, after drawing a huge dick shooting wads of jizz into the face of a political candidate on a city billboard.

"Wow..." I said, wheeling around.

"Do you like it?"

"You look real different. I mean, not in a bad way, just... it's very... it's gonna take some getting used to."

"I think it looks good," she said, striking a pose, with one hand cupped under her chin and that long, golden hair chopped to a boyish cut.

"But where'd my friend go?" I said.

"She ran away, she's gone." Judy wrinkled her nose in that way she always did, that never-serious-about-anything attitude that permeated every conversation, even when you wanted a straight answer or just the acknowledgement that some things, some feelings, mattered. "Say my name."

"Ju..." She mushed a finger against my lips.

"Melody," she replied, glowing, as though it gave her a kick just to hear herself say it out loud.

"Did you choose that, or did he?"

"Charlie." It was a rhetorical question. That's what he did, doling out new names like a sculptor scratching their initials onto the bottom of the latest piece, part of that Brand New, where old personalities and hang-ups were dismantled and rebuilt without all the pieces that held you back. Old names were a hangover from our parents' influence; the artist's signature on a soul that no longer existed.

I didn't mind, although it seemed like only chicks got the name-change deal. At least there was more dignity in Tom than those pricks with their self-given macho nicknames. A couple of weeks back, a new guy introduced himself to me with a wet handshake and faltering eye contact as Steve from Chicago. The next day, my "Hey, Steve," was replied to with "Oh, I'm called Snake-Eyes now, call me Snake-Eyes." Judy's haircut was another part of that ethos. People changed their looks all the time. Charlie was a chameleon, with each press-piece illustrated by a dozen photos of his various guises. Having anything but a free and easy attitude towards personal appearance got you pegged as someone who'd never really live. If you can't get a tattoo or shave your head on a whim, would you ever be willing to take a risk that really mattered? Someone who didn't understand might look at a beautiful young girl running a razor over her head and ask why, but someone who lived at Eden would ask, why not? It's like Charlie always said, no sense makes sense.

"I like it," I said, "it suits you."

"The hair or the name?"

"Both." Melody, as she was now known, pulled herself into me and fumbled with my wrist. I tried not to inhale her scent or think about kissing her. Attachments were bad. Relationships, monogamy; that's what they say. There is love, and it's all free, but it's meant for everybody, trading hollow fucks around the campfire.

"There. Later, skater." Melody gave me a sisterly peck on the lips and trotted away. A small, soft plait of golden hair was tied around my wrist. I waited until she was out of sight before lifting it to my nose and giving it a sniff. It didn't really smell of anything.

I was still unconsciously fiddling with it the next morning, as I sat hanging by the barn with Jedro Haze. Jedro, who could've done with a name change himself, was making out with a chick called Rosie. He went through skirts like pussy was going extinct. The guys who came to camp seemed to like the fucking most of all. Fucking and drugs, all for the low, low price of being Brand New. Jedro Haze loved both, but given the choice, he'd wear all the skin off his dick. Likewise, Clark's broken, little-boy-lost routine had made him into something of a mascot, like the school spaz adopted by the cheerleaders, and he was always getting dragged off somewhere to play.

"It's off the hook, man," said Jedro, briefly pulling himself free of Rosie's mouth, "finally got myself on an album, after all these years. Put myself out there so much – nothing, and *boom*! It just happens. Think we'll be on the liner notes?"

"Doubt it. It's just backing vocals and shit. There were, like, a hundred of us, they can't fit all them names on there. Be cool to hear it when it comes out though. Maybe we'll all go up there and listen to it." Jedro didn't answer, but he was right, it was weird to think of yourself coming out of speakers in people's bedrooms, even as one voice out of a hundred. I hadn't sung that loud anyways, at least, not as loud as the night we first heard that song. "*We got the love that'll open their eyes*" was the chorus to the closing track on Charlie's new album, *Free Inside*, recorded in the house at the top of the ranch, with backing vocals laid down by the big fire. They'd wanted it done in a studio, but Charlie refused, saying that would dilute the rawness and purity. He'd only make it on his own terms, so they brought in all this equipment and he laid it down right there. A week from now, it'd be released into the wild, spreading his message even further, and not just with words, but because of how music sticks a thing into your mind, like those little songs at the end of commercials. Oscar Mayer weiners, Uncle Poop-a-Lot's mini corncobs, and Charlie Manson.

The club gigs in LA never happened. Rats with too much time on their hands pressured the owners, kicking a stink with the press and getting the shows pulled. It didn't matter. Charlie didn't care. He was headed out on his own, supporting the new record all over the country. He'd got a hold of three old buses, for himself and whichever family members were along for the ride. We'd painted them up with slogans and signs, love-hearts and doobs, ready to roll through the streets of the United States. One cat called Max was a sign-painter at the funfair in his previous life, and he'd decorated the lead bus with the *Life* magazine portrait, with Charlie's eyes staring right out at the world as it went by, staring them all down. Except the logo now read *Lie*.

"Can you fuckin' imagine how many royalties he's gonna get?" said Jedro, extracting himself again, but with his free hand down the back of Rosie's pants. "The last two years have been one giant commercial. Bet Lennon wishes he'd been on trial for murder, or fuckin' Brian Wilson, raped a horse. You watch, once this hits, they'll all be trying that shit. Fuckin' courts will be full of rock stars copying the innovator, like they always do." I pictured Mick Jagger feeding a hooker into one of those machines that chew hunks of raw meat into sausages and laughed, and at that moment, a long, dark shadow fell across our feet.

"Tom?"

"Uh-huh," I said, looking up at the three girls staring down at me, hands on hips. Leading the pack was Freck, with a girl I'd seen around but never spoken to, and Amber-May, one of the chicks from that cooch-on-cooch action that night at the fire. As was her thing, Freck did all the talking.

"Charlie says it's time for you to move to the next level."

Before I had a chance to get nervous, we were striding across the ranch towards the entrance, drawing attention from anyone who was awake, with Freck tugging on my arm like a mother whose patience had worn to nothing. Passing a quizzical Clark, all I could do was shrug. As we got closer to the gate, I saw three dune buggies, with a girl waiting in the back car and the biker named Lowball leaning against the bumper.

"You're with her," said Freck. I climbed into the middle buggy, with Amber-May behind the wheel. I tried to read how it was gonna play, but she had that Eden girl wicked expression that gave away nothing but where she called home. Freck's buggy zoomed off out of the gate, with ours following behind and Lowball bringing up the rear. It was the kinda ride you'd pay a dollar for at the carnival, with the dirt roads that led out of camp pocked with bumps that shot you out of your seat. I clung to the roll bar just to keep myself from being tossed.

"Is Charlie coming?" I said, but couldn't hear my voice over the buzz of the engine. We finally got out onto open roads, where I could take in the gawps from the squares and the pigs of the city stopping what they were doing to watch us roar by. They knew who we were, and the grey worker drones and suburban moms would examine each face as it passed, in the hope of seeing Charlie himself, and even though they were doing their best to look offended at our presence in their world, you knew they couldn't wait to tell the story around the dinner table. "Darling, you'll never guess who I saw today..."

We pulled into a narrow road that eventually broke off to a dirt track leading out to the desert, the buggies keeping their tight formation, with me sandwiched in the middle. After twenty, thirty minutes of rickety off-road, Freck pulled to a stop, in a barren patch of rock and prickled brush, miles from civilization. Every direction looked the same, as far as you could see, like the background a cartoon character would run past, again and again, and where a man could easily disappear.

"We walk from here," she said, nodding in the direction of a bare sky that stretched off into forever. I was hit by a wave of dread, as I spotted the rusty pistol poking out the top of Lowball's pants. For the next couple of miles, we clambered across hot, cracked ground, with Lowball at my back. I wondered if they were trekking me out far enough to plug a bullet in the base of my skull and leave me to the birds. Gossip at Eden flowed like horse piss, and maybe some rumor about me had grown enough legs to run me down. Or perhaps I'd said or done something to cause upset.

Finally, we came upon a large rock, the size of a person and oddly shaped, like some shitty modern art sculpture that'd been hacked out by years of rain. The rock had a hole running through the middle, with a heavy-looking iron chain threaded through and around and locked into place. Without saying a word, the five of them encircled me, each with eager expressions I didn't much like, as though readying to yell "Surprise!" and reveal a candled cake made from human shit. Freck jostled me towards the rock with shoves, before taking me by the hand and snapping a metal handcuff around my wrist, with the other cuff locked around a link of the chain. A large plastic water cannister was tossed onto the ground by my feet. As I opened my mouth to protest, Freck roughly grasped my head with one hand and lower jaw with the other, while Amber-May shoved a handful of small green nubs inside; foul-tasting buds that looked like the heads of little cacti.

"Chew," said Freck, roughly clamping shut my jaw. The horrible, bitter taste would have seen me spit, had Freck not been holding on; her fingernails digging into my upper lip, as my body bucked and gagged. Lowball, gun in his belt, watched intently a few feet away, and alls I could do was whatever they wanted. Freck pinched my nose with her fingers, forcing me to swallow. It went down in one big lump that wanted right back out.

"Keep it all down," she said, "don't you dare." She forced my jaw together again, as I swallowed down the foul-tasting mush for the second time.

"Jesus God," I said, gasping for air, "what is that? Tastes like Death's cum."

"Here," said Freck, holding out another handful, "more."

"I can do it myself," I said, "let me do it myself." She stood waiting for the plate to be cleared, as I popped them in one by one, holding my nose as I chewed so's not to boke again. Twelve, in all, plus however many she'd stuffed in the first time.

"Open," she said, sticking out her tongue "blaaaah..." She examined the inside of my mouth and under my tongue. I pictured my insides boiling like a witch's cauldron, with green bubbles popping on the wall of my stomach. I'd done plenty of weed in my time at Eden, few hits of X every now and then, but I always skipped hallucinogens. I'd seen a couple real bad freak-outs during my first week, so I always found a way to say no. Until now.

"Is this gonna be alright?" I said, "cuz it seems like a lot."

"You're gonna let go of all that, boy," said the third girl, lightly slapping me around the cheek. She leant over, planting a small, wet kiss on my mouth, before backing away. I took a step towards her, but the chain jerked me still, holding me in place. Freck turned on her heel and began walking away, with the others following.

"Hey, what the fuck?" I yelled. Freck didn't even look back as she shouted –

"Best you sit tight. Shit's gonna kick in real soon."

"You're leaving me? It's hot as fuck out here!"

"You've got water," said Amber-May, "see ya!" As they disappeared over the rocks and out of sight, I swear even Lowball was laughing.

"Are you coming back?" No answer. A rising wave of panic crashed over me, and I tugged at the handcuff, yanking so hard that the metal dug a bloody clump of skin out of my wrist. The chain around the rock gave me about six feet at full stretch, like an angry bulldog in a Tom and Jerry, but it was so heavy that, when fully taught, it was like being dragged straight to Hell.

I found myself fingering at the soft, golden bangle that had been placed around my other arm the previous day, as I looked for an escape, or for a head popping up from behind a cactus with a "*Just kidding!*" Neither came. The glare of the noonday sun was so bright that I could barely keep my eyes open, and the old Outside Tom insecurities were coming right back. This was all just some cruel prank, where the nerd had been lured into the desert by the popular girls, and left to die like a stray, dusty-mouthed and tripping in the sun.

Stay calm. I just had to stay calm. It was obviously a thing they did. I'd seen people taken away before, and they always came back, or I thought they had. But it was getting harder to remember anything, harder to think. I could feel my brain loosening inside my skull, melting around the edges; the tissue unfurling into slender, sticky limbs, like stretching out after a nap. Out of the corner of my eye, something moved. A rattlesnake or scorpion, or just the trip starting to dig its dirty nails in. I became aware of other things moving; scuttling across the floor; fluttering across the sky. Shapes that broke ground to take cover under rock.

Fuck. Just be calm. Breathe. Focus on your breathing. In. Out. In. Out. Establish that rhythm. The most natural rhythm there is. In. Out. In. Out. Feel your heart beating in your chest, slow and steady. In. Out. In. Out. In. Out. Out. Out. Out.

Something else was with me; something inbetween my heartbeats. There was a pounding; distant, barely perceptible, but I could definitely hear it. I got on my knees in the dirt, sharp and rocky, and put my ear to the ground. There it was – the heartbeat of the earth. *Ba-dum. Ba-dum. Ba-dum.* I slowed my pulse until both were thudding in unison; synchronised like lovers; and oh, if my arms had been long enough to wrap around the planet. But what if it suddenly silenced, like the golden bell in the church where God hung himself? I could see it – a vision – like a dream that fled into the waking world.

The planet tumbled through space, keeling over and clutching its chest like my dead grandfather. Trees rotted in Golgothan poses, rivers still and glassy, skies choked black with the dusty rattle of coughing volcanoes. Would I die too, now that our hearts pounded as one? That horrible, terrible thought caused my heart to jolt against my chest, as though trying to escape. And the heart of the Earth began to race too. Harder and faster, building up steam, unstoppable, panic that begat panic, silver balls on my friend's dad's desk's dad's friend. I cowered foetal in the dust, as the universe shook itself apart around me. Animals and insects skittered from their holes, cities fell, island nations uprooted and tumbled into frothing seas. The sky smashed into the earth. I inhaled cloud and space.

Then –

Silence.

I don't know how long I lay there. Periodically, the Earth would tilt violently upwards, leaving my back pinned to the wall, and nothing above or below but a slide into an endless abyss. After many thousands of years, I was eventually calmed by the sight of the moon, hanging above. I remember you, from when I was a boy. That camping trip, my first night away from home, my mother told me no matter how far away I seemed, if I looked up at the sky, she could walk into the yard and stand beneath that exact same moon. Concentrating on its gentle glow seemed to push the madness a little further away. Very slowly, the wild colors and sounds and thoughts began to dull, edging the real world back from the beyond, brighter and closer. There, I found truth. The truth that I was thirsty. So fucking thirsty. I tried to prise open the jug of water, but the screw-top lid seemed complicated, and my hands were big and clumsy; a giant at the door of a dollhouse.

Later. My hands were smaller now, and I finally managed to free the lid, lifting the container high and glugging it dry. The water went all down my face and body, and onto the desert floor at my feet. It tasted strange, and as I moved I could hear it sloshing inside my empty gut.

I sat on the ground, watching the water seep into the dry cracks where the desert had split. Would things sprout to the surface? Long-slumbering seeds might feast on the sweat, spittle and water and push their way through to our world. Flowers with tongues that would call me brother. Out in the gloom, a coyote howled. A greeting, maybe, or a warning, or of aching for something to eat or fuck, or of missing home. I thought about my own parents, the family I'd left. My father's large, disapproving face, and my mom, who never thought less than the best of me, even if the only way she could show it was with a snatched look behind his back as he strode out of the room.

I stared at the moon for the comfort I'd felt as a kid, wondering if they were under that same sky that same moment, thinking of me. But the moon seemed to know; skittish and shy, it didn't want to be watched.

"I don't feel pretty today," it said, coyly flitting to and fro, and finally, blinking out altogether. Alone and shivering under the stars, I retched for a small vomit. Nothing came out but a winter's breath; a sticky fog that hung in the air and stuck to my skin when I brushed it with my fingers. I got scared it would smother me, and held my breath. Thoughts flooded my skull-pan of a cop knocking on a door and telling my parents that I'd breathed and fallen and fell and fallen and I can't remember.

I heard myself crying, although when I felt my face, it seemed like I wasn't; mouth not turned down at the corners, eyes dry. My head was so filled with bad and scary thoughts that my neck buckled under the weight, and I couldn't lift it without using my hands. I knew. I knew. I knew that if I wasn't already dead, that I would be soon. That's when I realized I wasn't alone.

Shapes, all about me, moving around out there on all sides. And out there suddenly seemed so huge, with me, a tiny, helpless dot, my brief existence soon to be stepped on or swallowed. A shadow darted past; a starlit outline flashing across my vision.

"Who's there?" I yelled. I hurled the empty jug into the darkness. A breathy laugh right in my ear flinched me all the way to the floor. I scrambled to my feet, pulling on the chain and seeing a flashed vision of myself with bloodied teeth, gnawing through the bone of my arm. "*Please, please, please, please...*" Noises all around; giggling, words, guttural sounds. I stood frozen as something approached – a being lurching out of the darkness. Inhuman and birth-naked, its arms streaked shapes against the sky; fingers that tore stars from the light of heaven. It stood before me with large, dark eyes and a bullish snout tilted to one side, inspecting me, regarding me like man regards the worm. I spoke in a voice of belched up hieroglyphs inside a Disney speech bubble.

"Who are you?"

"I'm your mommy, baby," the thing replied, pulling my mouth towards her tit, nipples plump and red against my lips, hard like erasers.

"No," I said, pulling away. "Not!" The thing wore the face of a beast, not of a mother.

"You'll never be free if you can't let go," it said, with a femininity, its claws exploring its body in a way that was revolting yet filled me with blood.

"Take it off and see," it said, snatching my wrists and placing my fingers on the edges of its face. It came away in my hands, revealing a new face underneath. My mother's. Or what little of it I could remember. "Once you do this, you can do anything..." I dropped its face on the floor and rested against the rock, prone. "No, no, *you* have to fuck *me,*" she said, and lay in the dirt, legs apart, unseen eyes watching from the darkness.

"Do it."

My cock was painful against my pants, a famished wolf, and as I loosened my belt, I saw something nearby, *someone,* familiar and masculine. I glanced to the figure on the floor and back, but he'd vanished. "Come..." she said. I pulled myself on top, and we fucked like brutes under a bleeding sky. When the end came, I began to scream, screaming that I'd cum my whole body out through the end of my dick, that I'd spaff all my organs and bones and be left an empty sack of skin, turned inside out. Under my shrieks, she laughed and pulled me closer, eye to eye as I painted her insides.

I lay inside for a moment, clasping handfuls of swollen breast, before the other figures came. Two bodies became a pile. Hands wandering, feet and backs and limbs and lips and lips, with no beginning or end; a formless, shapeless wraith writhing in a nest. There was a tongue at my shoulder, and something thick filling my mouth. It pushed my lips into an O, stroking the inside of my cheek and roughly sliding itself back and forth in intensifying pumps. It went off like a gun in the back of my throat; a warm, wet bullet that stickied on my tonsils. That explosion, that pop, was the signal for everyone to scatter, for the beasts to crawl back into the cracks and leave me alone with the male presence I'd felt before. He loomed over, horns protruding from his temples.

"I'm the Devil, and I'm here for your soul. You gonna hand it over, or do I have to take it?"

"What will you do with it?" I said. He slapped me hard around the face.

"Remember that."

"Okay..."

"Do you want to die?" He asked. "Do. You. Want. To. Die?"

"No."

"Aren't you afraid?"

"I've got nothing left," I replied, weakly.

"Yeah, well, you've got a soul, and you're gonna gimme it..." Satan reached down, grasping at my chest to pull it right out of me. I pushed away his hands, telling him "No!"

"I'll ask again – do you want to die?"

"No," I said, with a blankness that echoed the blankness I felt inside. Hollow.

"There's nothing left for you here. Look what they did; they left you, all alone. Chained you up like an animal. Nobody's gonna come help. You got no family, no friends. You got nobody. Nobody but yourself, nothing but what's in here." He crouched down and tapped a finger against the side of my head. Satan spoke in gentle tones, the voice that seduced Jesus in the desert, tender and truthful. "You want to be left out here to the scorpions and the vultures? Or do you want to be set *free?*" I felt myself sobbing, and this time, the tears were flowing, spilling down my cheeks like they had some other place I could no longer remember.

"Free..." I said, before snorting back the snot and the sobs and steeling myself. "Free."

"You understand what you're asking of me here?" he said. I shook my head. "Once we do this, ain't no going back. That soul will belong to me, for all times."

"Okay," I said.

"Okay then." I wasn't sure what to do, but it felt the natural thing to reach inside my chest and pull it out. The Devil's eyes were deep-set and hidden in shadow, and he nodded. I cupped my soul tightly between my hands. Though it was weightless, I felt lighter without it inside me. I passed it to him gently, as you would a butterfly.

"Wa-hoo!" he cried, snatching it away and crushing it tightly in his fist. "Now you're dead!" He span on the spot, whirling and kicking up dust, babbling in an ancient language. "Bloo-bala-ba-joop-a-cacar-cacar..." a dervish fed with the life he'd just taken. "You hear me boy, I said you're dead! Can't live without a soul. This right here is the afterlife!"

"It looks the same. Are you sure?"

"Course I'm sure, I'm the Devil, ain't I?" He slapped me again, right across the face. It stung even worse than the first. "You feel that?" Clutching my cheek, I just nodded. "Felt like it did before, right? Like it did when you were still alive?"

"Yeah..." I replied.

"That's the big secret, man; death is just an illusion. There *is* no death, only life. Your body, it's just this *shell*. It ain't no more you than the pants you put on. Everything you are, everything that's you, it's *inside*, and it's in the trees and the birds and the water, it's in all the animals and the bugs and the snakes, and the stuff so small you can't even see it. It's in the air all around us, the sky above our heads, the dirt that's a hundred miles beneath our feet. You don't die, you just go right back into that; back into the Earth, back into the universe, and they can't *never* get you, even if they kill you – and they'll waste their lives trying to kill ya – they can never stop you being free. If you know the truth, if you understand, and you embrace it... you see what I'm saying?"

"Yeah," I said, suddenly so fucking buzzed that I felt as though I was floating, "I get it, I see it now..."

"See," said Satan, "Charlie just wants to you be free, but you have to trust in him. Now you think on that. Rest up, close your eyes and think on that." So I did. I closed my eyes. Christmas Eve tight.

"You think on that, free man," said the Devil, and I lay back, feeling the cold of the rock against the flat of my palm and listening to the gentle tap of his footsteps as he walked away.

"Time to go."

I awoke some time later to the sight of Amber-May and Freck, illuminated by the morning sun; bright and cleansing.

"Find yourself?" said Amber-May, as Freck leant down and unlocked the cuff.

"Found something," I said.

On the walk to the buggies, I felt weightless, like that rock was everything that'd been holding me back, and when they unchained me, I'd left it all behind, forever. My back was scored with scratches, my body knotted and grazed, but the air against my cracked lips had never tasted sweeter.

I spent the journey back to Eden in a daze, exhausted yet euphoric, seeing the world as if for the very first time. We parked at a red light, and I looked at the banged-up stranger staring back from the wing mirror. Amber-May asked me how I was feeling, biting down on her bottom lip with anticipation.

"Amazing," I said, "I feel fucking amazing." A pedestrian stared at us from the pavement, giving it the old it's-the-Manson-Family hairy eyeball. I reared up out of the passenger seat, tugging down my shorts to show my crack. Index and pinky standing proud, I threw a pair of horns, holding them to my forehead with a maniacal "blalalalala!" as we sped away.

Back at camp, the first person I saw was Melody, idling near the entrance as though she'd been waiting.

"Hey, there, stinky," she said, "you okay?"

"Oh yeah," I replied, enveloping her in a hug both loose and loving, with none of that grasping desperation of hugs past.

"Someone's happy." I didn't answer. I just rested my chin on her shoulder until she wriggled free.

"Well, I'm glad. If you're happy, I'm happy. And I have awesome news too... this is so awesome..."

"What is it?"

"God, I can hardly believe it... I'm headed out on the tour!"

"Charlie's tour? Really? Man..."

"Yeah. I mean, it's super-lucky, 'cuz everyone wants to go, and there's only so much space, but I was talking to Charlie last night, and he said if I wanted, which I did..."

"That's great. You're gonna be gone a while, huh?"

"Yeah, little while. We're going all over – man to be a part of history like this. Not to read about it, or see it, but to live it! Right inside history!"

"I'm happy for you, that's... that's awesome. Gonna be quiet here with you gone – with all of you gone."

"Yeah, see, that's the other thing... you wanna come with?"

"You serious? He won't be cool with that, will he?"

"Ask him yourself," she said, as Charlie Manson silently emerged from behind me.

"How you doing, darlin'?" he said, grabbing Melody around the waist and lightly tickling her into doubling over.

"We're excited about the tour," she said.

"Ooh," said Charlie, looking me right in the eye. I'd never exchanged more than a polite nod with the man himself, but suddenly, I was nose to nose and chatting away. Funny, up close he wasn't so intimidating. "You comin' too?"

"Yeah... I mean, yeah. Hell yeah." I was mumbling like a schoolboy, but I think Melody found it cute.

"Alright, man. Good to have you on-board, it's gonna

be wild."

"I can't fuckin' wait," I said. Charlie loosed his arms from Melody's waist and slapped his hand into mine. I shook it firmly, and he fixed me with that magnetic gaze of his.

"I guess I'll see you later, brother," he said. With a wink at Melody, Charlie strolled away. "You know," he said, not looking back, and mouthing the words with his hand held high like a puppet's mouth, "you're a lucky guy. Most folks'd sell their soul to be comin' on tour."

"Told you," said Melody, "he must see something in you. I know I do."

I wanted to ask her something, but my mind was white noise.

"You need some sleep," she said. Melody threaded her arm through mine, brushing the hair out of my face, and we took a stroll in the high morning sun.

6 AT DAWN, WE ROCK

"Society's going backwards, that's the difference 'tween them and us. We're the only ones moving forwards, the only ones evolving. In olden times, they drilled holes in each other's heads. They just wanted to spread that knowledge. And now we're sending kids to shoot babies. You can't reach those people. You can't. They're too scared, 'cuz if you grow and expand, you have to *think*, and as soon as they think, they'll realize everything is bullshit. Fear to create wars; create money – I don't need money, I got all the money in the world. What do I need money for? A fancy suit? A big house? The trees are my house; the dirt, the rocks, the sky – that's my home. This ain't about money, guy, it's about waking 'em up. We're gonna get to those kids, man, let them see what's out there. And anyone who ain't worthy of saving, hell, they can sit there and choke on the smoke of their burning world..."

Fuck, that guy could talk. Not just important stuff; everything, from pop music to nature to transcendental meditation, Charlie's mind was on a whole other level, streaking through the cosmos, with us, these scurrying little ants, gifted the chance to learn at his feet. Even if you didn't catch on right away, if you had trouble keeping up with the ideas speeding by, you still felt that rush of wind and the invigorating roar as they tore past. I'd been talking to a new girl. Maybe fifteen, sixteen, walked in all window-eyed and with an image in her mind from the magazines of how it would be. Within a day, she was crying on and on about how much she missed her parents, and what would they think? I said it was a dumb question, and wouldn't they be proud?

"We have this chance," I'd told her, "to walk in the path of the disciples," but the next morning, she was gone. If you give up that easily, you don't deserve to be free. Go live your life beneath the muck. The thrill came from knowing we were there at the beginning. If man was gonna evolve to the next stage of enlightenment, then Eden Ranch was the cradle of civilization.

"Everybody git over here! I mean *everybody*, let's go!"

We hung off that bus like monkeys, with Charlie's painted face staring out like it could see through to the ends of the Earth. The man himself stood front and center, surrounded by his Family, like a great-grammy at her hundredth birthday. He held his guitar aloft like a warrior's sword, and poor Dutch Bobby had to fit near two-hundred posing, flashing, bird-flipping members of my Family into a single picture.

"Alright – everybody say 'blooloolooooloo!'" Charlie's happiness, his energy and excitement was a lift to all our spirits. His moods seemed to be reflected back by the world that surrounded him. If Charlie was down or angry, it felt like the skies had darkened, and even the cats and dogs that roamed freely did so with that animal sense of things not being as they should. But on those days when he was bursting with a mischievous, childlike spirit, it was all you could do to stop yourself from dancing.

He'd always wanted to get his music out there; of all the many things Charlie was, foremost he was a musician. Now he was finally about to head out, in spite of all the people who wanted to stop him, and share his music and his message with the world, and I was gonna be right there with him. Dutch Bobby clicked the camera, and there we stood, the Class of '71. Peace signs and middle fingers; painted tanks ready to roll through the cities and go to war.

"I guess I'll see ya in a month," said Clark, patting his hand onto my shoulder. He was clad in a faded t-shirt and jeans that, on him, out of all the people in camp, somehow always looked like someone going to a Manson Family costume party. God love him though, he was trying.

"Yeah. You gonna be cool, man?"

"Sure. Be weird all empty here. Imagine this place without Charlie. Be alright though. I'll be good."

"I'm sure you will," I said, "you and a couple hundred chicks. Try not to break anything." Even though I was kidding, there was still something unsettling about Clark's manner; this sense of some awful truth he had yet to share. Hopefully I wouldn't return to find everybody chopped into pieces because he'd started having flashbacks and I hadn't been there to talk him down.

"Yeah, don't worry about me. Just promise you'll tell me *everything* that happens when you get back, okay?"

"Sure."

"Everything, dude. I wanna hear all about it." He held

me with an intense look that made me feel guilty he wasn't coming.

"Hey," I said, "what I remember, I'll share..."

With that, it was time to jet. Melody grabbed my hand and dragged me onto our bus. We ran up the aisle as the convoy started to pull out of camp. Those left behind ran alongside the buses, banging on the sides and waving the little arms of the babies, everyone cheering us like a football team headed out to show the rival town what Eden Ranch was made of. We slapped back against the windows, craning out heads to shout goodbyes and woos, horns blazing. As we pulled out of the gates, I looked back at the ranch. It was still full of people, but somehow looked empty. It always did without Charlie. I wondered how Freck and Deezer would run things with him gone.

As the long, painted buses slowly twisted their way through the windy back roads and out into the streets, we were dizzy with excitement.

"I bet he'll be on *Carson*," said a wiry, wired guy called Jackson, with a constantly jabbering mouth filled with yellow, speed-ground teeth. He'd pitched up at the ranch a month or so back, and talked his way onto the back bus with me, Melody, and a shitload of girls. Just like camp, the chicks outnumbered the dudes something rotten. "Can you imagine that shit?" Jackson continued, "Charlie's gonna be the most famous man who ever lived!" He was right, and we were gonna be there every step of the way. "Oh fuck, we got an escort?"

"Wow," said a skirt named Spacy, "I feel like JFK."

True enough, flanking all three buses, and bringing up

front and rear, were the Judas Noose biker gang, a presidential motorcade that nobody would be crazy enough to fuck with. "I don't know if that makes me feel safe or nervous..." she said, looking out at the escort party, imposingly thick and tattooed, in black leather vests with the club symbol – a blood-soaked length of looped rope tightly clutched in a leather-gloved fist – stitched on the back. The Judas Noose didn't mix with the rest of us, mostly sticking with their own by the converted barn at the side of the house, and guarding the gate from any potential wacko rolling up to take a shot at Charlie.

"Nervous? Are you kidding?" said Jackson. "This is fucking awesome!" He banged his knuckles on the glass, aiming his piss-colored mouth at the small open window. "Hey! Hey, Rex!" Rex didn't even glance up, whether he could hear him over the growl of his Harley or not.

"You know that guy?" I said.

"Yeah... nah, not really."

We felt like royalty. People saw that fleet; saw his face looking out; they knew. It might have been Charlie's LP, but we were all rock stars. That first ride to the opening show was the road trip every itchy-footed kid dreams of. Each vehicle we passed on the highway was mesmerised by the procession; the rainbow circus train of painted flowers, roaring bikes, and rows of jiggling tits and bare asses. Sometimes they'd give you the finger, sometimes they'd wig out, instinctively wrench the wheel and swerve across two lanes of traffic, and sometimes, whoever was in back would push their ass out into the wind and flash you right back. The first time I saw Melody's bare breasts up close, they were squished against the window, getting a thumbs up from a car full of zipperheads. The best times though, were when you'd be waving at kids riding in their parents' cars, and you could see in their eyes how badly they wanted to bust out and join us.

Unlike the last bus journey I'd taken, this one was filtered through a glowing LSD-haze; a party on wheels that was all about the open road and open possibilities, and a bunch of horny kids trapped in a tin can with not much to do but look at the scenery and fuck around. That first night, halfway to the opening venue and parked up in a field in Riverside, was the first time me and Melody made love. There were others involved, but for a little while, it was just us. We slept curled up naked under a big ratty towel. I awoke the next morning alone, and watched her flirting with one of the guys from the middle bus. That's how it was. If you gave a fuck, get off the fucking bus and walk back to Shitsville with the rest of the piggies. Sure, thoughts would sneak in; the picket fence and the painted nursery, but you pushed them aside. You had to. The snatched moments we had together, they'd do. For now. Melody flirted with him, I made out with a girl called Cherie, and right after we were back to poking each other in the ribs and puffing out our faces against the window like bursting goldfish.

We were nearing the city for Charlie's debut, when the lead bus pulled over to the side of the road. The convoy came to a stop, and we watched from our position at the back as Charlie got out and paced the grass verge. He was obviously wigging out about something. Ronnie Eighty-Eight, acting head of *Free Inside* security, parked his hog outside our window and walked over to Charlie. Ronnie was built like Dick the Bruiser, with a neck like a fuckin' sewage pipe, and rumour was, the missing tooth was from a bare knuckle fight with a mountain lion some blackie had taught to walk upright.

"What's he saying, man?"

"Shut the fuck up and maybe we'll hear..." I said. Next to Ronnie, Charlie looked like a stick figure. Charlie wasn't yelling, or even raising his voice, but Ronnie had the beaten poise of that bald kid from *Peanuts*. Charlie got back on the bus, and all eyes were on Ronnie as he sloped submissively back to his bike.

"Yo, Ronnie," I said, through the window, "what's the deal?" Ronnie just shook his head.

"We missed our turning," he said, "been going the wrong way for a half hour."

So's not to come off like the hippie who doesn't belong with professional, *real* musicians, the Manson fleet flew down the freeway, way over the limit, other vehicles fearfully moving aside. Those rear views of the huge, colorful fleet barrelling towards the traffic must've really been something. We shot past a cop car so fast they were a blur before any of us had the chance to push our dicks against the window. The pigs were so afraid of Charlie and the Noose, that they didn't even follow.

Barely ten minutes late, the Manson buses rounded a corner, and we knew for the first time – not that we ever doubted – that *Free Inside* would be a monster. There were lines of people snaking down the street, throwing up their arms and screaming in a frenzy when they saw Charlie's enormous face rolling along.

"Jesus, look at the crowd."

"Jedro would have fucking loved this," I said, as we slowed to a crawl, moving carefully through the bustling throng, their hands clawing the sides of the buses, with Beatlemania squeals of "*Charliiiiiie!*" Outside the building was another group. This one smaller and gathered into a tight square, wielding protest signs, with chants that were drowned by the fans who outnumbered them 100-1. As we drew by the crowds, I reached a hand out of the window.

"Holy shit," said Jackson, laughing as screaming girls stretched up to my fingers, as though I was a star by association, and touching me would bring them closer to their idol.

"We are gonna get *so* much ass," said Jackson, as we pulled into the gates. "I gotta find a way to hang my cock outta the window..."

As we exited, Charlie stepped off with a weasely looking guy I'd never seen before. He walked like he had a wooden butthole and followed so close behind Charlie that he was never more than a few inches away at all times.

"Who's that guy?" I said.

"Road manager," replied Melody, "I don't think the label would let Charlie out on his own."

"Since when does Charlie bow to other people?" said Jackson. "Jesus, look at that little prick. Nice suit, Charlie McCarthy lookin' motherfucker."

"Our Charlie's hand right up his ass, too," I said. "See, he's not bowing to anything. He's playing him, just like he plays that guitar."

The first performance was magical; a Sermon on the Mount set to music. We all watched together from the side of the stage, waiting to see if he'd call us on to sing backup, but he went it alone like only he could. I thought we'd never be able to hear him over the screaming, but the second Charlie opened his mouth, that whole place became utterly silent. And then, his voice. It was as beautiful as he was, and now they'd all be able to see.

After the final encore, Charlie waded into the sea of hands, touching, grasping, signing LPs and magazine covers that touted him as a psycho-killer and a danger to your children, while we waited backstage, where there was a spread fit for a king. We all loved Eden, but they catered to a lot of hungry mouths, and mostly we ate whatever they'd pulled from dumpsters behind the bakeries and joints down in the city. One of Charlie's conditions for the tour was that each venue had to lay on enough for the entire Family, and boy, there were so many cakes, rolls, pastries, peach cobblers, fruit platters, weiners, pizzas, pretzels, donuts, beer and sodas, that you could almost hear the tables begging for mercy.

I'd barely taken a bite before an RC Cola was flying through the air and a face was being mushed into a cake. Venue staff ran for cover as it broke into a full-on food fight, their jaws on the floor as the feast found its way into hair, faces, and down each other's pants. It was a riot. I didn't know if I was gonna choke from laughter, or from the éclair Melody had pushed into my mouth. One of our girls wore two pizza slices as a bra; Jackson sprayed soda over the staff like he was cumming on them; and when there was nothing left to hock but a box of Krispy Kremes, the cry of "how many donuts do you think I can thread over my dick?" was our cue to leave. We went back to the buses hungry and messy, but owning the world.

We left, as we would each night, with more members than when we'd arrived; devotees who snuck and stowed aboard as we drove out, or been heaved through the doors as we pulled away, begging us to *take me with you!*"

That's how it went. Charlie would sing, we'd laugh and play around, and every night saw new faces who ran away to join the circus. Funniest was the show in Goldfield. This fucky old coot had to watch his innocent young daughter drive out of his life forever, wagging his fist and crying, and shouting her name as the bus got further and further away, and I shook my cock out of the rear window.

"Put that thing away," said Melody, "you'll hurt somebody!" I replied with a wink, "You'd know." About that point, almost everyone knew. We were having to leave all the bus windows open during the shows just to air out the stank. Some ways in, as we quietly trundled through some leafy suburb, out of nowhere Jackson, who was itching at his crotch like he was trying to pull a root out of the soil piped up with "Tutankhamun's got more skin left on his dick than I do..." I don't know if it was the close proximity, or the euphoric mood, or maybe we just felt the need to prove ourselves, to fly the flag of the free while loosed in that outside world, but even by our standards, there was a *lot* of fucking. Threesomes, foursomes, a-whole-lot-moresomes – the cheering section of that whole tour was held together with dick-sick.

We drove by day, across the landscape of the United States, taking in the scenery of the world we were conquering, piece by piece, like a great wind sweeping away the cobwebs. By night, we'd park up for these big barbecues, partying, more singing, skinny-dipping in lakes, and listening to Charlie. For newbies, it was an intro to the lifestyle to which they'd soon become accustomed. Most of us had never taken a real vacation, just grotty family ones where you're forced to visit Bumblefuck's world famous pencil museum and wake each morning to the sound of your old man pissing into an SS Helmet from dubya-dubya-two. Truly, these were the best days of all our lives, on the open road with our real Family.

The crowds that greeted us at shows were a mix of fans, protesters, and an increasingly heavy police presence. It was never us bringing trouble; it was the pigs trying to shut us down – trying to shut him up, but it wasn't working. The love was only getting stronger, and the buses only getting fuller. Ours started from home with less than a dozen, but as every show brought a new ass or ten, things were starting to become cramped. Charlie's was so full that he'd had to stash all his signing LPs in ours. One afternoon, a real young-looking chick called Belle who'd gotten on a couple of nights before, was staring into the cover – an artistic looking shot of Charlie gazing soulfully at the ground – hypnotised like a deer in front of a speeding Buick on a dark mountain road.

"Gosh, would you look at him," she said, "so beautiful."

"Wonder how many people have jacked off over it?" said Jackson, snatching one off the pile, sliding out the record and pulling the sleeve over his head like a mask. "How much pussy could I get if I went out wearing this?" Everyone laughed, and he put on a mock-Charlie voice, swaggering about the aisle. "Would'ya come and give Uncle Charlie a little kiss? Ah go on, guy, just a peck, right on the end of the dingus..."

"Not cool," I said, snatching the sleeve off of his head. "Maybe you need to remember why we're here."

Sat in the middle of the bus was a mother and daughter who we'd picked up at the previous show. The mom was old; late thirties; the daughter late teens, and such a younger, smoother version of her mom it was a visual diagram of the passage of time. I spent a while looking at one while covering the other with my hand, blinking back and forth, wondering how I'd look at that age. Having someone's mom on board felt awkward at first, like there was a chaperone, but once the beer and pills started flowing, she joined right in. You could never tell who'd hitch up. Some nights you'd look out at the wailing faces, knowing they'd all tag along if they'd fit, but often the ones who made it onboard were the most surprising. If someone really wanted to be one of us, if it was destined, they'd find their way.

One morning I found myself eyeing a familiar girl stretched out across the aisle, trying to place where I knew her from. I hadn't fucked her, I was pretty sure. Hadn't talked to her either, but she was definitely new.

"Hey," I said, "didn't I see you holding a sign? Ban this Filth or some shit?"

"Girl can change her mind," she said, shrugging.

"Yeah. He'll do that."

We were the hottest ticket in town, although we still hadn't been onstage with Charlie, like he'd promised. Every night, someone would ask that suited little anus from the label O'Beale "we gonna go?" and he'd reply "not tonight," sneering like he didn't want to dirty himself by dealing with anyone lower down the food chain than Manson himself, which he did only out of fear. Outside the shows, the presence of the bikers kept protesters at arms length, and they had no fight beyond chest-beating and empty chants. Film crews from the news hung around too, clamoring for a word with Charlie. He'd always give 'em something for the front page; some nonsense quote that he'd laugh about later, watching them try to find meaning in it, while they gave another few pages of free advertising. Today, concert halls, this time next year, arenas!

On occasion, someone would get left behind, after passing out, or hooking up with a local girl and missing the ride, but damned if this ragtag group of "brainwashed hippie killers" hadn't toured like a real rock and roll band without a drop of blood being spilled.

That's why the first flash of red and blue got everyone real excited.

"Oh shit, pigs..." That got everyone's hackles up in a flash. For all the talk of pigs and snakes and whores and The Man, encounters with those most wretched of creatures were rare, as none were brave enough to venture inside the ranch. Those sirens rang out like an air-raid warning, and I think we all hoped something was about to kick off. Maybe some dumbshit pig tries his luck with the Noose and find himself on the dirty end of a tattooed fist.

The piggies ordered us off the road, pulling the convoy up on the side of the highway. Up front, Charlie was jawing with a pack of bacon-boys. I stuck my mouth to the open window and yelled at Lowball, who was walking back from the set-to with the moustache twisted halfway up his face.

"What's going on?"

"They won't let us over the border."

"What?"

"State governor says he won't let us in, says he's not gonna promote a criminal. Outstanding warrant or some shit. They wanna fuckin' lock him up again."

"Can they do that?"

"I look like a fuckin' lawyer?" Lowball stomped off to the rest of the Noose, arms folded and throwing eye-fucks at the pigs leaning on a nearby squad car. The buses rocked with cries of "Bullshit!" and "Fuck The Man!" They didn't want him to sing, but sing he had, and they still wanted to take that from the people? I stomped down the aisle and out of the bus, with others following behind, dissent searing through our veins. Charlie was talking to the cops, at his most animated, hammily playing up to the audience watching from the windows, and from the traffic passing on the highway. The stupid pig couldn't even tell when he was being mocked.

"They just don't know how to cope with us," said Melody, watching the cops untrained in dealing with Charlie's prancing and 'Yes, Massuh!' hand-wringing. "They don't even speak the same language." The pigs finally gave up – I guess they had nothing to charge him with – and Charlie skipped back onto his bus. The engine hissed into life and the convoy pulled away, with row after mocking row of passengers politely waving bye-bye to the cops like dainty southern dames.

Though they'd let him go, we were still banned from crossing into state, so we had no idea where we were headed. But knowing Charlie, he wasn't gonna let anyone tell him where we couldn't go. We'd probably just plough across the border, fuck the governor, while the pigs pretended to be dignified, chasing down a row of pink flowery buses with tit-filled windows.

Later, the convoy finally came to a stop, and like the piss-break stampedes, we rushed the doors, half-expecting to find ourselves parked on the governor's front lawn. Not five yards from the front bumper of Charlie's bus, there was a big green sign – *Welcome to Texas!*

Waiting beyond the sign were three squad cars and a paddywagon, with a bunch of state troopers, nightsticks drawn. Charlie took a few steps toward the sign, and the five-o readied themselves. An older sheriff, with his nightstick cupped in the palm of his hand, figured he was about to bag himself a big ol' fish. A boyish trooper looked like he wanted to run.

"I guess if I step over this line," said Charlie, "y'all will lock me up." We all roared with laughter as he frolicked like a court jester, delicately inching his toes towards the line, in and out, and *almost*. He whispered something to a new girl, who patted off to the bus.

"This is fucking hilarious," I said to Melody, "look how pissed they are." You could tell those Texas bulls wanted to put a round in the head of every one of us, goading and teasing from behind the line, like poking a banana through the bars at the monkey enclosure. Away from the pack, O'Beale was pacing, gripping the bridge of his nose between thumb and forefinger.

"What if he puts his prick over the line?" yelled one of our guys. "Will you stick a handcuff on it?"

"Yeah, make a jail cell for my balls," said another, thrusting his hips towards the state line so hard that he overreached. The cops bristled as he windmilled his arms, teetering between states, a single breeze from toppling into a night in the cells and a beating. Right as he was about to fall, we pulled him back by his shirt, to more laughter.

"Thank you, darlin'," said Charlie, as the girl returned with his guitar. And that's when Charlie played the greatest show we'd ever seen. There was no crowd besides us, the pigs, and the cars that tooted honks of appreciation or anger as they sped by, and he only played a couple of songs, but it was fucking glorious. Charlie could always make something out of nothing. Once again they tried to stop him, and once again they'd failed. He used their rules against them, taking that fine print off the page, unspooling and straightening out the letters, and twisting them into his own signature. He sang his heart out there on the side of the road, a tongue's length from the state border, and those pigs had to stand there and listen. For the first time on the tour, his voice and our voices were as one, just like back home, united in the face of the oppressive shitheads who couldn't understand why their empty rules weren't enough to combat the power of love. I could have sworn I saw one of those pigs tapping his feet.

From such a high, things could only go downhill.

The roadside performance drummed up more publicity, and a photo of Charlie, eyes closed and mouth wide in peaceful song, across from the bulldog glares of Texas' finest, adorned front pages worldwide. A detour took us around to the next shot, a venue that was way more us than the cramped, dripping walls that'd housed previous shows. A small open air stage in the center of a farmer's field was a home from home, fenced on far sides by tall trees and with a fertile green floor.

"This is so beautiful," said Melody, as one of the bikers positioned Charlie's stool in the middle of the stage. "Can you see Charlie at Woodstock? Zeppelin opening for *him*, the Stones, the Beatles..."

"Helter Skelter, man," said Jackson.

"Shut the fuck up with that shit," snapped a tubby guy known as Zombie. Zombie was from Sacramento, and once told me he was so sick of his small penis, he was gonna get it inked with a tattoo of a much bigger one.

Zombie clouted Jackson in the shoulder with a solid punch. "If he hears you... Jesus. Why you gotta bring that shit up?"

Charlie took the stage right as the sun was setting, and in the stillness between the strum of the first chord and the opening line, you could hear the crickets singing in the grass. Nature and man, in perfect harmony. That atmosphere was something else – like a homecoming – open skies, fresh, country air, and hearts filled with nothing but love. I watched from the crowd, with Melody on one arm and a decent chick from Arizona on the other, soaking up the love from all sides. It really made me appreciate how blessed we were, to be out there feeling what the audience was feeling by being in his presence, something we were lucky enough to experience every day. Together, we sang our hearts out, and we swayed, and we hugged, and Charlie–

Crack!

I didn't realize what it was until the second pop, when people started hitting the floor. I'd never heard a gunshot before. In my mind, just one word, "Charlie..."

I never felt panic like it, not since I was a kid, when my dog got away from me and ran round a corner. The screech of tires had stopped my heart dead in my chest, just like that crack.

The air was filled with screams. I was too far back to see anything but people hurling themselves down, or running in a blind panic, and on stage, a bundle of figures tackling somebody to the ground. Melody cried out in fear, grasping me tight, but I shoved her off and made for the stage. Bum-rushing forwards, I pushed and manhandled and threw people out of the way; anybody who stood between me and him, knocking them to the ground, and desperately trampling through the stampede.

"Move, fucking move!" I yelled, punching a dude in the neck, and wrestling another to the floor by his face, as my ankle twisted on backs and limbs. I pushed through to the front, a foot from the stage, where I hauled myself up. Other Family members were stood around Charlie, who lay flat and face down, next to his stool. He never looked smaller than he did right then, lifelessly sprawled across the stage.

"I'm gonna get a splinter," said Charlie, lifting his head. He strained a look out towards the sea of fists and feet, and the Judas Noose dragging somebody off by the hair.

"Charlie, you alright?!"

"Are you hit?!"

"Charlie? Charlie?"

"I'm fine," he said, grinning. "Fuckin' cunts'll do anything to shut me up."

"Is he hurt? Are you hurt?" Ronnie reached down and offered his hand to pull him up.

"Get the fuck off-a me," said Charlie, slapping it away and shoving us all back. "Am I a man who needs any fuckin' help? Everybody back the fuck up." We parted the ways, and Charlie rose to his feet, slowly and firmly, showing the remaining crowd that it'd take more than a bullet to put him down. He didn't have a mark on him.

The shots had all dinged through the curtain at the back of the stage.

Then came the familiar catcall of sirens, as a fleet of cop cars screeched onto the field, just in time to witness the escalation into a full-blown riot. From the safety of the stage, we watched the violence below. There were no sides, just a good old fashioned shitstorm, with everybody wading in. Two shirtless men were in a violent embrace, thumbs in each other's eye-sockets; a guy warded off a pair of hippies with a broken bottle; Jackson gleefully kicked the cum out of a fat kid. Melody had made it safely to the stage, and watched from behind my shoulder, as the pigs advanced into the mass of bodies. Everyone was swinging or rolling on the ground in pairs, or aiming stamps and kicks at those already snared in combat. Some bled, others merely spat. Boots found ribs, fingers found eyes, and nightsticks met legs and the backs of heads. Near the front of the stage, a slip of a girl I recognised from camp was rattled from side to side by some fuckin' harpy trying to yank her hair out of her skull. I reached down and plucked her out of the melee, aiming a kick at the girl below and spitting in her face when she looked me in the eye.

Above the madness of the storm, we watched the pigs bring things under control with violence of their own. Those who hadn't fled into the woods soon lay on their bellies with arms cuffed behind their backs. Charlie moved to the mic at the front of the stage. There was a shrill whistle of feedback, and then he spoke.

"You lock those kids up for defending themselves, but where were you when someone tried to shoot me? Did somebody pay you off? Were those bullets from one of your guns? Or are you just so fucking incompetent?"

"Go home, Manson," replied some pork-smelling motherfucker with his hand tensed over a side-arm, "if you even have a home."

"My home is with my Family. But where were you to protect these kids? Look at this little girl..." Charlie gently clasped the waist of the chick I'd pulled from the crowd, one of her big blue eyes swollen shut and leaking, "you don't protect anyone except yourselves." The world bubbled and frothed, ready to boil. My veins were thick, and my skin felt too tight for my body, like I wanted to tear it off and rush out there to show them how uniforms and badges didn't mean shit. Staring down from the stage, we all knew that one word from Charlie, one nod, we'd swarm those motherfuckers, and not stop unless he said so. They were armed, but so were the Judas Noose, and the pigs were outnumbered ten to one, let alone outmatched. They had guns and hats, but they didn't have what we had; they didn't have freedom. You could see in their eyes that they knew it too. I never saw a situation that Charlie didn't have complete control over.

"Fuck 'em," said Charlie, "let's split."

That night, under a perfect, starlit sky, we examined each other's knocks and bumps, and talked through most of the night about how one piece of shit tried to ruin everything. Everyone agreed they wished they could have gotten their licks in on the cocksucker, but Zombie said that there was nothing of 'em left. The bikers just tore him up.

"You saw?" asked the daughter, eyes wide with images of the beautiful end that they'd dished out to the faggot with the gun.

"Yeah. Cunt got what he deserved. You gotta ask yourself, six feet away like that, how d'ya miss? There's something there, that's all I'm saying. Destiny. I bet he could'a put that gun right to Charlie's head and still... fate, brother." That night, Melody and I fucked, this time alone, and I slept under the stars with her lips tenderly kissing away the knots in my knuckles.

The next morning, the convoy sat outside a diner while O'Beale made a series of phone calls. As we waited for him to come out, I sneakily slunk closer to Charlie, so I could hear what was said when he came out, 'cuz from the look on his face, it was something heavy.

"It's over," said O'Beale, with a sudden and disgusting level of confidence, as though he figured nothing could happen to him so long as regular people were pumping gas and eating grits nearby.

"What's over?" replied Charlie. "What do you mean, *over*?"

"They've pulled the plug. The label. They heard about what happened last night. I mean, everyone heard. Go watch a TV." O'Beale snorted with laughter, and I could see Charlie's eyes blacken. "Word gets round real fast, especially where you're concerned, *Mister* Manson. The bottom line is this; no venue will have you, not now. You were almost impossible to insure before, but after last night, sheesh. You've got protesters, cops, and now there's people shooting. And riots... it's over. I'm sorry, truly I am. If you were shifting more units, maybe they'd have let this circus carry on, but the sales have been..." He hesitated, not out of politeness, or even fear, but because he was savoring the moment.

"Look, they're not good. None of the big chains are willing to carry you. First week was fine, there was a morbid curiosity about it all, and this *image* you have, but once the ads start getting pulled, and you've got stores being boycotted and picketed, the people at the top get itchy. All this... it's just not worth our while." Charlie roughly wiped at his own beard with a palm, saying nothing. Without a word, he turned his back on O'Beale and walked up the steps of the bus, closing the doors behind. O'Beale called after Charlie, "I guess I'll be making my own way back?"

From inside Charlie's bus, I heard the sound of a foot kicking hard against the inside of the door, over and over again.

The bummed-out mood on the long ride back home was a bleak contrast to the sunny, positive vibe of the tour, as though everything had been dirtied. Melody sat on my lap, pulling my arms tightly around her. Our world had been shaken, and we'd all had a glimpse of a horrible future – one without Charlie. Someone had taken a shot at him, and he was the one who walked away the tallest and the proudest, as an example of how he, and we, couldn't be stopped, that his love would win out, no matter what. But one phone call from The Man, with all his empty connections and money and power, just cut the fuckin' strings, and it all fell down. There was nothing we could do. Half our friends were in jail over the riot, and God only knew when or if they'd ever get back to us. Plus, not only was Charlie's tour done, but he no longer had an album.

"You know what though," said Zombie, his voice the first thing to cut through that sombre silence besides the rattle of the old bus in hours.

"Shut the fuck up."

"Yeah, I know," he said, "but seriously, think about it – even if they had shot Charlie, even if that bullet had got him right in the head, you can never kill his ideas, you could never kill *this*. It sounds fucked up, but as a symbol, maybe he'd have been even more powerful dead than he is alive. Imagine that; crazy sonofabitch thinking he can silence him with a pistol, man, he'd have found out real quick that, if Charlie died, his ideas would live *forever*."

7 KAYFABE

Though returning home early from a cancelled tour of an album that'd been dropped by the label, it wasn't the tail-between-the-legs defeat they'd surely been picturing. If anything, it demonstrated to all how afraid they were of Charlie's ideas getting out. Such terror, that he'd walk among their world and blow the sleep from their children's eyes; that their daughters and sons would climb into our buses and never look back. Charlie said every time the pigs did stuff like that, they were letting the world know that he had them on the run. He called it a 'tell,' like a poker player who unconsciously rubs on his earlobe when he gets a good hand. Taking all that trouble to shut him down, they were letting everyone know that they were holding a 2-7. It didn't matter. From now on, Charlie would play only for his people, for those who deserved to hear his music, and those who were capable of understanding. You don't take a worm to the opera.

The big news while we'd been gone was that there'd been a killing down in the city. A pair of young newlyweds carved up like badly-cooked BBQ, with 'something significant' daubed on the walls in their blood, so they said. Significant enough that the pigs hadn't released it to the public. It was no surprise that the snakes of the press had hinted and suggested and teased that the blame lay at Charlie's feet. He was hundreds of miles away, playing beautiful music to a theatre full of people when it happened, but they didn't care, with headlines of "*Manson Copycat Slaying*," and an old photo of Charlie positioned beside a picture of a taped-off crime scene, to tie those things in people's minds. It was just the latest in a long line of tells; fingers scratching at their faces, mouths that spoke of confidence and truth while twitching at the corners.

Jackson was back. He turned up about a week after we did, with no front teeth and a negress on his arm, which went down like a steaming bowl of shit soup. Poor bitch is probably still wandering the desert trying to hitch her black ass a ride back home. Speaking of people who go missing, O'Beale hadn't been heard from in weeks. Supposedly he never made it back from the tour, and his wife and all the suits were terribly worried.

Friendships at Eden shifted and flowed like the stray cats that climbed into the laps of whoever's clicking fingers they noticed first. It was like being a kid again, picking up temporary buddies as you cycled through neighboring blocks. Over the past few days I'd gotten closer to a girl called Imogen. Imogen was a country girl, with a hee-haw accent and chunky thighs, and we'd had a bunch of good talks and made out some, but I'd seen her getting close to other guys around camp too, until they or she got bored. She was pretty needy, and more than a little irritating, but I liked the way she'd hug into me from behind, resting her chin on my shoulder and pushing her boobs against my back. I'd even confided in her about Clark's increasingly distant behavior since I'd returned, which had been playing on my mind.

I hadn't expected him to leap into my arms and pepper me with kisses, but there was a sudden coldness that hadn't been there before. I wondered if he resented that I'd left him behind. We'd entered this world together, and not gone a day apart since. A guy like that craves stability above all else. Maybe I was imagining things. Half the time I was so fucking high on one thing, or coming down from another, making it hard to judge my own mood, much less other people's. But it'd been a dry week at the ranch, with little more than a few baggies of weak Larry Fine being passed round. Perhaps that was part of the problem, as Clark's appetite for drugs had started to go way beyond recreational, even though he tried to hide it, which he did badly. Without the love and support he'd found, he'd be one of those guys on the news; "*...before turning the gun on himself.*" Or maybe we'd both moved on from our days as virgin babyman and twitching wreck.

Across the way, Melody sauntered into view. We caught each other's eye, and she nodded a "hey," flinging up a wave and beaming across at Imogen and I. My gaze followed her until she was all the way out of sight.

"You love her," said Imogen, in a sing-songy, childish voice, lightly pushing and twisting the tips of her fingers into the dimples of my cheeks.

"I love everyone," I replied, "even you."

"Aww, well ain't that sweet?" I did, though, love Melody. Imogen, not so much. I could'a hung with Melody more than I did, but oftentimes it was tougher to be around her than not. No matter how many beautiful moments we shared, free love meant no emotional ties. That was uptight bullshit for the squares outside. But though we preached that, I'd still make myself scarce when she was fooling around with other guys or girls. It put a knot in my guts that'd put me off my food and keep me awake; not just the picture in my mind of all the things they were doing to her, but the shame of not being able to man up and shake it off.

It's then that I spotted a figure headed towards the entrance; a familiar shuffling gait and stooping posture, with that weird sense of anxious, eyes-to-the-ground urgency even when he's just walking back from the can. I watched as Clark passed through the gate and disappeared from view.

"The fuck's he going?" I said.

"I dunno," replied Imogen, "when you were gone he kept disappearing. First, I thought he was leaving, 'cuz I knew you guys were tight. Figure maybe he'd had enough. But then later I saw him by the fire. Comes and goes. He does that."

"Goes where?"

"He's out to lunch, man. Totally bongo."

Later that night I needed some space to think, and shook myself loose of Imogen. Though there were people everywhere, the ranch was big enough that if you wanted to go off and be alone, you could.

I sat on the grass, leaning against an old tree that had scores of heart-wrapped initials carved into the trunk from the various pairings who'd slunk off for some alone time, and truly, deeply loved each other in the five minutes following their fumblings under the branches. I traced my finger through the indentations, trying to put names to the letters, when I heard a vehicle pulling up the path outside. It wasn't one of the droning dirt buggies or guttural Harleys, and I wondered if the pigs had come to stir up more trouble. I followed the sound around the perimeter fence and up to the entrance, where a grimy old pickup slowly cruised inside, gravel crunching and popping beneath the tyres. A sketchy-looking dude got out, walking around to the back. One of the Judas Noose stood illuminated in the faint red glow of the rear lights, as the driver unhooked the tarp that covered whatever was in the back and slung it open. Guns. Lots and lots of guns. Rifles, from what I could make out, and aside from the odd 45, I'd never seen anything like that around camp. The biker – I couldn't make out who – shook hands with the skeezy guy, and soon, the lights of the truck were trailing across the ranch and up towards the big house.

I spent that night asleep and alone under the tree, hoping for nothing more than to not wake to a pair of star-struck lovers 69ing at my feet.

My mood had lifted a little the following morning, walking once again amongst my friends, the sight of Clark wafted a small parting in the dark clouds. I knew that I'd go over and say hi and everything would feel fine again. Clark was in the middle of a conversation, so I hung back, resting in the shadow of the barn.

I quietly watched him chatting to the mom and daughter we'd picked up on the road. They'd been dubbed Pear Big and Pear Little, because of their tiny waisted, big hipped, eight-shaped bodies. There was something about his hunched manner that felt familiar, a reverting back to the broken man he was that first time we'd met. It was clear from the body language of the mother and daughter, to the timbre of his voice, that something was upsetting him. I took a few quiet steps nearer, hanging back, just close enough to hear.

"I'm sorry," said Clark. His voice was audibly trembling. He paused for a moment, composing himself with a deep, shaking breath. Pear Big put a hand on his shoulder, and though I strained to see from my position behind, both women's faces were streaked with tears. Clark continued, "Do you know how fuckin' weird it is to hear myself saying all this out loud? I've never talked about that day before, not to a civ. You go home and it's just... I guess there's something to be said for the comfort of strangers."

Clark gently blinked his eyes closed for a moment, rolling out a drip that slid down his cheek. He didn't wipe it, he just let it be.

8 HEADHUNTERS

For once the ranch and the world outside were on the same conversational wavelength; both abuzz about the latest batch of murders – a rich girl and her two roommates, slashed into wet confetti in the Hollywood Hills. Never mind that all that crime and violence happened beyond the gates where we made home, in a grubby little world that we'd opted out of; that didn't stop the scuttle about the supposed evil puppetmaster who'd sent out his brainwashed death-cult to stir up the shit. It was all bullshit. Charlie reckoned the pigs were doing it to set him up. Some nights I'd sit and look at the far-flung lights gazing out from the stinking sprawl like the blank eyes of a brain-dead coma patient. A diseased murk of smog hung permanently above the buildings; above the families inside them, like a physical manifestation of their own oppression that they'd only be able to see if they could get far enough away. Down there, they trudged through life like depressed cartoon characters, with raindrops pittering onto their crooked heads, while the 'degenerates' up on the hill had their bodies warmed by sunbeams. Th–

"Come with me."

A gloved hand gripped my shoulder. Lowball loomed over me, stony faced, with his eyes behind dark glasses. I tried to play it cool, but felt a small panic pull itself out of my chest and down over my head like a plastic bag. I thought back to that thing I shouldn't have seen. Lowball lead me through camp and up the path towards the big house on the hill, and I thought about all the faces who'd come and gone, without a word. Far less goodbyes than there had been hellos. Maybe they'd seen something too. Maybe there was a big pile of bodies back there; a mass grave of poor bastards who'd stumbled on some shit, and could only be trusted into silence with a length of oily chain. With Charlie you always felt safe, but the bikers were unpredictable; dangerous. Look in their eyes, and you didn't see a whole lotta love.

"What's this about?" I said, breathlessly keeping pace with Lowball's long, heavy strides. He didn't answer. Each step took us closer to that place; so alluring, so mysterious. I always wondered what kind of things went on behind those windows, when the new girls would go inside for days at a time, especially considering the stuff we got up to in the open. But the nearer I got, the less I wanted to find out. As we reached the stoop, Lowball pushed on past and lead me round to the back. I half expected to be greeted by a pack of angry Noose, but nobody was waiting for us. Me and Lowball stood in the shade of the violently sloping hill that backed the property. He didn't speak for half a minute, and I sensed he'd smelled my fear and was getting a kick out of fucking with me. Finally, in that speed-addled drawl, mouth barely visible under the thicket of moustache that hung on his lip like the Happy Birthday banner for a kid-touching cousin–

"Charlie's got a mission for you."

Before I had time to think, the back door of the house crashed open against the outside wall, and three girls emerged into the sunlight, sauntering across the lawn and joining us. I felt like they could hear the sound of my brain spinning.

"They're with you. Here." Lowball pushed a stack of bills into my hand.

"Okay?" I said, looking at at least a couple of hundred dollars.

"You're going into San Fran to drum up some new business. Go mingle, hit up anyone who looks like they should be here. Bring back a bunch of new recruits. Young, healthy; you'll figure it out. Don't do anything dumb. Don't bring back anyone that don't belong. Right?"

"Sure," I said, "I'll..." Lowball slapped a meaty paw on the back of my neck.

"He's in charge," said Lowball, staring down the three girls. "He tells you to do something, you do it. And don't fuck this up. Go." Lowball thrust a finger in the direction of the exit, and like that, we were on our way.

Charlie always said the nicest bait hooks the biggest fish, so it was no surprise the chicks he'd picked were all lookers, each uniquely super-sexy in their own way. Maybe he was looking to bring some fresh male blood to Eden, which had a snatch-to-cock ratio I kinda loved, like being an endangered species. Hell, that's half the reason the guys who were there stuck around, particularly the Judas Noose.

All three were recent additions to the Family. The one I knew by face, Sue, stuck in my mind only through her denim shorts, and the way she sat with her legs splayed wide enough to give an eyeful of the sandy tufts of cooch hair peeping out. Shelly, on first impression, was a quiet girl. She had what we'd say around camp was one of them coon bodies; brickhouse thick without being fat, and a bottom half that looked like a capital P. Mia, on the other hand, was all legs, like a stork. A stork you just wanted to fuck until it broke. All three were eighteen, thereabouts, and given the sense of mischief visibly steaming from their pores, I figured I'd be spending the next couple of weeks like a stressed-out babysitter, trying to stop the kids from blacking my face with Sharpies and burning down the house.

As we rode the train to SF, Mia was impishly saluting and calling me sir. Maybe they were wondering what I'd done to get hand-picked and stamped with that Manson seal of approval. Other than the bubble of the tour, I'd never been further than the city since joining Eden. Watching the passing scenery through the train windows felt strange; not like the tour; as though we were viewing the world on its terms, with other passengers and normals going about their business around us.

"We're not the only ones," said Shelly. "Charlie's sent a bunch of groups all over. We're like them fuckin' Mormons, huh? He called it a... uh, what was it? A recruitment drive."

"Recruiting for what?" I said. She just shrugged. Mia tapped my shoe with hers to get my attention.

"You know, if we wanted, we could just book it and not go back. How much money he give you?"

"Like, three hundred bucks," I replied.

"Get way further than Cali on three hundred," she said, "right, girls?" Maybe it was a test, like Charlie had prepped them to tempt out the weak and the disloyal, and a "*sure, why not?*" would see me pushed out onto the tracks.

"Do it," I said, holding out the money and wondering if Mia was set to take a tumble herself, "but I'm going to San Fran." She hesitated, then, with a sly grin that said "*just fuckin' with ya*," she closed my fingers around the wad of bills.

As we pulled into San Francisco, I thought back to a middle-school field trip to a museum, and the trouble Marty Walker got into when he farted in the face of a stuffed Eskimo. We were representing the entire Family, Charlie included. If we fucked up, the shame would be on everyone, and I had three hellcats pulling on my pecker the whole way, but as we got off, Mia gripped me around the back like she was giving a massage and said, "We've gotta do what-ever you tell us."

"An-y-thing..." said Coochie Sue. Jesus. I let out a cackle of a laugh. Who gave a fuck anyway? Was that what Charlie had taught me, to give a shit about what others thought? *People?* This world, their world, it wasn't a classroom, it was a playground.

The indistinct charge to "drum up business" had us wandering aimlessly for the first couple of days, as idle sightseers on a working vacation. We rode cable cars and walked the Golden Gate Bridge, wondering how many people had thrown themselves over the battered red railings to their death. Mia bet me ten bucks we could talk someone into doing it. You could never be sure if she was kidding or not, but we hung around for a few hours, on the lookout for anybody with that sunken-shouldered look of defeat, casting a curious gaze towards the water. It'd started as a joke, but whenever someone looked over the rail, there was a hush of excitement, followed by disappointment when they carried on walking.

"I bet your eyeballs would come out if you landed right," said Mia, forlornly leaning over the rail. Nobody died that day, and she sulked so hard that it took an ice cream to get her speaking again.

San Francisco's windy streets were almost vertical at points, sloping down so steeply you could just see Evel Knievel setting up a ramp at the bottom and jumping over the bay. The first time we rode the slope and spotted Alcatraz off in the distance, we all had the same glorious idea about herding up all the pigs and locking them inside, leaving the rest of the city; the rest of the world; to the people who deserved it.

Eventually, we started getting down to business, and caught another tram to The Haight. I remembered seeing the same little intersection on TV in '67. Back then, it was so vibrant and alive that the pictures seemed like they were in color. But now, in person, it felt like a poster that'd been left in the window too long and gone yellow and faded. Our time with Charlie had taught us to recognize true freedom, and this place was not it.

We went into a crowded head shop, the towering shelves so close together that we had to squeeze through in single file, knocking our elbows into elaborate glass hookahs and novelty pipes shaped like a puss. The guy behind the counter wore his hair in two long plaits, flashing us a brown-toothed grin as we bundled our way back outside. A few doors along was a boutique selling old clothes. Most of the racks wore handwritten signs reading 'Second Hand,' while a few were labelled as 'Third Hand.'

In the far corner, tattiest of all, was a single rail of 'Fourth Hand', which customers gleefully fingered through, so fucking unique and hip to be buying threads that'd lived a previous life, which they couldn't wait to wear for a day, then bring right back, getting off on how *wild* it all was. I watched from the back of the store in pants and a shirt that'd been worn by fifty different people and would be worn by fifty more, not because it was cool, but because it was right.

Everywhere you looked, people who'd stuck around after the Summer of Love were rolling around in the wet patches. But there had to be those worth saving too, the ones who'd gone there to find something that would never be on offer in a place like that. We had to seek them out.

Hungry and almost out of buck, we dropped the last of Charlie's cash on cheesy fries and soda at a diner. I sat window-side, looking at the motel across the street, which was called *Frank's Mootel*, with a neon sign of a sleeping cow with a row of Z's above its head.

"Could'ya stop scratching yourself? You're like a fuckin' monkey," said Sue.

"I think I caught something," I said, "my nob's been tickling like a termite nest for a week now. See?" I poked the helmet of my penis out above the belt-line of my pants, like a soldier peeking over the ramparts, and Shelly leaned in for a closer look.

"I dunno, there ain't really the light for it in here. Scooch your head back a bit..." Other diners threw muttering looks over their shoulders. "It does look a little sore. Just leave it be, it'll be alright." A middle-aged couple at the next booth amped up their sneers, and I tucked myself back in.

"What? You don't got one of these?" I said. They didn't respond, but Shelly and Sue started giggling. Mia emerged from the bathroom, and sat herself down in the booth of some old dude who was eating alone.

"Hey," she said. He smiled back, confused at first, but didn't seem to mind as she helped herself to a fry off of his plate. He was a balding guy with a shiny pink face; typical uptight office drone nobody, reading the daily paper on the toilet, fucking his wife once a month; a three minute heave-ho with his grey underpants around his ankles. Mia twirled a length of hair around her finger, whispering flirty nothings we couldn't hear from across the diner.

"What's she *doing*? He look like someone we wanna take back? Look at that pink little motherfucker." Finally, Mia came back to our booth, with Pinky's gaze following her ass all the way across the floor. He slapped a check onto his table and headed out through the exit. Mia grasped Coochie Sue by the hand, dragging her onto her feet.

"Don't go anywhere," said Mia, as she pulled Sue towards the exit. Off my look, and way more loudly than was necessary, she yelled – "He's gonna give us fifty bucks to eat each other out while he watches." She mimed a little weiner being jerked, as me and Shelly watched the three of them disappear into Frank's Mootel.

Less than an hour later, the girls reappeared, without Pinky, skipping out of one of the rooms to join us outside. Mia flashed a roll of notes at me, with a credit card gripped between her first two fingers. She explained how they'd tied him naked to the bed with his own clothes, and rather than chow on each other's twots, they'd mocked everything from his dirty habits to his pink little pecker, before trashing the place like Keith Moon. Coochie Sue held a small photo in front of my face, a portrait of Pinky posing with his wife and two teenage children.

"Here's your fuckin' moral American citizen. Old perv!" As a couple passed us on the sidewalk, she put on a babyish voice of concern, waving the picture at them with an "Excuse me! Have you seen my daddy? He's missing and I'm so terribly worried!" With a cackle, she was off down the street.

That night, Pinky's dough bought us a room in a fancy-ass hotel, with the biggest king-sized bed you've ever seen. As I lay among three naked chicks, on a soft mattress for the first time any of us could remember, all we wanted to do was sleep. The next morning, after endless nowhere conversations with posers and idiots, we finally found one we just had to have. Sat on a bench in the square, the quiet, bookish-looking girl with the plain face was visibly startled by the sound of my voice.

"Take you for a coffee and a sandwich if you'll sit with me and my friends." She was nervous, but smiled, and seemed grateful for a friendly face. She told us her name was Mary and that she'd ran away from home a couple of weeks back. She spent her nights sleeping in the park and her days evading the creepy stoners hitting on her. It was obvious Mary had no street smarts. She was like a baby in a bear pit, and it was a wonder she hadn't been eaten alive already.

I told her we'd all take care of her, and that Charlie would love to meet her. She seemed surprised, even flattered, like "He wants to meet *me?*" and soon she was tagging along, like one of the Family. Coochie Sue and Mia held her by the hands, like a child that'd got lost at the mall. I saw in her so much naivety, but so much potential. Even if she had to be chained in the desert to find it, inside that meek little girl was a beautiful, energetic soul just waiting to tear its way out; a gift that Charlie would delight in opening.

Once we got into the swing of things, I promised myself that I'd return with only the very best recruits. Quality over quantity, every time, even if that meant we showed up with a handful while the others had a hundred, I knew that Charlie would take one Mary over a dozen Kips – Kip being a tool we'd met on our first day, who wouldn't shut the fuck up about baseball, and asked if everyone at Eden had their own toilet seat.

While I'd shoot the shit with someone to see what they were about, Mia had a more predatory way. She'd look at those lonely young waifs the way a fat man stares at a ham, stalking through the crowds and picking out her targets with a keen eye. Her ability to identify runaways was almost superhuman, and often she'd spot some delicate young thing and say to me "You want first dibs on that one, boy?" But afraid and alone wasn't always enough, and weeding out the ones willing *and* worthy wasn't so easy. Most were just happy to continue safely wallowing in that pretend freedom where you never had to think or learn or feel, and you could sit and listen to shitty beat poetry while passing round a joint and really feel like you were fucking The Man right in the mouth. We got so bored, we took to dropping tabs of acid into coke bottles and leaving them around for people to find.

Eventually, we got chatting to this guy who seemed like he might be cool. With four pairs of tits, we had the attention of any dude we chose. He was tall and rangy, with arms that were too long for his torso, and the dark, drooping eyelids of somebody who never slept.

"Where do people worth knowing hang?" I said.

"There's a place. I'll take you there if you want. You wanna party, pretty lady?" he asked Mia. The guy introduced himself as Spinner, and lead us on a meandering walk through the city, during which he never did stop fucking talking. Finally, we came to a wonky three-storey house, with the brickwork of each brightly painted in a different color, and stretching into the sky like a clown's boner. The front door was wide open and hung bent on a single hinge. A guy sat in a rocking chair on the porch, eyes closed and hands tented against his chest, rhythmically rocking back and forth. A unicycle with a deflated tyre lay on the unmowed front lawn, amid piles of empty beer bottles and scorched newspaper. As we crossed the threshold, the man on the rocking chair said "Jah provides," without opening his eyes.

Inside the house, there were people everywhere. Standing, sitting, laying around on the floor; each thoroughly lacking direction. One freak-o was laid on his back on top of a tall cabinet, with his stomach pressing against the ceiling every time he took a breath. A girl in an oversized tie dyed shirt sat on the staircase with her legs dangling through the rungs of the bannister. I felt like I'd fallen into a Saturday morning cartoon of Eden Ranch – *Charlie and the Manson Kids*, in glorious technicolor! – a corruption of everything we'd accomplished, with everybody trying way too hard, but not hard enough. Different music pumping loudly on each floor competed for ear space, with beats and voices muddying into a terrible sludge. Bob Marley, The Stones and The Byrds jostled for space on an overcrowded stage, three drummers and an ugly totem pole of amps. We were led up the staircase to the second floor and ushered into a large bedroom, where fools sat on rugs and walls were stained a bilious yellow from the constant belch of anaemic weed.

"Hey," said Spinner, addressing a jowly man in little round sunglasses like John Lennon's, "I ran into these cats."

"Sup," he said, with a lift of the eyebrows, "you from out of town?"

"Yeah."

"Way cool. You can crash for a while. Always got room for life's travellers. Sit." He gestured toward a circular rug with a spiral design and the five of us sat down on the floor. "I'm Moon-Ape. My name, it's Moon-Ape."

"Tom," I replied, "and this is my Family." Moon-Ape nodded in such an overly deep way as if to say 'I completely understand.'

"Where you cats from?"

"Eden," I said.

"Eden? Never heard of no Eden. That up in the Rockies, brother?"

"Ranch. Eden Ranch." Moon-Ape sat forwards, the floor creaking underneath him. A pinprick of light flickered in the dim of his eyes.

"Oh, you're with Manson? You're his people?" The whole room suddenly bristled. Eyes that were half-closed or lost in the middle-distance now fell upon us.

"Don't believe everything you read," I said, "guy like

you should know that."

"Right on," said the apeman, visibly relaxing. "Dracula!" He clapped twice. "Bring our friends some herbal tea, the one from my special jug." A skinny boy with dark skin clambered out from the corner like a spider from the woodwork. He was wearing a skirt made from the pages of a book and bent a small bow at Moon-Ape before scuttling out of the room. "It's brewed by the natives of the Ucayali River from the bark of the rubber trees. They pass it through their systems five times before it goes into our cups. It's loaded with their essence. You can't get that from the coffee shop, man..."

Supping on our jungle piss, Moon-Ape got to talking about his place. It was a stopover point, he said, for artists and free thinkers from all across the world.

"I'll introduce you to Lucy. She's from Sweden. She does these *amazing* silent songs. Don't make a sound, but it's the most beautiful music you ever heard." Moon-Ape's enlightened group hummed sagely. I told Moon-Ape some of the things Charlie had spoken about, seeing if maybe I'd judged him too harshly and there was common ground to be found beneath the clouds of incense. I spoke on John Michell, Dee and Kelley, and the Tibetan Book of the Dead, and of Charlie's soul transference theory, which sees the soul depart the body at the moment of death to spend a timeless eternity learning all the secrets of the universe, before seemingly-instantaneously entering a new vessel.

"Nobody's ever achieved that level of soul freedom before," I said, "but Charlie's gonna be the first." In turn, he told a story about a guy who'd been staying there, because the vibes were really helping with his astral projection. One night, his astral self floated so high into the sky that when he fell back into his body, he broke the bed.

"He was in the attic room, but we all heard the crash!"

There was a man in the doorway making eyes at Mia, and she was flirting back, just to fuck with him. There's nothing more dangerous than a sexy girl who knows it, and knows how to use it. "Try it, pleb," I thought, "she'd bite off your dick." I noticed a stack of magazines piled high behind Moon-Ape, reached over and pulled one off the top. They were all underground press; the *East Village Other*, *Bloop!* and *Jacobi's Cock*; and filled with rambling descriptions of drug trips and intricate drawings of women smothering tiny little men with their ridiculous pneumatic breasts; huge nipples like baby pacifiers glinting in the light. I held up a picture to the girls, snorting with revulsion. Then I found a cartoon of Charlie. It was grotesque, covering the middle pages, like it should be pulled out and stuck on a bedroom wall. His head was five times the size of his body, and he was blowing on a flute, with musical notes trailing the air behind him, where a long row of people followed, stretched off into the hills until they were just dots. I think it was meant to be insulting, but I figured he'd get a kick out of it.

"Can I keep this?" I said.

Another guy plonked down next to Mary, shooting her a "*Hey, you*," and looking her up and down. You could see what he was thinking about doing to her, and I felt an anger boiling up inside me. I couldn't have hid it very well, because that fucker took one look at me and made his leave. Noting it, Mary clung to Mia's arm even tighter. Funny. When we got back to camp, Mia would probably finger her so hard she wouldn't sit down for a week.

It was time to go. There was nothing in that house; no drive, no will to achieve, just burnt out posers who didn't want to do anything but get high and tell shitty stories to whoever blew inside. I told Moon-Ape we were leaving, and he said "So long then, friend!" in such a lackadaisical way, I almost felt sad for him. There was an open door, and nothing inside but closed minds.

The fat shaman's pretend commune was so depressing, we all just wanted to go home. We spent that night in a cheaper hotel, talking about Charlie and our friends back home, and all the things we missed from Eden, and felt better for it. Then Mia took Mary into the bathroom for a half hour and they both came out giggling. Come daybreak, we set about tracking down the best that shithole of a city had to offer and getting the fuck out of there.

First port of call was a street musician we'd seen playing to the passers-by from his spot outside a book store, and drawing quite a crowd. I'd had a good feeling about the guy, and even tossed a dime into his case, so we went back to see what was up.

"Hey buddy," I said. He glanced up at me, before casting his eyes over the girls. "What tune was that? I don't recognize it."

"You wouldn't. It's one of mine," he said, fiddling with the tuning heads and pinging a wonky note, "I'm a songwriter. Got enough for five albums. I live through my music. Robbie Ray." He extended his hand.

"Tom," I said, "and these are my friends."

"Your friends got names?" Robbie Ray plied his effortless, white-toothed lines with an in-built audience of Frisco girls cooing away. After months of hot and cold running pussy on tap, and chicks reaching up just to touch my hand through a tour bus window, the handsome dude with the honey voice and magic fingers had me feeling like the ugly nerd again. We chatted with Robbie Ray for a little while, although I'm pretty sure he wasn't really listening until I started bullshitting about connections in the music biz.

"We were out on tour a little while back," I told him, "Charlie's played all over the country."

"Yeah, I think I heard about that," he said. "Didn't somebody take a pop at him?"

"Take more than that to take him out. Anyways, maybe we can get something happening with your stuff?" That was all it took for Robbie Ray to pack up his shit and join us.

It wasn't always that easy. We got shot down more than once, with some ignoring us like we were crazy, or marching off, tutting like librarians. What those people didn't realize was that their saying no wasn't a victory for them; it was an admission that they'd never be free. But sometimes, you don't always find them; they find you. As the six of us were about ready to call it quits, a finger tapped me lightly on the shoulder.

"Excuse me, sir?" I turned to see a married couple, who looked to be in their mid-thirties. "Don't think I'm being rude or anything, I wasn't earwigging you, but are you... from Eden? Are you part of The Family?"

"Yeah, man. Why?" I said, ready for another lecture from the chinless middle-classes.

"It's just, did I hear right that you were taking some people back with you?"

"What of it? Got a problem with that, I suppose?" Behind me, I could feel the girls bridling, pushing out their chests and making themselves taller. The husband looked away from me and down at the ground, his wife touching his arm in a way that said, *let's just leave, now.*

"No, just..." he said, "can we come?"

I probably should have admired the stones on the guy, but there was a desperation that was kind of pathetic. I sized them up, deliberately taking my time, casting my eyes over their well-fed, unlived-in bodies, making them wait on my word, like a pound-puppy on execution day. You'd think it was all the husband's dream, but it was clear that she wanted it more. To look at them, you'd never see them fitting in with our lifestyle. There was nothing that would have singled them out, but then again, who can tell? What was it about me that suggested I'd have ever belonged there? And shouldn't everyone who wants to become Brand New be given that chance?

"Sorry," I said, "we're full. Fuck off." Though they tried not to show it, both visibly wilted. A grim acceptance fell over their faces, as they shuffled a turn and began to walk away. Stopping after three paces, the husband turned back, firmly holding my eye contact.

"There's nothing we can do?" *Got you*, I thought. I made like I was thinking about it, and then–

"Drop everything and come with us right now. Can you do that?" The guy started to get flustered, hands to his head and pacing, hammering out desperate mental calculations. The wife pushed her way past, speaking for the first time.

"My mother," she said, "she's old. Just... can we go and say goodbye? We have lives, we can't drop everything.

We'll need time. This was just a judgement call, we didn't..."

"We didn't plan this..." he said. "I mean we've seen you people on TV and talked about it, but we never thought..."

"Fine," I said. "Be at the train station in an hour. One hour. You're not there, you're not coming. I'll make sure they *never* let you in." They muttered thank yous and we'll definitely be theres, and jogged away, hand in hand. I'd have bet my life on them being on that platform before we were.

I was feeling pretty boss as the six of us took that steep walk back up to the station. As we crossed the street, the girls leading the way, and me and Robbie Ray behind, three friends – two dudes and a skirt – moved aside to let us by.

"Sorry, ladies," said one of the guys, sidestepping to let the girls past.

"Hey, brother," I said, to the taller of the two, feeling casual and friendly. "How's life treating you?"

"Geez, you're an ugly chick." he said. He was obviously putting on a show for his friends. "Get a haircut." We got a thousand jibes about hair every time we stepped beyond the gates, so I honked a laugh, but Shelly suddenly erupted.

"You shouldn't talk to him that way," she said, "you know we're the Manson Family?"

"Shut up, no you're not." The steel in our eyes told him otherwise, but he couldn't back down. "I seen you around," he said, pointing at Mary, "I see you at the park. What're you doing with these freaks?" He turned to me, "You stealing little girls to take back to a killer?"

"We ain't stealing nobody. You don't know what you're talking about."

"He's at it again from what I hear. Four more bodies, just last week." The douchebag kept his eyes on Mary, like a deer unknowingly staring down the barrel of a rifle. "You wanna be a killer, little girl? He'll brainwash you like he did them others." Mia started laughing, a real wild cackle, and one of the pricks, a sneering, pan-faced, blonde hag made a dismissive *pshh* sound, looking us over like we were trash. The three of them began walking away, and just loud enough for us to hear, the taller guy spoke.

"They deserve each other."

That's when something took me over, and I found my body lurching forwards, fingers gift-wrapped into a fist, muscles and sinews tight with rage. It was a clean, hard punch to the back of the head, dropping him to the hot concrete. His girl screamed, hands over her mouth, while his little buddy could do nothing but watch, too afraid to speak, let alone step in. Straddling Tallboy's chest, the impact of my fist in his eye whipped back his head and bounced it against the ground. My right hand rained punches, while my left swatted away the fingers vainly swiping at my face from below.

"Fuckin' pig motherfucker!"

His arms fell limp, but I kept beating out a savage drumbeat on his skull, again and again, hitting so hard that I felt sure my knuckles would break through and feel the road beneath. The dull smacking sounds were a morse code telegram of adoration to the Family he'd insulted, *my*

Family. After a final punctuation point that pulped his nose, I exhaled deeply and pulled myself to my feet, pushing off of his chest, which bucked and rose in staccato gasps. My girls stood wide-eyed, nearly orgasmic, and each, but the shell-shocked Mary, with that look a girl gets when she's hungering for the cock. Robbie Ray scratched a nervous itch on the top of his cowboy hat. Blood was streaked all the way up to my elbow, like a posh lady's glove, and my knuckles were uneven and oddly sized. The pig on the floor gurgled through a mash of gums, spittle, and splintered teeth. The red and white seemed somehow festive to me, evoking a brief nostalgia for the lost Christmases of childhood.

The piggy's piggy girlfriend knelt down and cradled him in her arms, while his little buddy stood with his arms wrapped impotently around his own body. A dark, spluttered mouthful of hog's blood splotched a mural onto the back of his lady friend's hand, causing Mia to double over with laughter.

"You're just fucking thugs!" said the girl, in that weird, hitching way people talk when they're crying so hard they can't breathe.

"You don't get it *at all*," I said, and we began the walk back to the station, leaving Tallboy to bleed downhill streaks onto the city below. "Not at all." Why couldn't she see?

With San Francisco done, the final tally of new Family members was a healthy five. There was frail little Mary, an unopened present under the tree. Robbie Ray, pretty boy with the guitar – he spent the entire journey giving Mia the goo-goo eyes, and I wondered if she'd be the one to take him out back of the barn. It almost seemed unfair; good looking guy who could sing and play, he could get girls anywhere. Mike and Linda, the married couple who were ready waiting at the station to shake my bloodied hand. And then there was Jessica. She was a bonus. Young and pretty, just how Charlie liked, she said she was a friend of Robbie Ray's, but he told me they'd only spoken one time, while he was busking. Figures she had a crush on him and tagged along on the spur of the moment. Around for five minutes, and already proving himself an asset. I wondered if Charlie would be proud of my haul, hoping that none of them would do anything to let me down, and that once invited into our home, they'd make it their own and stay with us forever.

Coochie Sue looked across at my fist, swollen and red. I tensed it, wincing from the pain. She smiled warmly, shifting in her seat and widening her thighs, a gift for my dedication, before gazing out of the window. Mary sat arm-in-arm with Mia, now fully in her clutches, whispering softly into her ear.

"She wants to know why you beat that guy," said Mia. The girls from Eden Ranch wore the smiles of those who'd peeked under the wrapping paper. They knew why.

"I did it for love," I said, placing my hand onto Mary's and tracing a heart on her palm with my fingertip. "Love, Love, Love."

9 LUCHAS DE APUESTAS

I don't know what I was expecting when we got back from San Fran. Maybe a high five and playful head rub from Charlie; a chair at the main table with two of his hottest girls wafting me down with palm fronds. All that awaited was a whole lot of unfamiliar faces. Some of the other recruiters were back already, leaving us fresh blood to get the measure of.

Mary had jumped straight up to the main house, and I'd glanced her but a couple of times since, clinging to established members like a sheet buffeted by the wind. Jessica, so smitten with the bohemian musician stylings of Robbie Ray now had her pick of cats all singing and jigging for her attentions, not least the biggest superstar of them all. Then there was Mike and Linda. Maybe they thought this would be the next exciting step in their marriage; that they could just shack up and move in like buying into a new neighborhood. They found out real quick that nothing could be owned at Eden, especially not people. There were no wives here, no husbands, no girlfriends, "old ladies" or better halves, and definitely no ball and chains. Charlie always said "We take the *why* out of Yours, and get Ours."

I said hi to Mike once in passing, but his eyes were vacant, and looked right through me. I watched two girls toying with him, pressing a joint between his lips, prodding him to inhale and hold for as long as he could, and laughing as he nearly hacked out his skeleton. It reminded me of the bikers blowing weed smoke into a kitten's face. Course, they did that when Charlie wasn't around, 'cuz if he'd seen it, he'd have gone apeshit. I once saw him uppercut a guy just for standing on a bug. Mike was like that cat. A dumb animal who couldn't survive in the wilds. He might have been smiling, but it was the smile of a guy who'd watched thirty different guys and girls fuck his wife and found that he didn't much care for it. Guess some people aren't willing to pay the price for true freedom. He'd learn. He'd learn or he'd leave, and leave broken. You couldn't go back into their world after that, not half and half.

My own moods grew strangely darker, and I felt myself becoming isolated from the rest of the group. My interactions with Melody were the one bright oasis in an increasingly barren landscape. Sometimes I felt like I only existed when I was with her. Feeling bad was in itself making me feel worse; selfish and ungrateful for all I'd been afforded; the love of an enormous Family, the chance to learn from Charlie, and somehow still not happy. Near the back of the ranch, way off to the side in a part where nobody really ever went, someone, maybe the cats and dogs, had dug a little hole out in the soil. It was more of a groove really, a circular burrow about eighteen inches deep. I'd go drop acid and sit inside the hole, surveying things from the viewpoint of a curious gopher or mongoose, in my grubby wallow. One time I was tripping and thought I was laying inside my own grave, but I didn't really care. Charlie's always talking about how death is just an illusion.

I put my spiralling outlook down to two things. First, was the sudden and shocking demise of my boy, Robbie Ray, and secondly, the nagging sense that Clark not only wasn't what he seemed, but that he'd had a hand in something awful. So awful, it could put a stop to everything we'd worked towards. Like those streets of San Fran, it felt as though the world was pivoting up at an angle, and all of us were sliding, faster and faster, with no way of holding on, down, down, and ever down towards some horrible end.

So, Robbie Ray. Before all the bullshit started, I came back from a piss one evening to see a large crowd gathered by the fire. They looked real jubilant, swaying and clapping, like they always did when Charlie pulled out the guitar and gave us a show. As I got closer, I saw that it wasn't Charlie, but Robbie Ray, belting out one of his own numbers. We'd been back for little under a week, and I'd seen him noodle around a little, but this was the first the camp had seen him really going at it. I watched with the pride of parent at a piano recital, Robbie Ray, so confident and poised, and connecting with each member of the crowd like he was singing to them and them alone. He didn't even have to look at his hands. What I wouldn't have given for a talent like that. We were all clapping, hands over our heads, swaying, dancing, and when Robbie Ray asked if we had any requests, everybody wanted to hear the one he'd just finished playing, all over again.

Right in the middle of that song, suddenly, Charlie appeared. He shoved his way through the crowd and stared at Robbie Ray. I say stared at, but stared *down* is more accurate. Most were so into the music that hardly anybody seemed to notice Charlie, rooted to the spot, and with fury smeared across his face like a slap. If they had, they'd have ran, but instead they continued to ignorantly dance and clap, with their elbows and feet nudging into Charlie as they lost themselves in Robbie Ray's little show. Charlie's mouth hung open, his eyebrows tensed in a downward V, but when he saw him, that poor fucker, cowboy-hatted and handsome, just kept on playing, singing out even louder now that the king, with all his connections, had come down from the hill to check him out, and beaming this big ol' smile right at him. Maybe it was the key change which put him over the edge.

Charlie steamed forwards, yanking the guitar from around Robbie Ray's neck so rough that he almost pulled him over. At first, I think he thought Charlie was joking, but those of us who'd been around long enough knew different.

"Get this piece of shit out of my home," said Charlie, with an anger that knotted my insides. The mood changed so fast and got so tense, like if a bride had said her *I do* and then dropped dead in the aisle. "Take a walk, boy, 'fore I fuckin' put one in your head!" Charlie was not fucking around, and Robbie Ray didn't help none by standing there with this stupefied look on his face.

"Just leave, dude," said Jedro, in the soft tones of peacemaker.

"And who asked you a motherfuckin' thing?" yelled Charlie. Jedro held his hands up in apology and skulked off behind the pack. Robbie started backing away towards the gate, in defeated, stuttering little steps. He got about ten yards, and stood looking back towards Charlie with a sick puppy expression. The crack of the firewood popped like gunshots in my ears, as for a few dreadful moments, they locked eyes.

"Come on, man," said Robbie, all confused and pitiful. I looked to Charlie, who was smiling with his mouth, but nothing else. With a deliberate, almost majestic motion, and not once breaking eyes with Robbie Ray, Charlie tossed the guitar onto the fire. Robbie grasped at the brim of his hat, as the flames devoured the only real friend he'd ever had, before he turned and walked out of Eden Ranch for the last time. Charlie tramped back up to the house, leaving everyone feeling bad just for being there. Whereas me, I was the one who'd brought that into camp in the first place.

I'd could no longer find respite from my troubles by hanging with Clark. His drug use had gotten out of control. Most of us were high off our fucking asses whenever God provided, which he usually did, but this was a whacked-out dude with enough demons crawling up his ass as it was. I'd even seen him scoring heroin off the bikers. I had no idea where he got the cash to be doing deals with the kinda men you didn't wanna owe money to, which was another thing best not think about. But it wasn't the usage itself that was the problem. It's not like we had to be up for work the next day, and if Eden had drug testing, anyone who passed would have been booted out. Clark's problem was that his cravings made him needy and desperate, and he was pissing everyone off by being a total Bogart, popping up like a dog at the dinner table, eyes on the sausages, and his little tail thumping against the floor. He had no shame, nor any idea how many feathers he was ruffling. He'd turned into the joke of the camp, and more than once, I'd had to step in and talk someone out of giving him a clout upside the nut, due to his inability to take no for an answer. And that wasn't just over the dope. His increasingly leery, grabby behavior towards the girls wasn't winning any friends, and I was caught between disassociating myself from Clark altogether, and trying to stop him from shitting off the wrong person and getting sent to live on the farm with O'Beale.

It didn't take a genius to figure his worsening behaviour was down to a deeper problem; a cloud so dark that even he couldn't live beneath its gloom. It made my bones cold to think about it, but before someone else discovered the terrible things he was trying to blot out, I decided to start tailing him myself.

Lately, I'd been watching from a distance, peeping in on his conversations like a horny kid ogling a showering neighbor from the bushes. Like so many nipple-soaping middle-aged women startled by the rattle of a garbage can, I was convinced that he knew. Clark's growing paranoia was such that even a simple "What's up?" would leave him rattled, so I'd backed off for a little while. But maybe it was me who was paranoid, with nothing but a butt-full of free time to get tangled up in imaginary conspiracies.

Was it better be right than crazy? No. Definitely not.

I'd noted his habit of buddying up to the newest recruits, telling them his story, and then moving on, and that day, I took the opportunity to loiter nearby as he sat with a teenage girl who'd arrived the day before, after hiking across from Arizona. I listened in on her tale of sun-dried trailer park boredom; an alcoholic birth mother and a thumb that took her down hot highways to the place she'd now call home. When she was finished, he spoke.

The first time I'd heard the story, I was worried that I might cry in front of a stranger. The second time, I was disorientated, but in a different way. And then? Leaning on the barn and hearing it come out of his face *again* – I felt huckstered; used. I heard him tell the girl all about his five dead brothers, about a pile of bodies and a little foot, and how fuckin' weird it is to hear himself say all this out loud, for the first time. I listened to the whole thing, even though I knew the words. I knew the words, the pauses, the parts where he'd take a deep breath and push his fingers into his eyes. Over time I'd caught snippets here and there, but by then I could have sang my sinking heart out, waving my lighter at the slow, tragic parts, and standing respectfully still during the immaculately placed silences. My gut span like I was falling from the sky, because I knew. I knew that it was him. I'd felt it, like a faint rapping at the door, that first time we heard about what was happening in the city. And now the door was being kicked in.

Arizona Girl, in tears like they always were, planted a sympathetic kiss onto Clark's cheek, and with a few gently whispered words of strength, left him to compose himself. As I approached, he was still twisting on the oversized football ring, prop that it was.

"We need to talk," I said, startling him. He quickly wiped that familiar drip from his cheek and seemed to immediately snap out of his grief, giving me a "Hey, Tom," with the urgent normality of a masturbating man tucking himself back in when someone walks into the room.

"What is that?" I said, ship out of the bottle and sailing over the edge of the world. "Some kind of patter? You're just hitting up every sap that strolls in here?"

"What do you want... what are you talking about? What?" He was stuttering and stammering all over the place, looking either for an exit, or to see if anyone was watching.

"Look, man," I said, pushing myself right up in his face, "you wanna talk to me, or to one of those crazy motherfuckers? Plenty of folks here who'll cut you up without wanting to know the why. You might be craziest of all, that's what worries me." In my pocket, my trembling hand was gripping the flick-knife I'd brought along to cover my ass. I didn't know what he was capable of. Hell, even if everything he'd told me was true, I was still out of my depth. I didn't know if I wanted to help him, or just tell him to get as far away as possible and never look back. It was bad enough bringing Robbie Ray into camp, but the guy who was fucking everything up for Charlie by murdering civilians? That would be the end of me.

"I'll talk," said Clark, "but not here."

He lead me though the camp and out of the entrance, with me two paces behind, clasping the wet handle of the knife. We stopped at the tree-line just outside of the ranch; tall, old oaks leading into a quarter mile of woodland and lining the other side of the dirt path that lead down through the hills and into the city. We sat inside the shade, a few trees deep. I wondered if both of us would walk back out.

"Was it you?" I said, my right leg jiggling ferociously.

"Was *what* me?" He was so wired, there was no way the conversation wouldn't turn bad. I could see myself having to stick him just to get out of there alive.

"You know damn well what – the killings!"

"*What killings?*"

"Jesus Christ," I snapped, "the fuckin' killings down in the city. People all hacked up, just like the last time, so they keep saying. It was you, wasn't it? Fuckin' sneaking around, with your fake war stories and fuckin' football ring."

"What? No! Hell, no. And keep your fuckin' voice down. Shit." Clark's hands were trembling badly as they fumbled with a carton of smokes.

"Then what the fuck is up with that story of yours? I know you're all messed up in the mind, but I heard you. 'I guess there's just something to be said for the comfort of strangers.' It's word for word, man. Not just once or twice, neither."

"Look... it's not what you think. I'm... fuck." With an unlit cigarette stuck to his lip, Clark picked up a branch and idly poked at the dirt. The fucking thing was going in my eye, I just knew it. *Give me a reason*, I thought, poised with the knife and praying my buddy was still, and always had been my buddy, and that–

"I'm a journalist."

Clark let out an enormous sigh, flicking open the lighter with his thumb and sparking up. A snake! A fucking snake! I couldn't even speak. We sat in silence for a few moments, with nothing but the sound of his slow, deep, inhalations, and his blowing out the smoke the way he always did, in a thin little column like he was whistling Dixie.

"How can you be a journalist? You're a fucking head case!"

"I'm really not, but thanks. You know how it is, I couldn't have walked in here as me. I had to look legit."

"Oh yeah, I *know how it is*. I clearly don't know a fucking thing about you. Thought I did. Where are you really from, Clark? Is that even your real name? Who do you work for? The *LA Times*? Those motherfuckers? They said Charlie went around 'seducing schoolgirls...'"

"I don't work for anyone." Clark was calmer now, like the weight that had been lifted from his shoulders finally allowed him to breathe a little easier, sit up straighter. "Freelance. I figured I could dig around for a month or so, tops, write some piece from the inside, and off it to the highest bidder. Big bucks. But real quick I realized there was a book in this. Five, six hundred page epic, easy. Book, movie deal, fuck, I mean nobody'd ever be willing to talk about him, about this place..."

"Except you, right? What's a soul worth these days? You know, I felt so bad about what you told me. Was any of it true?" Clark just shook his head. "Did you even serve?"

"In Nam? Nah. I got the bandy legs. But if you're going undercover, your story is your backbone. If he got off, I knew Manson would set up somewhere new, but I didn't think I could just walk on in like we did. He made it too easy. I wrote that thing and just learned it off by heart. I am a writer y'know." Yeah, I thought, you look like a writer. Pupils like blobs of ink dropped in a glass. "Must'a read it a thousand times, over and over. Figured if I had nothing else, I had that. Anyone probes any deeper, just start crying or shaking or whatnot. Crazy is a good alibi. Took some drama classes at The Y. Gave it one last read when you were sleeping on the bus, right before we talked."

"Jesus fuck... wait, what about that?" I poked my finger hard into the gnarled skin that trailed up his arm and across the side of his neck. "How'd you get that, if you're so full of shit?"

"Oh, this?" he said, tugging at his collar. "Pulled a boiling saucepan on myself when I was a kid. Don't even remember it. Mom never forgave herself. Use what you got, you know?" And use it he did. Dude had gotten so many sympathy fucks with the crying and the scars that his dick must have sizzled like a blacksmith's poker whenever he took a wash. I felt so betrayed. He'd manipulated everyone, playing with our feelings and trust, building everything on a foundation of lies. It was the exact opposite of everything Charlie taught us. It was an aberration.

"Fuck you! I fell for all that shit. Jesus, I had nightmares about what you told me, and it's not true, not a goddamn word of it. All your buddies, the dead babies, *the fucking hand*... what kind of a sick mind comes up with something like that?"

"It's all true. Probably. Just... not for me. That kinda thing happens all the time. You seen how people come back from there? It breaks you, man. Interviewed this vet once, homeless guy, and he just walked in a circle, all day long, marching in the dirt until his feet bled, round and round and round. Groove was so deep it was up to his knees, and at nights, he'd sleep curled up in the center of it like a baby. That was all the peace he could find. Maybe that's what put it in my head."

"I wish you had've been the killer," I said, slumping back hard against a tree, and relishing the knotted bark digging painfully into my spine. "Be better than this shit."

"I never killed anyone. Not in any war, and least of all out here." For first time I thought I saw the real guy lurking beneath the character. The mannerisms, even the voice, seemed to slip a little, just for a glimpse. For a second, I wondered if the real Clark and me could have ever been friends. But I could never be friends with a cunting snake. "Don't feel bad, nobody else figured it out. I guess old Charlie's snake sniffing skills aren't as great as he likes to make out."

"You got no right to speak his name!" I said, jumping to my feet in anger.

"Simmer down. You wanna get us both whacked?" He nodded towards the gates, where guards from the Judas Noose were permanently posted.

"Fuck off, narc," I said, but conceding his point by dropping my voice. "You're right about getting whacked, though. You know what they'd do to you in there? What *he'd* do to you? There's not a person in there that wouldn't string you up by your dick and feed what was left to the coyotes. Not that there'd be anything left. Ranch cats wouldn't even wanna touch that."

"That include you? You gonna string me up, huh? Feed me to the scorpions?" He was getting cocky. He knew I couldn't ring the bell without making myself look the pig fucker.

"You gonna write about all the drugs and fuckin' you've been doing?"

"Look man," he said, suddenly defensive, "you don't know how it is. I had to be so into the *character* of Clark, that it could never slip. Never. What was I gonna do, say no? You can't be 'that guy' around here, you know he don't stand for that. That fuckin' chick who'd never do anything? Remember that? Week or two after we got here, cried when he tried to give her acid, all nervous and shit? She got away with it for a while, but much as he preaches individuality, if you ain't one of us, you're one of Them. Ran out one morning, never to return, saying someone had touched her. It's fuckin' Eden Ranch, man, everyone's touching everyone! I had to be one of Us. You see that, right? I couldn't afford to be seen as anything but, even for a second. You can sit there with that look on your face, but you've no idea what it's like. I have to be *on* twenty four hours a day. It's not enough to put on an act, I have to *be* that guy, wear the skin like a suit. Sometimes, you tell the same lie enough times, it becomes the truth. You wanna know something really fucked up? After like three, four weeks, I started having nightmares about the story. The bodies, the explosion, all of that, so vivid it's more like a memory than a dream. Made me wonder if it had happened and all *this* was the part that I'd imagined. Like maybe I was some war fuck-up, hallucinating another life as a writer. I've woke up weeping for my buddies more than once. It's no joke, that's real pain. Like when you have a dream about being in love with a girl that don't exist, and when you wake up, you feel that love, just for a minute. It's there and it's warm in your heart, as real as anything you felt when you were awake. I dreamed that so real, so often, I've really been there. And I've mourned those guys, I really have. Some days I feel as much loss for Remmy as I do my grandpa."

"Jesus, you're a piece of work."

"Yeah, I know. And I know I fucked up, I know I went too far, got sucked into that whole lifestyle, but fuck... it's gonna make a hell of a story."

"You're disgusting. Honestly disgusting. You can't be using your real name. What is it really?" I stared into his eyes, with their dark, hooded lids and yellowing whites. The endless months of living on Eden time, the partying until you pass out, the staying up all night to do acid and fuck under the stars; it had taken its toll. He might not have been a frazzled burnout when he stepped on that bus, but he sure as shit was now. He was barely capable of holding a book, much less writing one. "Guess it doesn't matter," I said, dusting the dirt from my ass. Suddenly, Clark reared at me, clasping the fabric of my shirt in his fists. The panic in his voice was pure jonesing junkie.

"Stop fucking with me! Are you gonna rat me out or not?"

"Get off, you dick," I said, separating his fingers one by one. Now I knew he wasn't a killer, in the city or in Saigon, I wasn't afraid of him. But I didn't know what to do. I felt I should tell him to leave, and never come back, but I didn't.

"Just let me ride it out a little while longer," he said, "I swear, just a little while. I won't fuck things up for you, and I can walk on out of here straight into a Pulitzer..."

"You ain't doing much walking. Look at yourself, swivel-eyed motherfucker." He was in no condition to be doing anything but slumping against a wall and sweating. And undercover or not, when you left our world and went back into theirs, you did so with the Mark of Cain, especially with LA still dark under the shadow of killings that everyone thought was us. He really thought he could stagger into a publishers and get past the front desk? And what did he even have? There was nothing going on, at least that goofs like us were privy to. Not that it was anyone's fucking business what we did or didn't get up to.

"Seriously, man," he said. He nodded towards the entrance with his eyes. Johnny Dingo was showing off to another biker, rolling a little knife over the edges of his fingers, flipping it up and safely catching it as the blade flashed through the air. "Something big's brewing, real big."

"What's brewing?"

"Can't you feel it? Everything got a little more serious lately. Charlie more careful about who goes in and out of that house. I heard Amber-May tried to leave, but he wouldn't let the baby go, so she's stuck. Once you get in that inner circle, ain't no way out. Little thing like that, dumb little skank, not allowed to go back out. Makes you wonder what she knows..."

"And what do you know?" Nothing. He knew shit. Just the shattered wreckage of two half-imagined lives, bobbing on a sea of spilled brain fluid. "You want a free pass, you'd better let on."

"Okay... but alls I know is there's something called The Wave."

"The Wave? The fuck is that? You're talking out your ass."

"It's true. And I don't know what it is, not yet. But I think it has something to do with all the guns."

"Guns?"

"Yeah. There's a shitload of guns buried in a pit out back. Guns, ammo. I think I saw some riot gas in there too. I caught a look once when I was smoking a duster with Jeanne. Not just handguns neither; rifles, automatics, big bastard shooters with telescopic sights..."

"That's just for protection."

"Come on, look around you. All these people, your little trip to SF." I just shook my head. "He's building an army."

That night, I held on to Melody as though she and

everything precious could be blown away by a foul wind. Or a Wave. Under brooding skies, I slept, with her soft hair against my face, lost in vivid dreams of melting children and severed hands clasping ballpoint pens.

"Get up, you piece of shit!"

A foot to the stomach was how I found the morning; a rooster with spittle-flecked lips and a metal badge, crowing a sunrise chorus of "Hippies!" and "Faggots!" A pair of thick, hairy hands pulled me across the dirt by my hair and dumped me at the end of a handcuffed row of wriggling spastic caterpillars. Breathing dust, I began to cut through the underbrush of disorientation. It was a raid. A big one. Fleets of cop cars and a pair of black FBI ranchers. Piggies everywhere, swarming like someone had kicked the top of a cockroach nest, and right at dawn, when those who'd bothered to do so had just bedded down. Most were too half-asleep or too apathetically familiar with the ways of the pig to put up much of a struggle. Those who did took a nightstick to the back of the legs and went down the hard way, with arms wrenched up their backs, and the boots of LA County's finest leaving prints across their cheeks. Jimmy Jizz slipped loose and ran, giggling and barefoot, from the clutches of the filth. A hard tackle brought him to the floor, and a winded Jizz was tossed onto the heap with the others.

"You're hurting me..." Melody. From the floor, I watched helplessly as big paws clamped roughly around her wrist, yanking her across the grass. She was giving it up quietly, but those bastards never missed a chance to rough up somebody small and unarmed.

"You fucking cunt!" I yelled, from my helpless position face-down in the dirt. "Fucking let her go!" He dropped her like he was putting out the garbage, and walked back into the fray. Melody lay beside me, sobbing. I wriggled as close as I could, touching her foot with mine; a little human contact in an inhuman moment.

"It's okay," I said, "we're all in this together." She took a moment to compose herself, bravely emboldening against the horror of watching the only Family she knew tied up like cattle.

"Where's Charlie?" Yeah, where *was* Charlie?

"Charlie? Charlie?" He didn't answer, and others took up the cry, calling his name and bucking their bodies to try and pick out that recognisable figure among the chaos. Freck lay across the way on her stomach, hissing like a wild beast, completely crackers. Her ankles were bound in handcuffs to stop her feet from kicking, and her face was flushed a deep red. I stared at the wonky line of cop cars, with their screech-mark scars carved into the dirt, picturing how they'd fall into the split in the Earth when Charlie saw what was happening. "Charlie?!"

And like that, there he was, with a pig on each arm, leading him across the ranch.

"Charlie! Char-lie!"

He was so calm, so dignified, giving them nothing. I bet they'd expected him to thrash and wail, to open himself up to the brutality of resisting arrest, but they didn't get it. He was so placid that he reacted to a full blown FBI raid at his door like others would invited guests. With his Family laid out before him, or being wrestled into submission by men who did so purely because they could, the piggies pulled open the door to the squad car, and Charlie turned towards us.

"It's that Man again," he said, a disgusted acceptance in his voice, "can't leave a peaceful guy be."

"Where you taking him?"

"Charlie! Charlie?"

We could only watch as Charlie was roughly bundled into the back of the car, his head slamming against the frame as he was thrown onto the back seat. A unified cry of pain rose from the pits of our stomachs.

"Where are you taking him?"

"He's done," said a fat piggie with sunglasses, his chubby cheeks contorted into a grin, "we've got him this time."

"For what? He's done shit to you."

"You smelly bastards don't get the news up here? We know he did it. We *know*. Didn't even need your help this time – did it all by himself, all those murders, every one of 'em. We got our sources. Solid-fuckin'-gold sources. It's all over! You freaks'll all have to go back to momma, if she'll have you. Your boy there, he's going to the chair..."

Somebody cried out – "Lying fuckin' pigs, that's bullshit!" I didn't realise it was me until Officer Fuckface hoofed my ribs with a size ten steel toe. Across the way, Clark was being pushed into a seated position with his hands cuffed behind his back.

"Did you do this?" I yelled. He mouthed the word "no," and I could see, even from there, that he was being true. The whole thing stank. They weren't searching for drugs or weapons, they just wanted him. And when the car containing Charles Milles Manson was halfway down the drive, they'd let us all loose, and we'd wander aimless and lost, pacing out Vietnam Vet circles in that valley between anger and grief. But as the siren sparked and it cruised towards the exit, my friends – my Family – watched from where we lay, bleeding and beaten and pushed into the dirt, and by who? The people in power. The ones who'd put hand on heart and sworn to protect the public, to stand up for the little guy; the innocent; to uphold justice and truth. The Man.

Charlie was right about everything.

10 SANTIAGO!

Nobody slept. Nobody partied. Nobody fucked. We did sing though; songs of support for our fallen brother, in a day-long midnight mass that had us linking arms and searching for that unifying spirit that came all too easily when he was leading us, guitar in hand, love filling the air in musical notes that flit about our faces like fireflies.

Charlie's presence over camp was all encompassing. He cast a long, deep shadow that shielded us from the glare of the world, where we could see clearly, without having to blot our eyes from the spotlights of careers and rules and expectations, beamed into the faces of everyone born into the system. Without him, without the planet round which we found our orbit, we clattered and drifted. All we could do – all it was right to do – was to keep vigil for his return. Briefly, once uncuffed, there'd been chest-beating talk of busting him out, galvanizing us to the point of tooling up with knives and planks, but it was a rudderless rage. Charlie had often talked of spiking the city's water supply with LSD, and we found a moment's hope in filling their streets with freaked-out pigs and chumps while Charlie danced through the door of his cell, except none of us knew how.

What we did know, was that he hadn't done what they said. Though we all agreed that if he had, he'd have had his reasons, and they would be well-deserved. If you're going to get the blame for something, why not do it anyway? Those fucking pig pricks waltzed in to a man's home, all because they had the badges and pieces of paper that gave them the right to do whatever they liked.

But their lies weren't playing. The tricks to drive a wedge between us were glass; brittle and transparent, grubby with the fingerprints of sweating hands desperately snatching for whatever weapon they could find to take Charlie out. Pointless. Useless. Laughable. You can't spread filth on man whose soul is laid bare for all to see with every word he speaks.

A full, long day later, like they'd rolled the rock away from the door, there he was; that small, slender silhouette, slightly stooped, arms folded behind his back, long hair fluttering in the wind, and framed between the two posts that marked the entrance to Eden Ranch. He came towards us slowly, savoring the walk back to his people in measured steps. We all wanted to run over and sweep him up in our arms, but everybody stood rooted, breaking out in a typically Eden, typically Manson applause and cheering. Many wept, with each of us lovingly grasped by those around us, a Family once more, everything as it should be.

"Honeys, I'm home!" There were gasps and fucks of outrage as we saw for the first time Charlie's face. It was bruised and cut, with a welt across the bridge of his nose, and a raspberry swirl of color smeared inside the white of his left eye. Then he talked, and we listened, explaining how things were, and how they were going to be.

"This is what they do to me." He touched the bridge of his nose, rubbing off a fine red crust. "Three armed men; four, five. They beat me like Romans, with my hand chained to a table. An unarmed man with nothing but love in his heart, and this gang of jackals..." Girls covered their mouths, distraught at the brutality against one they so loved. Tears welled in my eyes.

"These *pigs*..." *Pigs*. That word had never been spat with such righteous venom, "...they swear an oath to protect the people who live on this land, to serve the citizens walking the streets. Who's protecting us from them? Who, if not ourselves? The pigs who punched and kicked and beat on me, calling me the Devil and a pervert, a stealer of children, a corrupter of minds. They looked at me as if to say '*why aren't you fighting back?*'" Charlie paused, a small beat for us to ponder on the same question, something he did to encourage us to think for ourselves. "I didn't have to. They'd already lost. You raise a fist to me; a gun, a nightstick, a badge, you're admitting that you're weak. You may as well be beating me with a sign; a confession. I'm weak and you're strong. I'm wrong and you're right. I'm afraid and you're the thing that haunts my dreams. You're what keeps me awake at night. You're the shapes I see in the eyes of my children when I first see that glimmer; the look that says *they know*, they know mommy and daddy's word ain't carved in stone. This is what I'm saying, man, they bring it on themselves. They can't even see how fragile it all is. The cages keeping the animals at bay, the locks on those chains they slap on your ankles when they snatch you out of the womb – the harder you hit us, with your fists and your words and your warrants, the faster it's all gonna break, the quicker you're gonna set everything loose. Every blow puts another crack in the padlock."

In my belly, something was rising. My blood bubbled under the skin, my cells jostling like prison inmates with the smell of revolution on the air. The others could feel it too, we all could. Something was happening. Something was stirring.

"Five of them and one of Charlie. But I tell you something; you take *one* cop, and anyone out there'll tell ya, that cop has the muscles, the resources, the training, the power of right on their side – with all that, they *still* have to cheat. Five on one, handcuffed. The Man just can't help himself! The Man. The pig. The kike. The nigger. The spic. Ain't a one of 'em knows any other way to play than dirty. But they don't have the power. We do. We have it all. If they had the power, I'd be in a cell right now, or laying in a hole getting dirt shovelled on my face. If they had power, they'd have torn this place down and none of you would be standing here with me. They don't have the power, man, power comes with love and truth, and you can't hit me hard enough to have made me done anything wrong. You can't beat the guilty into me."

Those fucking motherfuckers. Charlie was the only one who knew, the only one who saw the world like it was, like it *could* be. As he talked, I wanted to climb the highest tree overlooking the city and yell "I love this man!" for the whole world to hear.

"I'm sat there, bleeding, chained like a dog, and they pull out these pictures... crime scene photos, the new ones and that stuff from ways back. Bodies, blood. I look this piggy in the eye and I say 'Why are you showing this to me? Does it excite you to force these images into my brain? Does it get you off? Is your little pecker doing handstands and cartwheels under the desk?'" Somebody giggled, but Charlie was in full flow and serious as a heart attack.

"All the while they're telling me again about the things I did, like they know my own actions better than I do; strangers and fools rewriting my history in front of my eyes, going back over that old ground, ploughing it up to plant poisonous weeds where I only ever laid beautiful flowers. They show me this one picture. Three corpses laying on a kitchen floor with 'Three Little Pigs' written across the wall in blood. 'Is that what you are, Charlie?' they say to me, 'Are you the Big Bad Wolf?' So I do what they said and I become what they wanted and I climb up on that table and howl. Howl at the moon! They're too stupid to see the lesson. A fool never learns. They think, "There goes that crazy guy again, playing the jester," but you call me these things I'm not; call me crazy, call me a killer and a murderer and a wolf, well, maybe you'll see me howling at the moon. You want to label me and tell me I'm something I've never been, see how it feels when I become that thing. You beat a dog enough times, tell him he's a bad boy, eventually, that dog gonna come up and bite ya."

I wanted to bite. I wanted to snarl and scratch and maul those who wanted to wrong us. Fuck, if there was only some way we could–

"But of course they don't see. They're too busy telling me how I'm going to go to the gas chamber, how they'll throw me in a cell with twenty other guys who'll take turns raping me. Niggers so big they'll use me like a condom to fuck another nigger in the ass. Do you know who I am, guy? Put me in there with thirty guys; fifty, a hundred, *ten thousand.* You'll find me standing on a pile of bodies and whistling a tune. I'll do what it takes to survive. I'll do what another man won't and not give it a second thought, and that's why I'm here. There is no right and wrong. What's wrong? Is it wrong to take a loaf of bread to feed my Family? Is it wrong to stab another man if he comes at me with a knife? Is it wrong to take the lives of those who've been taking mine, piece by piece, since I was ten years old? Don't you see? You take away my rights, take away my life, and don't be surprised when I do the same to you! You can't beat me; can't beat this," Charlie slapped his hand against his chest, the loud cracks threatening to spark the tinder we could all feel dry and yearning beneath our feet.

"I see, I said to them, I see what you're doing. You're trying to set me up, trying to set up my whole Family. You're going out and killing these people and making it look like it was me, trying to twist the beautiful thing we have here into something ugly and wicked. 'You wrote on the walls in blood! Just like the last time!' That's *you*, that's *your* image of me. Your devious, devilish plans couldn't be no clearer. See, they'd have all this ended. Our quiet, peaceful, beautiful little world. This world of love. The Man wants us ended because he fears what we know. They don't want word getting out to the rest of God's Earth that there's a better way. Why you think they do all this, man? Come on, *think!* They're terrified of what happens when their kids hear what we're saying. That's why they bring themselves to our doorstep. They're the aggressors! We chose to walk away, knowing us and them belong together like a rattlesnake in a baby's crib, but they keep wanting to pull us back in. They don't want us, yet they want us, because they fear what happens when we think for ourselves. And they *should* fear us. You keep trying to throw a leash around my neck and drag me into your cage, and you'll learn that you don't wanna be locked up with me. You don't go dragging the grizzly into the petting zoo, 'cuz when the shit goes down, ain't but one beast gonna be left standing. They knew if they rolled on in here, everyone out there's gonna think old Charlie's guilty. No smoke without fire, that's what they're thinking. Well they want a fire, we'll burn their city to the ground! *We'll burn the whole world, if that's what it takes!*"

"*Yeah!*" Fists in the air; a cheer so loud that Christ himself must have felt his throne shake. I was so fucking energized, I could have shot into space like the Silver Surfer.

"Take a look around you. We are two-hundred-fifty strong, and getting stronger by the day. Stronger, smarter, freer. Two-hundred-fifty free minds, no fear, no chains of "moral code" holding us back. There's nobody who can stop us! They came into our home and showed us exactly what they wanted. What they did; beating us, tying us, dragging us through the mud by our hair, laying boots to the faces of the men, women and children you see around you – it was an invitation, and I tell you all as I stand right now, on behalf of every member of my Family, it's an invitation I accept, gladly. They're gonna get exactly what they want, and what they want is a *war!*"

"*Yeeeeeeah!*" And the denizens of Heaven and Hell scattered.

No longer just a Family, we *were* an army. Say it, Charlie. Say the word.

"Let's do it!" said one, unified voice, two-fifty mouths strong. "Let's go, right now!"

"No," said Charlie. "We wait. We're smarter than them, so let's act that way. Soon though. Soon. But y'all think on what I said, and think about what they did. Look at the bruises and welts they laid upon you. When you go to sleep tonight, curled in the arms of your brothers and your lovers, remember what it feels like to be chained. That's how it is out there, even for the ones worth saving."

Later, as we basked in the sleepy glow of impending revolution, the post-Charlie euphoria, with our bond never tighter – us against the rest of the fucking world – I lay sandwiched between two girls; Melody at my back; smooth, tanned arms around my chest; Rae to the front. I spotted a dishevelled figure lurking in the distance.

"Be right back," I said, prising myself free and planting a kiss on Melody's forehead as I strolled over to Clark. Had he been there for Charlie's return? If he had, I hadn't noticed. Since his admission of snake-dom, I'd been keeping an eye on him, for the good of the Family, but hadn't wanted to dirty myself with his presence. But now, he didn't even feel a threat. The full weight of the LA County Police Department couldn't do more than borrow Charlie for the day, to have them chase their tails and dance to his penny-whistle, what could a doped-out schizo 'writer' do?

"Behind the stable," he said, "I got something real fucked up to tell ya."

"What's that, man?" I said, whipping my arm around him and half-hug, half-wrestling him close, "you been down in the city fucking them hobos again? Got yourself a little dumpster dick?"

"Not now," he said, shoving me off.

"Are you fucking... straight?" I said, laughing. "Shit, you can almost keep focus ..." I moved my finger back and forth like at a boxer who'd been knocked fucky, but Clark wasn't playing.

"Not for long. When we're done talking, I'm gonna get all fucked up. You'll probably wanna join me."

"Pssh, come on, man, be cool. Ain't the time to be

getting all heavy. Charlie's back, didn't you hear?"

"Yeah, I heard he was getting out..."

"Fuckin' A, man! They couldn't charge him with shit..."

"Yeah, *they*..." said Clark. "No charges. So what did he tell you? That it was The Man, right? Trying to keep him down? Trying to silence that eternal truth? Guy's a fuckin'..."

"Fuckin' what? Ah fuck it, " I swished my hand through the air, swatting away the bad vibes and snakey bring-downs. If there ever really was a time for Clark's which-lie-am-I-in bullshit, this wasn't it.

"He's not what you think. Whatever he says out there, whatever he's feeding you..."

"He ain't feeding us nothing," I said, "nothing except truth, brother. Life, love. And where do you get off talking like that about a guy who took you in and gave you everything you could never find out there?"

"Look, I know a guy in the Bureau, he was my hook-up when I did write-ups in the local rag; homicides, suicides, people whose bodies lay rotting for weeks with nobody to find them. Real bleak. Anyhow, we kept in touch, and I had him advise me. On going undercover; on Manson. He got me copies of the case files for that shit that went down in sixty-nine. Trial transcripts, photos. Risked his fucking ass for me. He's a tight source, man, trust me."

"Yeah," I said, scoffing like a bastard, "I totally trust you. This going anywhere, Sgt. Rock?"

"I know who set Charlie up."

The world around us fell away like peeling wallpaper.

"Who?"

Clark eyeballed me, perhaps inviting a guess. He was a liar and a junkie and many things between, but I felt certain that, likely for the first time since we met, he was telling nothing but the truth.

"Who was it? Oh fuck... is it someone here?" I was almost afraid of the answer. Faces flashed through my mind. Friends, lovers, Family – not a one in that camp that I didn't love with all my heart and who I wouldn't lay down my life for. Clark's frog-eyed, granite expression filled me with dread. Who was it? Not Jedro? One of the girls I'd brought in from San Fran? Fuck, what if I'd somehow lead the treachery to camp? Another name too, one I daren't think of. Not her. She wouldn't. Clark wore the face of a man with a terrible burden.

"Yeah," he said, "someone here." The words were barely free of his mouth before a murderous rage was coursing through me. How *dare* somebody betray Charlie? I'd kill them myself. I imagined the faceless wretch, the squealing pig, crucified on the Hollywood sign for the whole world to see, nailed to the big white H, a head-on-a-pike warning, their shit-filled guts spilled across Sunset Strip. In my rage, I tore my shirt at the chest, yanking myself open like I'd do to the rat. "Who was it? Who set him up?"

"Dude, listen," replied Clark, grabbing my arm. "It was Charlie."

"What was? What?" The swelling of my anger deflated into dull confusion.

"He put the call in himself. It was him."

"Goddammit, you loopy fuck. I thought you were serious. It's just crazy guy talk again. Who's your source this time, one of your imaginary friends? Frenchie Le Frog?"

"I am serious. He called them from a payphone 'bout a half-mile from the end of the track."

"I don't..."

"It was him for sure. He brought up something only he could know, from another time they'd pulled him in, said that he was willing to confess, to *everything*, with one condition. They just had to come and get him. So that's what they did. It was him, no fucking question. He made the call."

"Fuck off, dude, that makes no sense. Why would he do that? You're the biggest liar in here. Your whole life is a lie. You wouldn't know the truth if it dragged you into the desert and fucked you in the face."

"I'm a hundred percent positive on this, a hundred percent. I'd stake all our lives on it. It was him. Manson squealed on himself, and when they took him in, he refused to cooperate. Just played around, denied everything. Denied he'd even made the call. Look, I know he's got you all wrapped up in this little ant farm..."

"I don't get it. Why would he do that?" Clark didn't answer. His eyes trailed over towards the rest of the camp, everyone riled and ready to burn down the world, ready to do whatever their persecuted king told them, without question; the one person The Man was so afraid of they had to get him to the chair just to quiet him.

"He's got all these little sticks of dynamite running around. He just needed something to light the fuses..." I opened my mouth to respond, but nothing came out. "This is all building towards something terrible, I can feel it. The whispers on the wind, they're not speaking of love. He's got an end-game somewhere, and it's built on lies. It's all lies, man, all of it. He's just preaching whatever he needs to to get everyone on side; to get you thinking how he thinks. You're into it, I can see that. I mean... I get swept up too sometimes, but step back, man, look at the guy." I did. Charlie was back from the house, guitar in hand and surrounded by disciples, ready to sing his words and listen to his gospel long into the night.

"No," I said. "No. Your boy has it confused. Didn't you hear him? They're trying to shut him down..."

"That's just what he needs you to think. Open your eyes, there is no Man. The Man. Not like he wants you to think. You wanna see The Man, turn your head six inches that way, 'cuz he's right over there."

"You take a look! Do you fucking *see him*? Look at his face! You see that, right? You're not so fucked up you can't see the beating they laid on him? Five on one. You can't deny that. That's proof he ain't a liar, right there; evidence of what they did!"

"Yeah," said Clark, his voice hollow and blank, "look at what they did."

Clark peeled off his shirt and dropped it to the ground, revealing his scarred, seared body; itself a lie sold on a different truth. The first jangling chord rang out as Charlie strummed his hand across the strings. Through the gate, a half-dozen Brand New members walked into the ranch.

Look at what they did.

11 DADDY'S GIRLS

I hadn't seen hide nor hair of Clark for over a week. Right after our talk, I watched him share a handful of pills with a guy I thought of as Freddy the Fly – so filthy I always pictured flies buzzing around his head – but after that, he seemed to vanish.

At first, I convinced myself he'd left to write his story, and the seeds of discontent he tried to sow in me, hoping I'd spread them around camp, were a final fuck-you. For a couple days, I waited on someone rushing in with a newspaper, with a photo of a cleaned up Clark Clarkson, or whatever his name was, talking on his months living down and dirty with the junkies, sluts and thieves of the Manson Family. Yeah, right. They'd have to prop him up with a broom; grey-faced, smoke-belching cocksucker. As time went on, I figured maybe he'd been sussed, and someone, most likely the bikers, had driven him out to the desert and sawed through his neck-pipe with a buck knife. Though I shouldn't have cared, the latter possibility did not make me feel good.

Much as I tried to forget, I was still bothered by what

he'd told me. There was no way it was true, but say that it was, what would that mean? Clark was wrong, and Charlie had won. He'd stopped The Man from trying to shut him up, because they feared the truth. But if, if, if, if there was no Man, and no conspiracy, than what? Fucking Clark. He deserved to be left to the scorpions for putting that poison in me, and the dull ache of it haunted my days. Maybe that's why I took to the kid.

A tiny character, evoking coal-faced strays from a Dickens story, with a small bag of worldly possessions hugged to his chest, he caught my eye. He was maybe fourteen, but a young looking fourteen, especially among the kind of people that lived at Eden Ranch.

"Dude," I said, "you alright?"

"Is Charles here?" replied the kid, in a voice that hadn't broken. "Charles Manson?"

"He's around." Hands on hips, I motioned towards the house. "But he's a busy guy."

"It's okay, I can wait."

"Alright, man. You hungry?" The kid nodded. His eyes didn't meet mine once, too busy flitting over the candy store of sights and sounds, like mine had those first few weeks. I caught myself looking around too, as though taking it in for the first time. A dirty German Shepard with no collar ran in a big, bounding figure-of-eight. A girl daubed a smiley face around the nipple of another with a small piece of charcoal from the fire, tongue lolled in concentration. A pasty, dreadlocked putz smoked an eighth of Spanish Barry through a hollowed-out apple. All around, people lay like the dying on a battlefield, either resting off the night before, or just lazing with no purpose, until Charlie gave them one. A pack of four girls, best, best, oh the very best friends forever for the day, wafted across the lawn like dandelions towards me and the kid. One of them was tall and rangy like a model, flat chested with hips that got lost in her waist. There was all but four years between them, but she stooped down to speak to him like Santa's helper at a Walmart grotto.

"And who is *this*?"

"Shank," said the kid. The girls practically cooed at the puppy that had found itself among the rabid dogs and slaver-twatted bitches in perennial heat. Fresh meat.

"Shank, huh? That's a tough name. Wanna come hang out with us?"

Before I could speak, they were already gone; little Shank being led away, two girls on each arm. Not that I wouldn't have loved that when I was his age, but it gave me the same vague unease that had tinged everything of late. The next time I saw him, he'd probably have the weary eyes of a thirty-five year old.

I cheered myself like I always did. Weed and fucking. I couldn't find Melody, but sharing a little blowback with Lizz progressed into my listlessly penetrating her with a soggy cock that didn't so much cum, as half-heartedly sneeze a cuntful of jizz between her legs.

The conveyor belt of faces had long since started blending into one, and you associated more with an experience or an encounter than you did a name or a pink plate of eyes and lips. I perched on one of the old hitching posts, off-balance because my feet didn't reach the ground, and searched out someone, anyone, who could make me feel at home again. Kadie was sat alone, taking potato chips out of a paper bag and holding them towards a disinterested tabby. She was familiar, in a nice way, in that I'd once had a rad conversation with her about UFOs. We both agreed that there were aliens inside, but Kadie thought they'd be flat, like something that'd been cut out of a book, 'cuz of the heavier gravity on their home planet. I freaked her out by saying they'd be able to slide under your door and take you back to Venus, and I forget what happened after that, but anyway, sweet girl.

"Tom!" she said as I approached. "What's up with you? You've got a face on like a butthole chewing on an ice cube!" That's right, *Kadie*, with the weird potpouri army-brat accent. Spent the first ten years of her life in Germany, I think. Comes out more when she's drunk.

"I dunno," I said, "feeling a bit out of sorts, I guess."

"Aww, what's bothering you?" she said, patting the ground next to her. "Come tell Auntie Kadie all about it."

"Hey puddy," I said, gently scritching the cat behind the ears, "you been eating chips?"

"Nah," said Kadie, "he's not interested. Usually can't get enough. Put the bag down and he'll stick his little head right in, won't you Mister Kitty?" Kitty didn't answer, and when Kadie pushed another chip in front of his whiskers, he turned away, in that bored, snooty way that cats do, like they're above it all.

"He sick?"

"I hope not. Maybe he's just not hungry." Kadie crunched the chip into her own mouth, and the cat wandered off, brushing beneath Kadie's outstretched hand as he went. "So," she said, wiping her mouth, "what's up? Anything that can be fixed with chips?" I shook my head.

"People I guess."

"People? Someone here?"

"Yeah. No. Nobody here. Not now."

"Figures. Those normies, huh? Zipperhead pricks."

"Pretty much. Messin' with my mind."

"Those *bastards*," she said, with a sudden bile that unexpectedly jolted a little extra life into the conversation. "Some fuckers just don't know how to behave. That's what's so precious about living here, babe. Just a bunch of souls who want to live as we want, nobody telling us what we can or can't do, or how we should think. Out there, they're just..."

"Liars," I interjected, with a little less conviction and a little more sadness than I'd hoped. "You never know where you stand with people like that."

"That's gonna change, *real* soon."

"Mm?"

"Just wait until they see The Wave." Her face wore the words 'am I right?' and mine, the embarrassing blankness of someone who knew nothing. But those two words made my heart recoil. Did Clark's story suddenly have a character witness; a barefoot girl with European vowels who was about to pull my world apart? "It's coming."

"Nobody tells me anything," I said, only half-joking.

"Seriously?" I nodded. "Well, fuck." A small, hard

laugh ricocheted out of her mouth. "It's getting cleansed, baby. This country, the whole world; everything's getting washed clean. All the pigs and the niggers, and the cunts who're happy to walk around in shackles, they're all gonna drown. It's The Wave, man, it's beautiful..."

"Pretend I don't know," I said. Kadie shuffled forward on her haunches, planting herself in front of me cross-legged, the kindergarten storyteller reading from her favorite crinkled old book and hoping to inspire that same love in her audience.

"Okay, dig on this. On the day it goes down, The Wave, we'll all start out from here, everybody, all in one big line, marching out of the entrance for the last time, 'cuz where we're going, we ain't *never* coming back. Out of the Garden of Eden to start the second Genesis! On the sixth day, Charlie recreated the world, ya know? Each of us is gonna be armed; handguns, rifles, shotties, m80s, grenades, World War I mustard gas; fuck, you should see what he's packing. We got enough for an army back there, and that's what we'll be, a fucking army. Soldiers of the truth. Got me dibs on a fuckin' kevlar tit-vest. So, the babies are safe on the buses that'll be trailing us from the back, stocked up the ass with extra ammo, and with shooters on the windows. From the ranch, we march, unbroken line, arm in arm, singing, with love and fire, right along the coast till we get to San Diego..." Her eyes were wide, with this crazy, ecstatic look, Charlie's words from her mouth – his love and passion and rage rising from her body like heatwaves on a summer's noon.

"And if you're not with us, you're against us. Anyone getting in our way is getting deaded, no matter who. Anyone who's not willing to join The Wave is getting swept underneath, getting popped, man. Boom, right in the head! Once we get to San Diego, we start heading east, sweep our way across the whole goddamn country, till we hit the other side. And it's gonna grow so fast, like a snowball rollin' down a hill. At first, they won't be expecting it, and by the time the first cops show up, they'll be way outnumbered. We'll take those motherfuckers out like nothing. They ain't prepared for something like this. The time those dorky fucks get their shit in gear, we'll be even stronger; larger; people taking up arms to stand by our side and fight for a new world, a world of *love*. The FBI'll roll up, more cops, army – fucking bring it – the further we go and the longer we march, the stronger we become. While they're getting mobilized, there'll be thousands of us. They won't stand a fucking chance, man." She started laughing, a real deep, hard, from the pit of the gut laughter, the kind of laughter that's rooted in absolutes, of enemies whose last meal is a 10lb humble pie served with a big side of spilt milk. Settling herself, she continued.

"Do you know how many guns there are in this country? How many stores and stockpiles we can loot as we're passing through? Think about it. Charlie says there's a gun for every home, and that's just the regular families. Then you got these people holed up waiting for the apocalypse with stove-pipes and flame-throwers, a crateful of dynamite in the basement, and we're exactly what they've been waiting for. Hell, look at that shaky guy you hang with, that hobo who got all wacko from killing slopes. There's plenty like him out there, all fucked up by the government and just waiting on their chance to get revenge. And then you've got all these kids, kids like us, and they wanted to be here but for whatever reason, they couldn't take that final step, or they just couldn't get away, or they don't know we're here. Just imagine, dude, they're watching us on the news, helicopters filming the whole thing, cities on fire, and this army, the Manson army, getting closer and closer to their homes, and they know there's that gun in a shoebox under their parents' bed, and fuck if by the time we get there they ain't already waiting to join that love train. That's the beauty of it, there are so many people out there who feel the same, and as we go along, mowing down the ones who don't want to join the revolution, taking on the ones who want to be free, that line's getting longer and longer, the links in the chain getting stronger and more unbreakable. When they see us coming, the people are gonna grab those guns and knives, and either stand in line next to their new brothers and sisters, or die in the streets where they stand. We're gonna wash it all clean, babe, burning the cities as we leave them behind, setting *everything* on fire. We're gonna light a fire so big, God's gonna be choking on the smoke. The streets are gonna flow with the blood of the unbelievers..."

It was as though Charlie had dressed as a teenage girl for Halloween; his end of days rhetoric in valley girl falsetto.

"Be like a fucking abattoir, man, ten million useless, worthless pigs all getting a bolt in the fucking head. As long as we're together, nobody can stop us. The power of one. We'll be like a giant – a monster – one single being comprised of hundreds; *thousands* of bodies. And the brain is Charlie, and he's gonna surf that wave, ride it all the way to the White House. By the time we get to Washington, we'll be fifty thousand strong!" Kadie's voice was fire and brimstone in a burning pulpit, and had drawn the attention of a couple of girls – Redhead Emma and Mary – who pitched up and joined us.

"I wanna feel their blood on my feet," said Kadie, lifting her feet from under her and pushing the grubby soles into my face.

"Wha'chu talking about?" said Emma, but Kadie was lost to the fantasy, keeping her heat-vision gaze locked on me, as Emma playfully flicked at her earlobe.

"What do you think?" she replied, lingering for a second before turning to the others. Her orgasmic look was repaid by both and suggested many long, detailed fireside chats about all the things they'd do when it all finally went down. Kadie rocked back onto her ass, pulling up her knees either side of her head, with her feet high in the air. "Look at these. It's gonna be up to my thighs, man. I'm gonna splash around in it, paint a fucking mural. I'm gonna write my name across the highway, fuckin' thirty feet high."

"Swim in it," said Mary, "think we could do that?" Mary, no longer the fragile waif I'd plucked from Haight-Ashbury, but a woman of the world, albeit His world. Redhead Emma looked more like a pixie than an actual human being.

"Hell yeah! We're gonna do whatever we want."

"Yeah," I said, "I'm all for shutting down the pigs. Shit's been unbalanced for a long time..." The *but* didn't make it out alive.

"You ever kill anyone before?" said Redhead Emma. I answered matter-of-factly, giving nothing of myself either way.

"No. You?"

"Yeah."

That was the moment it all became real.

The distant whispers of girls with knives and gut-spilled home-owners; of a twisted leader that brainwashed corrupted young minds into psycho-hippy slaughter. That stuff that had been no more real to me than campfire ghost stories about murderous fishermen with hooked hands, or the spectral cows Friar Fuck swore he saw down in the valley. When you saw Charlie dancing, gentle and carefree, pulling Kung-Fu poses and speaking that funny gibberish talk, just to make us laugh, just to keep things interesting, you could never imagine him doing the things they said he'd done. Terrible things. Violent things. I was looking at Redhead Emma, but the only face I saw was that of the old man who'd looked so disproving as we marched towards the ranch that first day. It seemed like a lifetime ago. That old man had thrown that look at another person entirely.

Whether any of it was true or not, for the first time, I could *see* it. Pictures of death; everything that'd skirted around the misty edge of my imagination, in a brain too busy with distractions; it now stood clear and center of frame. The day I felt the Earth shake under my feet through Charlie's will, through his rage at what they were doing to him and the Family for whom he'd do anything, everything else had gotten pushed out of my head. But the ground had lay still for a while, fat with the half-asleep forms of those no longer knew anything but how to smoke and toke and drop and fuck and suck and play, because he said it was the right way, the free way, and who now said they'd shoot and stab and kill and laugh as the falling bodies pounded the streets like a heavy rain. This girl, who I'd watched lovingly feeding and playing with the motherless babies; was she capable of such things? Were any of them capable of the things they bragged about? It happened the first time. Really happened. That's what they said anyway. They. Us. I couldn't remember where the I fit anymore. The Me. I just knew I couldn't picture myself splashing around in the remains of another living person. All these thoughts came in the long silence that followed the last time Redhead Emma had uttered a sound, and ended with the laughter that broke it, the laughter of all three girls.

"No," she said. "No, I never killed anyone, not really. But real soon. And once I start, I just know I won't be able to stop."

"Was it you who was talking about keeping score?" asked Kadie.

"What about the innocent people?" I said, butting in. "Kids and old people. The ones who're just living their lives and letting everyone else get on with living theirs. What happens to them during The Wave?" It drew looks of suspicion from all three, looks that filled me with a strange and brief feeling of nostalgia for the old days, when I felt like I didn't belong.

"The fuck is an innocent? There are no innocents." Kadie laughed at such a preposterous idea, the other two joining in heartily. "You think there were innocents in World War II? You live in this world and you don't take a stand, you're fuckin' guilty. And we ain't got need for the lame. It's a brave new world, you dig? Fuckin' food chain, man. Those are sacrifices, target practice. Time the army shows up, we'll be able to blow a piggie's head off at five hundred paces..."

"You are a pretty good shot though," said Redhead Emma.

"She is." Mary, forever a music box mirror of whoever's around.

"Oh, you know it, girl. Charlie took us out into the desert a couple times to shoot off rounds. *She* was all over the place."

"I was not!" Emma gave Kadie a playful shove, "them big ones just got a kick to 'em, that's all."

"Yeah, yeah..."

"You had a little pistol, I had this huge thing that was half-way down to my knees..."

"That what you've got?" said Mary, to me, "a huge thing that hangs down to your knees?" an aren't-I-naughty grin plastered across her face. Everyone was always playing to the cheap seats.

"He did alright," said Redhead Emma, "I had a go on it." She patted a hand down on my crotch. "He ain't no Irish Jake though. That boy got a champagne bottle down there..."

"You should have seen her, you'd probably have gotten hot."

"Oh yeah!" Miming with her fingers, Kadie picked off imaginary assailants, future victims in the cleansing. "Take that, blackie. Pow! Here's one for you, old timer. Bang! Nigger. Nigger. Nigger. Reload."

Three teenage girls with painted toes and puppy fat hips, talking holy war.

"I hope we go through my old town. There's a few cunts there I wanna stick. Oh, hey, mom." Click. "Nothing ever was good enough for you, was it, daddy?" Click. Mary, angel of vengeance.

"What about your sister? You got a kid sister, right?"

"Uh-huh. She's welcome to join us."

"And if she doesn't?" I said. Mary shrugged and mimed firing for a third time, her left eye scrunched for better aim, wrinkling her forehead and pushing out her lips. The invisible gun bucked with the recoil of the shot.

They were so deep into their fantasies of who was getting ended come judgement day, reeling off lists of popular cheerleaders and overly-strict teachers, ex-boyfriends and the guy from down the street who'd looked at them funny once, that none of them noticed when I got up and left.

Day by day, the camp seemed to be shifting by small degrees, into an unfamiliar place populated by faces I began to recognize less the more that I saw them. Most that I'd found interesting or quirky or fun were now just irritating or crazy. Everybody, Charlie most of all, had spent countless hours talking about how we were going to change the world. But all you ever heard was the *why*, and never the *how*. Until now. And that *how* seemed like the furthest thing possible from the love we all lived by. Everybody spoke as though part of a single, greater being. One in, all in. If you're not with us, you're against us. The Wave would apply that unity to the rest of the world; a natural progression of Eden's mentality, formed into a rising flood that would surge out of the gate and down into the world. Were my friends part of it too – was I? Flesh-cog limbs in a giant that was mutating into a monster? Part of me wished I felt that same casual blood-lust; able to laugh about slitting a throat or bombing a school bus; knowing I wouldn't hesitate if it came to it for real. Were that me, then at least I wouldn't be back to feeling the outsider. Perhaps I was just weak, or a phony like Clark, and when it came the time for action, the day to stand with my brothers and sisters of the Brand New, everyone would see I was still the same old Tommy. Maybe I deserved to drown.

Amid everything, there was one constant, and I sought her out.

We clambered up the hill on the eastern side of the ranch overlooking the city. Melody was 10-tabs unsteady, laughing as her hands sank into the grass, and fascinated by the sharp incline that she swore kept changing direction. It was nightfall when we sat looking down on the world like gods.

"All this stuff about The Wave... what do you think?"

"The what?" She was so high, she would have replied "The what?" if I'd asked her about the toes on her feet. "Here," she said, opening my mouth and placing a blotter on my tongue. Things began to fade around the edges. Hard lines blurring. From our position on the hill, I couldn't see the campfire, for the first time in I don't remember. In its absence, the sky was bright with pinprick stars and far-off galaxies; a clean, inky black with glimmering wishes.

"Probably just talk," I said.

"Everything's talk. It's all talk. Charlie says you can leave yourself, when you die. Leave yourself, and come right back into another body. And out there, time, like, doesn't even exist. To you, you're out there for a billion years, learning all the secrets of the cosmos, conversing with deities, then you come right back, land in a new body, and you know *everything*. He says nobody ever did it yet, 'cept some Tibetan monks and Chinese mountain people, but if anyone can, it's him."

"You spend a lot of time with Charlie. Up close I mean, in the house." Melody settled back, her head resting on her hands. I instinctively reached out to catch her, as though she was going to fall or float away, but she didn't. "What's he like?"

She looked at me as though she couldn't fathom why

such a question need ever be asked.

"Charlie is love," she said. I lay the back of my head on her stomach.

"You ever think about what else is out there?"

"Yeah. I mean, God, there's so many planets. I bet whatever you can think of exists somewhere. Like, right now I'm imagining an alien with a head that's on the inside. And all the stuff that *should* be inside, like intestines and guts, all that's on the outside, like our ears or whatever – and I bet there's something exactly like that out there, you just have to fly far enough. And if he met us, he'd be all grossed out at the disgusting Earth men with their faces on the outside of their bodies. Or there's these big, like, toad-men, and they've got fingers that all have fingers of their own..."

"Yeah... I meant more here on Earth, you know, outside Eden. Out there."

"Oh. Like, other cultures?" she said.

"Yeah. Coming to Cali's all the travelling I ever did. If you could go anywhere, where would you go?"

"The Pyramids. Paris. London. Japan. India."

"That's not one place."

"I couldn't pick one. If you want to expand yourself, spiritually, you should see everywhere. China."

"China?"

"Do you think they really they eat dogs over there? Imagine eating a *dog!*" Melody laughed with a loud *"ha!"* that reverberated through her stomach and into my head.

"Yeah, it'd be kinda gross...." I said.

"Think of how big it'd be on the plate though. Black lab, just sitting there, eyeballing you. Man, I couldn't eat that. I can't eat anything with a face..." She reached down and roughly caressed my face like a blind man would.

"Could you eat me?"

"You'd have to get in a big bun," she said through laughter, "just lay in it like a casket. I'd eat you right up." Melody rolled on her side, crunched in two with the giggles, the bone in her pale back poking out between t-shirt and jeans. I rolled over and gently spooned, our backs at the ranch, and nothing in front of us but the rest of the world. "I wanna see London. Be like Mary Poppins. You ever see that?" I shook my head. "Aw, man, it's amazing. There's this nanny, and she's *magic*. She flies on an umbrella..."

"We should go to London. Me and you."

"I'd like that."

"Oh yeah?"

"Yeah."

"You know you're my favorite person..."

"Even if we went to London? You'd meet some pretty British girl and forget all about me."

"Never," I said, softly. "We could go to all those places, see the world together. See the Pyramids, the Taj Mahal, tread the paths that Jesus walked. We can go wherever we want."

"Sounds wonderful." She reached back with a hand

and brushed my cheek.

"We're gonna go up the top of the Eiffel tower and float down on an umbrella…"

"And just keep on going…" We were both speaking in near-whispers. "We'll do it."

"You promise?" I said. "For real I mean. Leave here and see the world?"

"Sure, baby."

"Just you and me, we'll take off, hit the road."

"It's a big world out there."

"We could explore it together."

"Nobody I'd rather do it with," she said, rolling over until we were nose to nose, eyelashes tickling. "You just come find me one day, whenever you're ready, and we'll go. Won't look back."

"What about all this?"

"What about it?" she said, kissing me. She pulled away with a smile, stroking her fingers through the air, entranced by some unseen playmate. "Fireflies." There were no fireflies, but it didn't matter.

"They're beautiful," I said, and I pictured myself beneath a red umbrella, Melody tightly clasped around my neck. And we were soaring.

12 UNFIT FOR PUBLIC CONSUMPTION

There was something in the air. Not the deep-rooted bouquet of body odor that newbies would remark on, or the promise of impending revolution, just... a buzz.

Though we were unrestrained, camp life often fell into monotony, and anything that broke the routine, even for a moment, was a gift. Most of these gifts came from Charlie's of-the-moment, do what thou wilt free-wheeling, from spontaneous outbursts, or requests for some randomly chosen member to make up a song on the spot, using only words they'd invented, to outings into the city to freak out the squares with minor acts of mischief. In the row of identical days, these were often the things that stuck out. I still remember the girl with three nipples, the dog that could ride a horse, and the day somebody broke their wrist falling off a penny-farthing. Today had that feel, with scurrying to or from whatever it was that'd colored up the day.

"What's the deal?" I said, collaring San Francisco Mike, who was stumbling back, arm around a girl twenty years his junior, his face now wrapped in a bushy, grey-flecked beard.

"They found something behind the old shitters." Ah, the shitters. Many a newcomer had fled at the first sight – and smell – of the double-wide shack, where you'd squat over one of two circular holes cut into a plank, hovering above a warm pit of piss and turds. I ambled over for a looksee. Probably nothing, but you'd be kicking yourself later if it was. Few weeks back, I missed the guy who'd fallen asleep while jerking himself off. I heard the cheers, but missed his being tossed into the air like a football hero, with his pants still around his ankles. Seems kinda silly now.

They were coming out from behind the outhouse with their arms over their noses.

"Fucking stinks, dude. That is *rotten*."

"Hey," I said, "what y'all looking at?"

"See for yourself, man. But it ain't pretty." I bustled my way past the half-dozen gawpers. When I saw what they were looking at, a sound came out of me that drew their eyes from the ground and onto me.

It was the boots I recognised first. Scuffed and worn, like he'd done a lot of walking. His eyes had been pecked out by crows. The flesh of his face was picked clean by the mewling cats that roamed Eden Ranch. Clark. Some days gone, sun-baked and devoured, his sunken body had lay unnoticed; likely stepped over by those who thought "there's a guy who knows how to party!"

"Overdose," said a voice.

"Shit, mang. He fuckin' raw," another, coughing through the stink.

"He chased that thing so hard he ran right into a wall..." Clark's open mouth was black with flies; his chest alive with maggots that called a dead man home. The fingers on one hand were splayed and eaten to the bone. The highschool football ring sat untouched, red and gold on skeletal white. Those who find a loved one gone in the night often say they have a peaceful look, as though they're asleep. Clark looked like he'd found himself in the fires of hell and still hadn't stopped screaming.

"Probably been there a day or two, maybes a week. When'd you see him last?" I just shook my head. My legs were denim-clad mist, barely keeping me from joining Clark flat-backed on the dirt.

"Could see this coming, eh? Fuckin' guy was always hitting me up for something."

"Did he have any shit left on him?" said some guy, making no attempt to hide the shuffle of his feet towards Clark's jeans pocket. "Who got it?"

"That look like a guy who had anything to spare?"

"Well, shit."

I noticed a small figure peering around the corner of the outhouse. Shank, looking every bit the child, had his big eyes fixed on Clark's body. Just when I thought I'd never speak again, I heard myself yelling–

"Get the kid out of here! Fuck me... he don't need to see this."

"It's natural," somebody replied, "way of the world. It's okay, son, you take a good look."

"Natural?" I said. "Full of dope and rotting behind a communal shit-pit; nobody finding you for a week? That's natural? That how your grandparents are gonna be found? Jesus…"

"Shit, my gramps would probably enjoy that. Might lighten him up a bit." I threw eye-daggers at the shaggy haired chucklefuck, his cheeks pinched inward on the tiny remains of a joint, trying to catch the gaze of anyone who'd heard his terribly witty aside. Who was this fuck? A straight-through-the-door young-blood motherfucker, telling me how I should feel about a dead man whose name he didn't even know. Just another part of the hive. Suddenly, I could no longer shake the sense of being surrounded by echoes. Bees. Drones. Hollow-headed ventriloquist dummies.

"He was a person!" I said, my voice cracking with emotions I hadn't felt in a long time. "He was a person, and he died. A person with a name and a family, with a mother and father who loved him, and–"

"Oil your butthole, man," said Chucklefuck, snickering, "death is just an illusion." Charlie's words; an unwelcome intrusion. In that moment, I needed something real, not another repetition of a repetition; spoken so often that it stops becoming language, like the sounds of a skipping record. When was the last time I'd heard something real? Nobody ever talked anymore. We just tugged the strings on each other's backs to hear His voice coming out.

This wasn't an illusion. He'd walked and talked and laughed, and now he was a stench in the back of my throat; the stench of bad meat. Of death. Real, solid, lonely death. All anyone had was fortune cookie wisdom written by a fucking chimp. *Give me something real!*

A girl placed a hand on my shoulder, speaking into my ear before strolling back to the weaving of daisies in her friend's hair, from which she'd been so rudely distracted.

"At least he got to be free. Most people die before they've even lived..."

That was it.

I was done.

I couldn't be inside that place for another second.

I strode on a rubber body towards the entrance. No. Not entrance–

I strode on a rubber body towards the exit.

"Got a quarter?" I said, to a kid so fresh through the gate that he still had money on him, and snatching it out of the air in one smooth motion so's I wouldn't have to look back. Down the path I walked, with the dirt below my bare feet seeming to bend and buckle with each step, but becoming gradually steadier the farther I got away. I didn't look back, I didn't think. I knew that if I let him back inside, even for a heartbeat, I'd turn to a pillar of salt, and what little of myself remained would scatter to the desert winds.

I barely held it together as I walked through the city, caught in the spotlight of a thousand glowering gazes. This time, there was no grandstanding; no waving or flashing. It was all I could do to shuffle by, suddenly shamed. They all knew where I was from. I wore the Mark of Cain in my very attire; long-hair, mix n' match clothing, and no shoes; the uniform of Charlie's slacker army. But it didn't matter. I had my mission. My mission was to get to the one thing that makes it all okay, no matter what you've done; the thing that picks up all the pieces and puts them back together – your momma's voice.

It's not that I hadn't thought of them. I had, but in the past tense. Charlie taught us that to find freedom, you had to remove your past selves, including people. You can't take possessions with you when you die, he'd said, just like you can't bring along your baggage when you want to be Brand New. Baggage. When I came home in tears because Stevie Bundell had blacked my eye in study hall, and my dad, for whom the loosely-gripped bearhugs of Bruno Sammartino were considered gratuitous violence, offered to go over to Stevie's house and clock his dad while I stood and watched, an eye for an eye. Baggage. When I was running a triple-figure fever and peppering the bathroom floor with hot vomit and dribbly shit, and she cleaned up after me. When they raised me from a helpless baby to a man, a man that died the moment he walked through that entrance. Baggage, all of it. Fucking Charlie. He twisted everything.

I'm not sure how long I walked, but eventually I found a payphone. On a billboard across the street, a man with a tight face offered personal salvation at the calling of a number. I thought about using my quarter to ask how he planned to reach somebody like me, and started laughing. Or crying. Maybe both.

My memories had become splintered at Eden. There was nothing to mark the days or months, and no real seasons in the heat of the hills. Events and conversations could have been last week, or last year. Every memory before Charlie was seen through the wrong end of binoculars. It was all just lights and shapes. A sound, a scent. I don't know if it was Charlie's various therapies, or the sheer amount of people passing through, or just because we were completely fucked off our faces most of the time. We all did enough acid to kill off the dinosaurs. But while most of the footage was gone, the one thing could never be wiped clean were the feelings. Maybe the faces of my parents were blurry, but I remembered how they loved me, and me them. And they always would. They might not be proud, but when the door closed behind us, guns and bikers and rotting bodies, and *him*, would be left outside, and I'd be home.

I dropped the coin into the slot and dialled. Of all the things that had been lost, the number went in without even thinking. It never goes away. I couldn't be sure, but I thought it was a Friday. It felt like a Friday. My dad would be working out of his home office, and he'd answer in that practised, professional way that made me laugh when he broke off in the middle of an argument with my mom to pick up the phone and politely recite back the number, and with his best telephone voice, "*Holder residence, Jim Holder speaking.*" As the dirty receiver rang in my ear, a random fragment of memory sparked, of school crack-up Ronnie Milber doing an impersonation after calling my house. "*Holder residence, Ji–*

"*The number you have dialled is not in service. Please hang up the receiver.*"

When a puppet cuts its own strings, all that's left to do is fall. I lay there on the sidewalk, sobbing, crying like I never had before, crying like I'd only just learned how, with no idea how to stop. Who was I even crying for? For myself? My parents? For Clark? His body sat rotting in the sun, eaten by cats that had licked my face. He tried to tell me the truth, but I didn't listen, and in his death I saw the thousands that would come as a result of The Wave.

"*Don't sweat it,*" they'd say, piling the bodies high enough to climb a stairway to the stars, "*death is just an illusion.*"

I had only one thing left. The thing that made me snort back the last of the tears and heave myself onto my feet to drag myself back into that place once more.

If The Wave really kicked off, there wasn't nobody who could stop it. Me and her needed to be far, far away, where Charlie and his poison could never touch us.

Fuck. How long had I even been at Eden? I couldn't remember. It felt like a year, but could have been two. Three? Charlie equipped us all to be free, but it was the kind of freedom that only worked in there. The only rule was there were no rules, he always said, and that applied to everything; time, boundaries, morality. None of it worked on the outside, in the real world, and I couldn't survive out there alone. But together, explorers on an alien planet, we could colonise, re-learn, and start afresh; create our own utopia, where we could truly, finally be free.

I stepped back over the threshold, desperately clinging hold of my thought; my objective. I mustn't lose it; mustn't sway or forget, mustn't be pulled into games, whirled in circles for days with my screams mistaken for laughter. Maybe I'd come to this point before, bags packed and ready to take flight, but I'd forgotten, like I'd forgotten so much else. But then, there she was, like she was fated to be, drying her hair by the fire, wearing a wraparound white dress that looked like something from a painting in an old country house.

"Let's do it," I said, firmly taking Melody's arm, "right

now." I started tugging her gently but resolutely toward the gate.

"What are you doing?" Melody said, half-laughing and wriggled free of my grip.

"What we spoke about. I'm ready now." That beautiful face was paper-blank. "The pyramids? Mary Poppins and the Eiffel Tower? Come find me, you said, whenever you're ready, come find me and we'll go. Well I'm ready. Come on."

"Ooh. Yeah. Dude, I was pretty fuckin' high..." Melody laughed, catching the eyes of others nearby. Once she realized I was serious, the smile dropped off of her face. She wasn't happy, she was... offended. "Why would I leave? Why would *anybody* leave?"

"Come on, *please*," I said, aware of the ugly desperation in my voice, drawing more attention; making a scene. I had a vivid flash-forward of Tom the turncoat rat being bum-rushed and tossed onto the fire. I grabbed again at her wrist, but my desperation made me clumsy; made me rough; nails digging into flesh, fingers against bone.

"God, let *go*," she said, yanking herself clear. "Stop being weird."

"Y'all cool over there?" yelled over some guy called Cramp. The hair-bracelet she'd tied on me lay on the ground, torn loose when she'd pulled away.

"It's fine," she said, waving away Cramp.

"You love me," I said, feeling a hundred eyes on me, but not caring. No wasn't an option. "That's what you said. You'll come if you love me."

"I love *everyone*."

Fuck it, then. Let them throw me on the fire. I wanted to hear the crackle of the flesh melting from my bones, like Clark's roasted child, just so I could feel anything that wasn't this. Melody's voice was hard, robbed of the connection I'd felt that night on the overlook; words backed by a layered Phil Spector chorus of '*Why do boys have to be so silly?*'

"Just take a chill pill, man. Maintain. Go get your dick wet or something. Why'd you have to get so heavy?"

"I just... Clark died." I brushed a hand under my eye, expecting tears, but there were none left.

"I know," she replied, with a genuine sadness, but covering herself with folded arms. The three-feet between us was a thousand miles wide. We stood trapped in an unfinished paragraph, before she silently turned to walk away.

"Wait," I said, "I have to know..."

"Have to know what?" Even through her impatience, there was pity.

"Were you there?"

"Where?"

"That night they took me out in the desert. Was that you?"

"No," she said, shaking her head. "Not at yours. Now I gotta go. New guy." I watched as she and another girl headed over to a couple of new arrivals; two guys with woollen hats and heavy camping packs. Then came that familiar dance of Eden, the seduction, the laughing and body contact and 'I think you'll settle in just fine.' The girls each helped one of the guys off with their packs, leaving them to one side to be emptied into the kitty. Melody paired with the taller of the two, sharing a joke I couldn't hear and tipping her head back with laughter, her eyes alive and bright. She took his hand and lead him out behind the barn. Thirty seconds from now, he'd be convinced this was the greatest place on Earth.

She was lost. They all were. Everyone who came through those gates. Clark had tried to fake it, tried to merely pretend that he'd fallen under the spell, but whoever the 'real' him was had been swallowed whole; devoured until all that remained was the lie. A lie which became the truth. Charlie's word spread through camp like a disease, passed down onto each new arrival like an old recipe. He was remaking their worlds in his image, and meant to do the same to *their* world. The Them of out there. And now I was trapped in a world in which I no longer belonged; a dream I couldn't wake from no matter how hard I pinched myself. I could have left, but I'd have been leaving those I cared about to be devoured too. Melody, Jedro, all those folks who weren't bad people, just people who'd made a bad decision, who'd gotten lost and wandered into a trap, like I had. And if I did leave, I had nowhere to go. He ruins you for anything else. But worst is I knew what was coming. The Wave.

Much as I wanted to jet and never look back, I'd just be waiting for those first news reports to roll in, knowing I could have – should have – done something to stop it. I could scrounge another quarter, but who could I call? Even if I ratted, and the pigs actually bought it, then what? The feds roll up again, cocked and loaded, and catching

Charlie unawares for real, that's just gonna kick the party off early. I could picture it happening, every bullet, clearer than I ever could being free of that place. Being free of him.

The growing sirens would prick Charlie's ears like a coyote's, and he'd be ready before the first car was through the gate. His lieutenants; the bikers, anyone close by; they'd get tossed rifles and pistols, or home-made pipe-bombs from the secret cache. He'd hunker down near the house and fire off a few rounds from cover. A couple of cops would get tagged and drop, and then everyone on the ranch would start screaming. Chaos. People running in every direction, looking for somewhere safe, trampling on those who'd slipped or been clipped. But Charlie, he'd love the panic, thrive on it, fire and brimstone for the end-times pulpit-basher he really was.

He'd stalk out from behind the house and make his way down the path, under the wild covering fire of his disciples. As the only love he has is for himself, his only desire self-preservation, he wouldn't blink at his Family getting caught in the crossfire. Sacrifices for the greater good, and anyone who caught a bullet or a grenade, well, if the universe meant for them to be by his side at the new dawn, then be they women, children, or just too slow and un-fuckin-lucky, they were falling into graves that fate had already dug. The feds might be wrong-footed enough by sheer fire-power for him to survive the opening salvo, so it'd be round one to Charlie. He'd step over the corpses of the pigs and of his own and head out into the city. Sure, he wouldn't survive beyond an hour or three, and he'd know that too, but those hours would be enough, they'd be all he needed; to lay his dying body down on the concrete at that Walk of Fame and never be forgotten.

The Family was comprised of devotees who'd flocked to be by his side off the back of the trial, and grew more extended by the day. If he managed to drop a couple dozen police and a handful of regular American citizens, they could cut off his fucking head and still not hold back the tide. Publicly martyred for the next generation of crazy fucks who'd look to him for inspiration on how to break free of their shitty lives, Charlie's philosophies would never die; his call to burn down the world would see the flames flickering long after the cities went dark. "Why were they trying to silence him?" they'd say. "What were they so afraid of?" The press would run with it until all the clocks stopped ticking; until their buildings were razed.

There had to be another way. But what could I do alone? If I revolted, ranting, raving, and gathering them round the fire, telling everyone how they've been used, and "come on, let's all leave together!" they'd jam an apple up my hole and roast me like a hog. Snitches get stitches. I had nothing except for that place, and him. The life that belonged to that other me, the outside, out-there me, the one who worked a job and laughed along to Cosby, the Tom who found pleasure in regular people shit, like Coca Cola and superhero books had been slowly digested. Nobody to talk to, nobody to listen. Nobody who wouldn't kill me if they knew where my head was at. Those who knew about the oncoming Wave wanted nothing more than to be in the center of the maelstrom, and would defend its right to exist with their last bullet.

How can you stop an army? Three hundred bodies. Three hundred strong, but all thinking with a single mind. Fuck. *Fuck.*

I was the only one. I was the only one who could do what needed to be done.

I had to kill Charles Manson.

13 APPLE FOR THE TEACHER

Slowly, I'd been inching my way up the food chain. When you got down to it, these weren't businessmen with hierarchical, members-only structures built on secret handshakes and old school ties – it was simple balls and bullshitting. I'd gone through life with the idea that it was better to blend in with the wallpaper and watch from the outside. Once you lose that, even if you have to fake it, it's not so hard to climb. If Clark taught me anything, it's that you can become the lie.

Once I'd set my mind on getting close enough to Charlie to kill him, suddenly my life took on a new focus. That became my full-time job. To finally have something to do was exciting. Days took on individual identities again, with targets to be met, be they small, like being on nodding terms with one of the Judas Noose, or seemingly out of reach, like getting up in the house by the end of Spring. I started simple, sitting a little nearer to Charlie during his talks, just to get my face seen, so people, newcomers especially, would feel that I belonged; that I was part of the lead pack. Become the lie. I had at least one thing in my favor. Being around since the day the gates opened had given me a familiar face, even if there were barely a couple dozen out of a few hundred that could tell you my name. I'd blended in with the background so long that I was a part of it. A permanent, unimpeachable fixture.

The Wave was my ticking clock. When Charlie was at his most mobilized, riling everyone up, it seemed like it might go down at any moment, but other times, he'd be laughing or lazing like he'd be happy to spend the rest of his life as the biggest fish in the smallest pond, training crows to land on his arm and fucking girls young enough to be his daughters. Just like his speeches, his thinking tended to fly off on tangents. One second he'd be saying how the whole world was just a train, riding down on the tracks he laid, then he'd be off free-forming about the waffle house and the rainbow, the cat and the rat that chased the little girl off the swing set. He'd also started disappearing, often for days at a time, holing up in that house, or in the little shack that sat alongside. One night, we didn't eat at all, as nobody wanted to start without Charlie, and he never showed. Then one night became more.

I kept these observations to myself, even from the few that I'd go as far to describe as trusted, or to call friends. At Eden Ranch, everybody loved everybody, but the love for Charlie overrode all others. Having taken a step back, I could still see why, and sometimes you'd find yourself falling back under his spell, just for a second, like a sheet billowing over your head. Laughing at a joke, or unconsciously nodding along with a piece of wisdom that always sounds like it makes sense if you let it waft through your brain unbothered. But that was what he did, and I had to keep reminding myself. It was all a game; a trick, and if he had an inkling of what was going on inside my head, he'd saw it off with a sling blade. But with the loss of everything came the loss of fear. Well, mostly. It's liberating to not give a fuck about anything any more. I'd let it all go on the sidewalk by the payphone, an empty vessel that had walked back into camp and once again become Brand New, this time, not the square who became the cool kid, but the broken prey who'd turned hunter. My single reason for existing was to hunt that motherfucker down; to tear down his world, slaughter the queen and cease the buzz of her gathered drones. If not, then I may as well head back out there and hang myself with the cord of the phone, pleading sympathetic passers-by to push their knees into my back until my eyes turn milky.

My grandfather used to hunt. Deer, mostly. I asked him once why he never kept any trophies. There were no heads on the wall, and he told me it was because deer were so stupid. "It'd be like wearing a medal you got punching out a retard," he'd said, and he couldn't respect any creature that'd stand there while a man shot it in the back of the head. The problem with Charlie was that, literally or figuratively, he never stood still. There were no drinking holes from which he'd sup while you got off a clean shot, no nest of eggs to which he'd return, nor could he be lured into a rusted trap with cup-handed mimicry of the female mating cry. How do you predict the behavior of a man who once declared himself, with the sincerity of a wedding vow, to be the Pope of the mountains and sky? I'd seen him singing a song to a pig; a gentle ballad that he'd crooned into its hairy little ears with no idea that anybody was watching. Half the fun, and danger, of being around him, was never knowing what he'd do, from one minute to the next. Brand New was an ethos he lived by, minute to minute. There was no pattern.

So, unable to get close just yet, all I could do was to get closer to the ones who sailed on his winds. The hangers-on, the security, those sat by his right hand for the dinnertime whispers and loudest whoops, "*Yes, Charlie, that sounds great!*" It helped to be one of the few with a clear head. Everyone was so caught up in the mindlessness of it all, perpetually gorging on weed and acid, while I was just trying to stay straight and sane after living like a crazy person for too long. Fuck it, maybe a little crazy was what was needed. Not Manson-level crazy, smoking frozen turds and planning the downfall of humanity, but just enough to be able to break bread and shoot the shit with career criminals and psychos, and seem like you belong.

Eden's population was growing all the time. People came and went, but mostly they came. And the longer they stayed, the harder it was to leave. Anyone who'd arrived with a child found it wasn't so easy to pluck them back out of Charlie's free-range, group-rearing system for a hug, much less a stroll out of the gate, so those who'd brought their kids or pushed them out in the dirt of the ranch with midwife Manson either stayed, or left their children behind.

"Man, how we gonna keep feeding all these mouths?" said Jedro.

"Dunno," I replied. "The veggie patch would probably do better if they kept the animals off it."

"Yeah, no shit. Fuckin' dogs eat better'n we do. When they brought that cow in, I figured we'd be in for steak or some shit, but you know Charlie. I don't think they even milk it. Check this though..." Jedro pulled up his t-shirt, revealing a stomach without an ounce of fat on it. "Sit-ups or not, I never got a body like this back home. Even when I was broke. Kinda makes me wish I was auditioning again."

"When's the last time any of us had a burger?"

"Fuck, yeah. My mom did the *best* Sunday lunches. We should get her up here, huh? Maybe I'll give her a call." I tried not to remember that divine scent of the gravy boiling on the hob that came wafting through from the kitchen every Sunday. Always the last thing to get made, the gravy. You didn't need a gong or one of those hillbilly triangles, just that smell on the air. You'd attach yourself to it and float straight into your chair. There was nothing so subtle at Eden Ranch. Nothing so pure. At best, one of the girls would clang a stick around the inside of an old pan while yelling "chow time, cocksuckers!"

"Don't think I'd remember how to eat at a table now anyhow," said Jedro, "we're like monkeys. Chimp's tea party. Ooo-ooo-ooo!"

The newest mouths through the gates huddled and flapped like a flock of overexcited birds. They were a group of five Japanese girls, all long dark hair and huge brown eyes that looked way too innocent for this place. One of them had Charlie's LP under her arm, and it was all they could do to keep themselves from screaming as they took in the familiar landmarks they knew already from TV shows or magazine layouts. There's the big fire. Look, the house on the hill where Charlie lives. Longhairs and hippies and wild dogs, just like in the photos and badly pantomimed news re-enactments. It took me back to the tour, and all the crazy fun we'd had, people banging on windows like we were Ringo Starr.

"Goddamn Japanese pussy," said Jedro Haze, stretching out on the grass like a cat on a sunny driveway, "you ever had any of that?"

"Naw. This keeps up, this place gonna need a translator. German chicks, Limeys, that one dude from Italy or wherever it is. Think they speak any English? Actually, probably better that they don't..."

"You might be right," he said, pulling himself to his feet, "although there is that one universal language, we all speak it. The Language. Of. Love." He thrust his hips forwards with each word, doggy-fucking the air, spanking an invisible, Asian butt. "Their coochies go sideways, ya know. It'll look right at ya."

"How's that whole Hollywood thing coming along?" I said, Jedro lost in his pumping. "Those the moves you're gonna show off?"

"Hell yeah, casting couch, baby!"

"Yeah, well you should probably get a wriggle on. We're none of us getting any younger."

"I'm still young." He stopped mime-fucking, and desperately tried not to look out of breath.

"Got time enough to live the dream, huh..."

"This *is* the dream. Pussy on tap, grass, booze..."

"Anyone gonna remember you for that?"

"Eh," he said, making a noise like a Jewish grandmother, and brushing my words aside with a wave of his hand. "That's all ego, man. Fame, all that. Charlie could'a been the next Elvis if he wanted. But he's here, with us. There's more to life than fame, man. You think any of those motherfuckers are really happy? I bet Jerry Lewis goes home every night and weeps. He's got the big grin and shit, but how can they be happy on the inside? That million dollar house of his is more of a prison than the one I got out of."

"What?" I said. Jedro had never done time.

"He, I mean. The one Charlie got out of. Why'd you think he jacked in the music? All the contracts and people riding you like leeches. Who needs that? That's their prison, they just pretty it up and make it look like a palace, make you think you're the one in control, and all the while you're dancing the steps they laid out all across the floor. Fuck that, man. I don't want that. I thought I did, but now I know better. Besides... look at this shit." Jedro waved across at the Japanese girls with a shrill whistle. They looked over at the long-haired American hippie boys; Manson Family boys; giggling like high school girls getting a wink off the star quarterback. "Sometimes I feel like a fuckin' celebrity anyway," he said. With the international gesture of c'mere, Jedro motioned the girls to come over.

Jedro Haze was right about one thing. It was all ego, and it didn't take much for me to tumble back down into mine, and a pair of exotic girls saw me lose my footing and fall back into the black. At least down there, it was too dark to see the future or the past, only whatever filth was trapped down there with me. We led the girls to one of the many make-out spots to lay down with them. Mine made squealing noises that made me stop and ask if I was hurting her, but I think it was a cultural thing. Part way through, I caught Jedro's eye, and mouthed at him "*it don't go sideways.*" It was good to get lost; to feel emptiness instead of fear. Maybe I couldn't pretend to be human, but I could pretend I wasn't inhuman. Down there, there was no Charlie; no lost mom and dad; no massacres lurking over the horizon, or cat-gnawed corpses; just two Japanese girls, probably old friends way back to middle-school, who'd played in the sandbox together, and excitedly taken their first flight to the United States, and who were now being nudged into kissing each other between the thighs, by some empty fucking deviant who'd learnt from the best.

...

Days came and went like moods. I'd sit with my kin, collecting honey and flitting from flower to flower like all the other drones, but with one eye always on the queen. I was still just a lie becoming a lie becoming a lie. I moved in a direction so vague that sometimes I could barely see it, like the early-morning grasp at wisps of a beautiful dream that started vanishing as soon as you looked at it. Maybe it was just fear; fear at what would happen if – when – I really did find myself sat at his right hand. Telling myself I needed to be more proactive, I started volunteering for stuff; the kind of tedious shit-duty others would hide from, and found myself going into the city on food runs. Like the children we were, nobody thought about where it all came from, as though Charlie would raise his hands to the sky and make it rain nachos.

Occasionally we paid for something with the petty cash that'd been shaken out of the pants of the new arrivals, but that was just a distraction tactic, while another of us raided the next aisle for a shirt-full of cheesey nips and pork-in-a-pots. The revolving door of faces made it hard for shop-keeps to scout us, and there was an unending selection of legs, tits, and asses with which to divert cashier boys. Sometimes we'd saunter out of a store with as much as we could fit in our arms before booking it in one of the buggies. What were they going to do, send the police up to root around in our shit for evidence? Still, I preferred it to the dumpster runs. I'd gone on one with Melody, thinking it might be good to spend some time together, since we barely spoke any more. We'd sorted through cold, smelly garbage like raccoons, stepping on diapers and rejoicing at a stack of old pizzas less edible than the boxes they'd been left in. Nobody had ever been further from Paris.

"Can you believe they just throw this out?" she'd said.

Eventually, I'd found enough focus to tick off the first of my bigger goals, and gotten myself on nodding, and then speaking terms with the biker Lowball. Nothing deep, just a couple of quick shit-shooting sessions. We'd had encounters over our time at Eden, but the Judas Noose kept themselves (or were kept) pretty distant from the rank and file, halfway between Family and security. They were often loitering, but you'd catch them dead before you would at a sing-along or dancing round the fucking maypole. Christ knows what Charlie was paying them, or maybe the drugs and girls were enough to keep them around. Like they were for everyone else. Lowball always seemed the most approachable, so I'd set about the dance of platonic seduction.

Many of the bikers were intimidating to be around, and none more so than Deezer, the obvious leader. Deezer wasn't even that big of a guy, but tales of his brutality were exchanged in whispers only during excursions outside of camp, for fear that he might overhear and add a new victim to the legend. I heard he'd torn out someone's eyes and eaten them, just for looking at his bike. The last thing they ever saw was the yellows of his teeth. Talk was, he'd been a champion biker bar fighter, in headbutt contests where the contestant's arms were tied behind their backs. I personally witnessed one stupid motherfucker who came into camp with the wrong idea and paid for it. He got too rowdy, too gropey; taking the free love ethos as an open ticket to do whatever he wanted to any girl that caught his eye, because 'no' was for squares. "Come on toots, lighten up. It's free love!" That boy got so broken up, he looked like a swastika. Fucking Deezer. Didn't matter who you were or how high you were, the giggling stopped when his shadow got within jizzing distance.

With cats like that, the only way in, the only way to get close to the Noose, and then, to Charlie, was through Lowball. Not that he was a joke either. He could fuck someone a new ricker with the best of them, and you wouldn't wanna get on his bad side, but at least I could throw a "*sup?*" in his direction without getting cut for it.

I was sharing a joint with Lowball when I spotted the kid, Shank. I don't know how long he'd been there, as I'd been lost in the vision of the house, now a mere twenty yards from where I stood. I wasn't in the door yet, but I had made it to the top of the hill, looking down at the rest of camp; ants who must be wondering what it's like to be a chosen one. I felt another queasy swell of pride growing in my gut like a tumor. Seemed like nothing could stop that ego from pushing its way in.

The house stood three floors, tall and wide like the one on *The Waltons*, and was tattier up close than it was from the aspirational bottom of the hill. A side window was smashed, and the main bay windows were covered from the inside by shredded drapes that were closed even though it was early afternoon. The remnants of small fires sat around the edge of the stoop in black, circular char. The stoop itself had a broken rail, and I wondered if Charlie ever stumbled out into the morning sunshine and leant on it, only to find himself in the dirt below.

At the side of the house stood the converted barn

where the Noose hung out. I didn't know what it looked like before, but apparently they'd made it into their own biker bar. A pool table, barstools, even a jukebox running off a diesel generator. Most nights, their bikes would be lined up outside like greasy dominoes, and sometimes their noise would carry down on the Santa Ana winds. Drinking, speed, and gang-fucking some girl so bad she'd need stitches. Never could see where they fit in with Charlie's ethos.

"Want some?" said Lowball, snorting a bump off a loose knuckle.

"I'm good. What's with the kid?" Shank was sat on the top step of the stoop, arm wrapped around the rail, head resting against the wood. *Shank.* Another self-given nickname that didn't fit. He looked more like the kids in that movie with the Jew and his gang of thieves.

"He's been sat there a couple days," said Lowball, "I told him, I said 'Charlie's a busy man,' but he said 'I'll wait,' and put himself down there. Ain't moved since."

"And you let him?"

"He's just a kid. What's he gonna do? Rochelle's clit's bigger'n he is..." Then, like a fly traversing the turns of a hallway to shit on your birthday cake, a growing buzz, off in the beyond, signalled the arrival of the man himself. My first, panicked instinct was to take off, and something about it set off a sudden, and very intense sense-memory from childhood. There was a buddy I hung out with after middle-school, but always hoping that his dad hadn't come home from work yet. His father, so big and scary to an eight year old, sat in his armchair like an ancient king, immovable, the God of absolutes inside those walls. I dreaded my friend going to the bathroom and leaving me alone with the silent giant, and eventually, after he yelled at us for blocking his view of the box, I stopped going over altogether. If I met him now, I bet he'd be a tiny old man.

Charlie roared up the path on a dune buggy, with Freck riding shotgun. As he came to a halt, Freck clocked me right away, holding me with the skunk-eye all the way out of the buggy and up to the porch. I held my nerve, and her gaze, firm but friendly. Just some guy, with no murderous intentions, that's me. Charlie saw me too, but paid no mind and kept on going. As he got to the steps at the front of the house, the kid was waiting for him, standing in his path so he couldn't be ignored.

"Mr. Manson?" Shank's voice was that hee-haw, ejaculating donkey crackle of teenage hormones. He didn't seem afraid or intimidated by Charlie, facing him down with the rehearsed bravado of a job interview. Or maybe he knew the first rule when encountering a predator in the wild. Show no fear.

"Mister?" laughed Charlie. "Only people call me Mister are lawyers or niggers. Which are you, boy?"

"*Charlie*," he said, firmly and proudly, like it felt good to say it out loud, to have that permission. "Charlie, I've gotta tell you something."

"What's that, kid?" Kid. Slightly hunched with one hand resting on his knee, even though they were the same height, playful uncle tone in his voice.

"I just wanted you to know that *I* did it. I did it for you."

"Did what?" said Charlie.

"Killed all those people."

Well, fuck. Charlie's eyebrows disappeared into his hair, like when he's doing one of his big double-takes for yuks; Lowball, even Freck, who barely acknowledged anyone beside Charlie, were gawping at the boy, throwing looks at each other like "say what?" An amused exhalation of air puffed out of my nostrils, but then the door to the barn opened, with Deezer filling the frame. His cauliflower ears must have pricked up at the mention of killing. My blood stood still in my veins as he walked across and stood at my shoulder, glaring in the direction of Charlie and Shank. The kid spoke again, calm, humble, a schoolboy delivering A+ results to his high-flying parents.

"They talked about it on the news, I saw. That was me. I just... I did it to show you what I can do."

"Bullshit," said Freck.

"Hold on..." The kid reached into the pocket of his oversized barn-found jeans and pulled out something small and dark. Deezer stepped forwards for a closer look. From my vantage point I couldn't tell what it was until I heard the familiar click, and saw the glint of sunlight on dirty silver.

"This is what I used," said Shank. "I know it's only small, but I'm just a kid so it's pretty easy. I rang their doorbells and told them I was lost, and they let me right in."

"They?" said Freck, with an authoritative venom in her voice. "And who are *They*?" Charlie waved her quiet with his hand, and the boy continued.

"Three families. And a homeless guy. But they never talked about that on the news. Guess they never found him. I started with the hobo, just to see if I could. It's not so hard, huh?" There was an odd sense of unity in the moment; me and Charlie, the bikers and Freck, equally thrown by this waif who'd yet to suffer the full wrath of puberty, confessing to a series of grisly home invasion murders; a moment that could only ever make sense inside that place.

"Let me see that," said Charlie. In one smooth, cat-fast motion, he palmed the blade out of the boy's hand and had him spun around, Charlie's arm around Shank's neck, the knife at his belly. It was one of those reminders of how dangerous he was. You forget. He was so weedy, a strong enough fart would've blown him into the sky, and he was goofier than a shithouse rattler, but man, he could and would fuck you up. They said he leapt twenty feet in that courtroom.

"You killed all those people?" said Charlie, speaking softly into the boy's ear. Head cranked tight in a chin-lock, face getting flushed, he nodded as best he could. "You lyin' to me, boy? Trying to impress old Charlie? Or someone send you up here to say those things?" Charlie was hard to read at the best of times. You never knew if someone was about to get cuffed round the jaw, or if he was just playing, and holding in the giggles. None of us knew where it was heading, least of all the kid.

"I thought you'd..." Shank said. Charlie's grip held tight and close, his mouth breathing into his ear. I was tense with the feeling I should step in and do something. But what? Lowball and Deezer would have my head, and Freck would wear it like a hat. My face wore the mask of Family.

"This don't even look like it could cut somebody..." said Charlie. He pushed the knife into the boy's belly, not hard enough to draw blood, but enough to suddenly make the kid seem like a kid again; small, afraid, wanting his own, real family. Tears dribbled down his reddened cheeks, but I don't know if it was fear, or from his hero taking his thoughtfully wrapped, lovingly selected gift and stomping it to pieces in front of everybody. "Why would you make up a lie like that? You ain't told me nuthin' to make me believe you..."

"Th-th-three little pigs..." He squirmed as though wanting to say more, but the grip around his neck was tight. Charlie's expression was granite, his lips curled down into a horseshoe, eyes out towards camp, as he squeezed against the kid's windpipe. There was no more sounds from the boy but a gurgle. Fuck, I thought, he's gonna choke him to death, right in front of me, and I have to watch like it ain't nothing, or I'm next. Manson abruptly released him, placing his hands on the boy's shoulders, as he gulped down panicky mouthfuls of air. Ever so quietly, his voice dropping into near-whisper, Charlie spoke.

"You tryin' to tell me something there?"

"Round my neck," replied the boy, the words caught on that hic-hic reverb of somebody trying ever-so-hard not to cry. Charlie reached the blade inside of the boy's collar, grazing the steel against the white of his throat. My own heart was beating so hard, I felt sure he'd turn to me and yell to keep it down. Shank's eyes were closed, too afraid to move, as Charlie slid the knife down inside his shirt. A dark Rorschach blot seeped across the front of the boy's pants. Manson paused, lifting the knife back out, now with the silver chain of a necklace hanging across the blade. He placed the necklace into his other hand, still around the boy's neck, pulling him close as he examined it. The point of the knife sat poised, half an inch from Shank's chin. From where I was stood, it looked like one of those pendants that flips open to show a photograph. Pictures of loved ones, or black and white portraits of sour faced, long dead great-great-aunts. The contents of this necklace were all over Charlie's face, which took on a rage unlike anything I'd seen in all my time there. Part of me feared the skies would blacken and lightning bolts would pierce the earth.

"I thought you'd be pleased..." said the boy, weakly.

"You know how that makes me look? You set me up! Why would you do that? Had the fuckin' pigs up in here; motherfuckers out there all assuming it was me, talkin' 'bout all that nonsense from way back, man... all that smoke's from fires *you've* been startin'..." This time, Charlie's fury had no crowds to play to, but he was so lost in anger, all he could see was the boy. "Goddammit it, you little motherfucker," he paced like a chained animal, "rat at the dinner table, shakin' your hand but pulling you towards the edge of the cliff. Here." Charlie tossed the knife to Deezer, who snatched it out of the air blade first, gripping it in a bloodied palm.

The boy made a break for it, sprinting back into the direction of camp. Within two steps, he was bundled to the floor by Deezer. I looked for my own exit, but only saw the same fate. I shot a look at Lowball, whose eyes were wide and fixed on the scene in front of him. Charlie moved up onto the steps of the stoop, as if to get a better view, as Shank crawled, desperately, along the ground, fisting handfuls of turf, but with Deezer standing on his ankle, he was going nowhere. With a swift, simple movement, Deezer knelt on the boy's back, reached underneath, and slit his throat.

His neck opened up like a zipper, revealing the red flesh underneath. Blood streamed from the wound, and I was oddly struck by the practicality of it all; the hard boiled facts. To kill a human, you only need empty their body of blood. Though I wanted to look away, as he gurgled and twitched on the floor, in spite of all he'd done, I felt he deserved a sympathetic audience; a futile mercy. Nobody ever looked more like a child than Shank did at that moment, his last.

The boy fell still. Crimson pooled on the patchy grass beneath his body. There was no great final cry of pain, nor rattling wheeze or final thrash of the limbs, just quiet. A terrible quiet. Deezer pulled himself to his feet, casually pushing off one knee in the way that middle-aged men do, wiping the blade against the hip of his pants. My breathing seemed so loud. Charlie looked at me from up on the porch, that black-hole glare of his meeting mine like sticking wet fingers into a light socket. He seemed to give me a short once-over, and I could hear his voice inside my head, "I'm straight to the chair if he tells what he saw..." I was next. I was fucking next. I made the decision to run, but my body didn't agree. Charlie came down the steps, passing the boy without glancing down, and walked over to me. My limbs felt full of rocks.

"Get rid of him," said Charlie.

A small "How?" squeaked out of my mouth.

"I don't care! Just get it fucking done."

14 THREE CHORD FUNERAL MARCH

We wrapped the dead fourteen-year-old boy's naked body in a layer of black garbage sacks held together with electrical tape. His clothes were cut off using the same knife that had opened his throat, and burned in a small fire by the side of the house.

The task of getting rid was assigned to me and Lowball, victims of circumstance. Had I been down by the campfire, or fingering a German girl in a barn, I'd have been blissfully ignorant. Who knew how many gutted children's bodies I'd missed the fun of disposing while I'd been bored out of my mind, away from the action? Lowball had a small polythene bag filled with all different pills, some brightly colored, but most a murky grey. We both quaffed a handful, just to put some distance between ourselves and what was happening. Even for him, this was an unpleasant day's work.

There was a lake some ninety minutes out of camp; small, but well-covered on all sides by a heavy tree line. Charlie wanted the body as far from home as possible, so we loaded it into the back of an old Camero, being that every 5-0 in the state routinely pulled over our buggies on-sight. If that happened, Lowball would shoot his way out rather than take the fall. We drove to the chassis-shaking sounds of a jacked-up KROQ and the Edgar Winter Group, not exchanging word one. I rested my head on the window, gazing at the dull streak of warmly-lit, distant homes, and gripping onto a length of rope. I wondered if I'd soon find out how the course material would feel around my neck, with my feet gently swaying beneath me.

Charlie had made us wait until nightfall, so we'd sat guarding the body round the back of the house until the sun went down. Just two guys making small talk, and the corpse of a child. Once we parked up by the water and unloaded the body, we set about lassoing it and tying the other end of the rope around a rock; heavy enough to keep the evidence hidden underwater. But the rope was too thick, and we were clumsy. Our great plan suddenly seemed like something that only works in cartoons. We'd have done as well trying to anchor the body to an anvil. On the fly, Plan B saw me holding the body still while Lowball sliced little openings into the garbage sacks, before pushing as many rocks and pebbles as we could find inside. Each time I slid one in, my hand brushed against the cold, dead flesh, but it had to be done; an errand that's not there to be enjoyed, like taking out the trash, that's what I told myself. Become the lie. Even then, like some red-eyed Laurel and Hardy, we found we were standing in a shallow part of the lake, where the water lapped against the shingle, and would not cover a corpse. So, we dragged it, now weighted down by stones, up a hundred yards of slippery embankment, rolling it off with a splash, as it disappeared down onto the bottom.

When we got back to the house, I noticed the inside of my fingernails were black, either with dirt, or the boy's blood. I thought about how many times on the ride home

I must have put them in or around my mouth, and ran straight out back to the hose, which I fired directly into my mouth so forcibly, I'm not sure if I was rinsing or vomiting. I hosed myself down until the wind was raw on my cheeks, shivering and dripping, and thinking about the dead boy I'd dumped into the lake, to please the man whose actions had caused the boy to do those things to please the man... a snake choking to death on its own tail. But fuck, if that wasn't an *in* to Charlie's good graces, then nothing ever would be.

"You look like you need a fuckin' drink," said Lowball.

"And a towel."

He pushed open the door to the Judas Noose barn, and I was immediately hit in the face with a blast of sounds and the spicy tang of beer and BO. The music was rockier than the stuff we played in camp, with jangling electric guitar and bass you felt under your feet. It wasn't quite the stranger-in-the-Old-West-saloon, just a few turned heads, as the dozen or so bikers and pair of ranch girls didn't pay us much mind.

"Chuck us a couple," said Lowball. A rakish cat in the leather vest uniform opened a stained refrigerator and tossed over two bottles of beer. It'd been so long since I'd held a cold drink in my hand that I almost dropped it. This was another world.

"What is this place?"

"Barn. Was. Way before we got here though. Think the people who had it before used it as a rec room for their kids or stable-boys or whatnot. Pool table was already here, we just dirtied it up a bit, just how we like it."

The floor was grubby wooden boards, with three bare light bulbs hanging from the ceiling, illuminating the room in bright patches. It hurt your eyes if you were right underneath, but gave the corners a shady, private feel, with a pair of bare female legs extending out of the darkness and into the edge of light. I peered into the gloom until the whites of four eyes; two less than friendly; came leering out, causing me to look away. The walls were papered in pornography, plastered on all four sides like a ransom note. It was all pretty graphic; a step up from the happy-girl virginal poses of Playboy; with thick, wrist-like cocks, and dripping faces buried under a snowman's head of cum. With the music and atmosphere, it felt like a more adult version of what went on at the bottom of the path; a trip through a shattered looking glass where the thin, smooth, sweet-smelling girls got switched for hairy men with oversized boots and meth-dick.

Like any regular night winding down from work at the bar, I just sat and drank. On a chair. I couldn't remember the last time I'd sat in a chair. My ass barely knew what to do with itself. There were also tattoos, lots of tattoos. Some were plain and clearly inked with the end of a burning prison bedspring, while others could almost be hung in a gallery, albeit in the toilets, above a festering urinal. As I sat and drank away my troubles, taking in the scene around me, I began to mentally compile a list of favorites, among the generic white power symbols and faded names of ex-lovers.

An elaborate tableau, set across a broad back and shoulders, of Christ and the Devil in a tug of war over a noticeably younger and slimmer depiction of its walrus-faced wearer, each yanking an arm and angrily eyeballing each other.

A roaring, toothed vagina, with a ringed-clit for a nose, on the shoulder of Rochelle, the lone female Noose, who somehow managed to spend more time talking about all the pussy she'd had than the cooch-obsessed dudes who wouldn't stop talking about fucking even if they were drowning. Honorable mention for the tat along the inside of her bottom lip reading 'CUNT'.

A unicorn fucking a mermaid in the ass. That was on some guy's chest. If you forced me to pick, at broken pool cue-point, I'd have to say that was my favorite. I didn't even know if mermaids had asses, but the expression on the seaweed-haired fishgirl's face was definitely "Holy God, I'm getting fucked up the ass by a unicorn!"

As the night went on, I started to feel more and more at ease. Maybe it was the booze, or maybe my actions earlier in the evening, with fresh child-blood under my nails, gave me the sense that I'd earned my place. Fuck it anyway, let them gang rape me to death.

Some bikers were more approachable than others, and eventually, with the Lowball seal of approval, hands began to extend towards mine; tattooed knuckles testing me with beefy shakes that cracked my fingers. Among all the Lowballs and Mad Dogs and Shittypants Joes, I couldn't claim a bad-ass sounding nickname, but the frequent squealing of my name like the black nanny in the cartoons – "*Tho-mas!?*" – made me feel oddly part of the gang. A thin, grieving widow's veil of booze had put enough detachment between me and the world, and I tapped on the table to get Lowball's attention.

"You a pool shark?"

"What?"

"I dunno, just...'Lowball.' Thought it might be a pool

thing." Instantly, the room dropped into that stranger-in-a-saloon silence I'd been dreading when I walked in. First time I'd opened my mouth and everything had fallen to shit. Lowball slowly placed his bottle down, eyefucking me all the way. A lone burst of crazy laughter shredded through the silence from someone hidden in the shadows, and was slapped down with angry shushing. I shrugged out a "What did I do?" but a powerful grip onto my shoulders pinned me to the seat.

"Show him," said Deezer.

Lowball stood, kicking away his chair. I'd have jolted were I not held in place. He began to unhook his belt; thick and snakeskin, with a huge metal buckle bearing his name in silver letters. The barn funeral-silent and all eyes on me, I sensed a test. Either I was fixing to get whupped, or really was about to have my back door smashed right off its hinges. Eyes drilling a hole through mine, Lowball dropped his pants past his knees, before whipping down his underwear.

"My *God*..." I said, "okay, that makes sense." Beneath his bush of greying pubes, beneath the stubby little rotten strawberry cock, hung a pair of sagging testicles, dangling a full foot in length. The sack stretched out like wrinkled gum, salmon-pink and decorated with hairs, with two normal sized balls sat low at the bottom. The hands around my shoulder slapping me upside the head and the barn shook with riotous laughter. It was a party piece they'd seen a thousand times, which would never lose its freakshow appeal. Lowball squatted down, until his balls hung a couple of inches from the floor, and wiggled his hips to swing them side to side, like the clanger in an old grandfather clock. "Were you born like that?" I said, not even sure why I was asking, and possibly hypnotised by the rhythmic to-and-fro of the bollocks.

"Nah," replied Lowball, finally hiking back his pants, "got 'em caught in the seat of my ride one time. I came off, bike and balls just kept going..." I looked at the others, waiting for the hard faces to crack.

"Really?" A beat, and then – laughter.

"What do you think, you dumb fuck? Balls don't work that way." Lowball laughed his way over to the back door for a piss, and a finger tapped my arm. It was an older biker, who pulled up in a seat next to me.

"It weren't no accident. He got in a fight with this queer boy, and the queer figures he'll grab hold of them balls and keep on pulling 'till Baller says uncle. Took four of us to prise the little fag's hands off, but Lowball never did say it. Ain't the Judas way."

"Yeah," I said, chugging back a mouthful of beer, "right."

"Well, you ain't gonna forget that sight in a hurry, boy." This particular gentleman, with arms like two fat pythons, introduced himself as Big Terry. Big Terry was so haggard from the years of beer, speed, and the toxic LA air hitting him in the face as he roared down freeways, that he resembled a (regular length) scrotum in a bandana. The bags under his eyes had bags of their own, like the staircase chins of a fat man, with creases in his forehead you could stick quarters in. He regaled me with tales of a pissing contest where he'd peed on the ceiling, and the times he'd spied on Rochelle bringing ranch girls to eat her pussy while he watched through a crack in the wall, jacking off with "a pecker that works a third of the time." "She knows," he said, "but she still lets me watch."

Later, at the close of a very long, very strange day, Lowball cornered me outside.

"Listen man," he said, "I got some shit to do tomorrow. You want in?"

"Sure. Like what?"

"Need some backup. Couple of us gonna meet with a Mexican that's got a package. Nothin' heavy, but there's always somethin' with them beaners. I can get one of the others if you ain't down."

"No, I'm down."

"Alright, man. I'll come get you round noon."

Noon came, and so did Lowball, rolling through camp on his Harley, with another bike following behind. He stepped off and called me over, and even through my hangover brain-fog, I wondered who, if anyone would be watching; seeing me with genuine hoods like the Noose.

"Shouldn't I be packing?" I said.

"Packing?" He laughed in a way that made me feel action-figure sized. "No, you don't need to be *packing*. Here." He reached into his pocket and tossed something at my chest. It hit me in the solar plexus with a solid thud and I fumbled it in my hands before it fell. Brass knucks. "That'll see you for now, cupcake."

I'd love to tell you it was a *Bonnie and Clyde* rampage of lawlessness, where we fled through the city with a dozen cop cars on our trail, but we were back at Eden before we knew it. I hadn't done a thing but sit in the buggy and watch a friendly enough conversation between the bikers and a pair of Mexicans. If anything kicked off, I was to leap out and help my brothers, but it was all pretty amicable. Nothing but handshakes and shoulder to shoulder hugs. Christ knows what use I'd have been if shit had kicked off, but I figure it was a job not even worth bothering the others with. Maybe he was just humoring me.

So was I a criminal now? Had I been one already? People always use that moral metaphor about stealing a loaf of bread to feed your family, but what if your family had deliberately opted out of all the things that would allow them to legally buy that bread in the first place? At what point was the line crossed? Sitting with a duster around my fist, one whistle from having to use it to beat in a Mexican's head, might not be the regime of peace and love that Manson was selling, but at least I was finally living in the real; the scummy, brutal truth behind the beautiful lie. Getting behind the curtain was the biggest step towards ending that fuck.

Charlie's late night sermons became a different beast entirely when you appreciated that he was completely out of his mind. The same words, the same wheeling of arms and chewing of lips, just viewed from a slightly different angle. I saw a card once in a magic shop. If you moved it one way, just a little, the sweet old lady's face became a skull, and her wheelchair turned into a speeding hot rod that spat out columns of flame. That's what Charlie was. You look at him straight on, taking him at his word, and blocking out everything but what's directly in front of you, you're looking at Jesus; the returned messiah who wants everybody to love everybody, so he can lead them into the light. Flip it a smidge, take a step to the side, and there's horns and hooves, a forked tail and a forked tongue. For the latest performance, I was barely a few bodies away. Moving up, up, up, with Melody at my side as though nothing had ever happened.

"Don't worry about me, only worry about yourself. You're the only one you have to live with..."

I'm going to kill you.

"Only you can know if you done anything wrong, ain't nobody else can tell you that..."

I'm going to end you.

"They try to tell you. Try to push their guilt onto you with the things *they've* done..."

Stab, shoot, strangle; tie you to a bike and run you through the desert till your skin tears off, like the snake that you are.

"It's all the mind; it's all in you. The whole universe is in here; the whole world. When they locked me in that prison, they didn't realize I've got ten thousand galaxies in here..."

Fuck you. Fuck. You.

"That's what you need to learn. Wherever you are, you can't run away from *here*. You're always here, wherever you are. Go to New York, go to Africa, you're not in New York, you're not in Africa, you're *here*. You see what I'm sayin'? Here is where you are. *You* are where you are. And if you done something you're ashamed of, or didn't do something you wished you had, don't matter where you go, all that's gonna be right here with you. The world moves under you – the universe – you're always at the center. I'm at the center of mine, you're at the center of yours. They lock me in a prison and think that the *here* in a cell is any different from the *here* in the Australian bush. They're sitting there laughing, thinking they got me. Well I got you, man, I *always* got you. You can't beat this. I go wherever I want. I'm already there. I'm the desert and the sky, I'm the oceans, the mountains, the poppy fields and the great plains..."

"They're not so great," joked Melody, whispering into my ear. I cuffed her across the face with an open hand that cracked so loud it drew everyone's attention away from Charlie and onto us. I don't know if I expected a look like the girl who'd taken the back of Charlie's hand when I first came to camp, but she really didn't seem grateful at all. In that moment, I swear I caught his eye, just for a second, and I imagined his voice in my head – "*That kid's got something.*" Without missing a beat, save that split second, he continued.

"It's all so shallow, guy. Think they're sitting around like this; open air, playing with their friends, big fire keeping 'em warm? They're not. They're locked inside their own prisons, and their minds are so closed, there ain't even a bathroom in there, much less a universe. Sat slowly killing themselves, with their tee-vees and their movies, and their microwaves and their macrowees, and their Elvis Presleys and their Shelvish Sheblees and shoomablooma ackasa mablasa..."

Sometimes that was all it took to get dragged back in, just for a breath. The vocal gymnastics and the spiel that he sold on pure passion and delivery, slipping it through the keyhole of your mind and making itself at home if you weren't careful. Even his face, always so expressive and clownish, was part of the big bag of tricks I always had to be on guard for.

"Aleister Crowley knew, and They said he was evil. Wicked. He knew it though. One of the few men to figure that shit out, and when you die, that's what I'm sayin', if you're pure... but nobody ever got to be that pure, besides a few, and they *could* be right here, sitting by this fire talking right now..." Charlie giggled, pushing his shoulders up and poking out his tongue like a naughty little boy. "Ol' Jesus, he knew. *I* know. Everyone gets distracted with that poison they pump into your minds. Jump from one body to the next and just keep on rolling..."

Guy wasn't just evil, he was fucking crazy. Out of his cunting mind. He seemed even crazier than normal, mentally deteriorating by the day, and even if it got to the point where he was no longer in control of himself, he'd still be in control of all of them. That was the scariest thing about Charlie. That a guy so obviously dog-dick insane could be so smart and calculating. It was focussed insanity.

Everything wound down, and Charlie hung around playing chase games with the girls and spitting more babble about reincarnation and the cosmos, and a fish in India that had learned how to speak. I stood nearby looking suitably wowed but trying not to listen too hard so's I wouldn't risk getting sucked back in. I did this by looking at the tits. I could sense Melody nearby, and wondered if she'd come over and join in the fun, but when I turned around I caught the back of her disappearing into one of the barns. So much for love.

...

I thought that'd be it. I'd done my dirty work, pressed the flesh, and now I had my in with the main man. Now I could get close enough to finish the job. Except that's around the time he started disappearing. Gradually, his treks down into camp; his speeches and mingling, became more sporadic, and each day he failed to put in an appearance was a day spent in fear that he was strapping himself up with grenades, ready to lead the charge. But he was just holed up in his little shack by the house, flying around the universe inside his brain, leaving class unsupervised, and with spitballed ceilings and a genital-covered blackboard. The kids who waited patiently at their desks were the old hands of Eden, who'd never be swayed, while many of the newest members, still straggling through the entrance on a daily basis, had yet to see him in person, yet to hear sermon or song. Left alone, the playful, blissed-out nature of Eden had taken on a more aggressively rowdy air, as the young strays living without rules for the first time made the most of it. Some nights, there'd be an unshakable sense of uninvited guests; friends of friends spilling beer on the couch and knocking over your grandmother's ashes, and refusing to leave. Part of me wished Charlie would come down and show everyone who ran things, like he did in the old days.

The Judas Noose, after years of loitering and merely looking the part, finally earned their keep by tossing out the dickheads and douchebags, and breaking up the nightly fights that sprung up around camp, mostly – but not always – involving greenhorns that were getting too loud and too heavy. Everything began to feel disjointed, as if an externalising of my own deteriorating view of the place, as though my Lobsang Rampa third eye was projecting outwards into the world. Even some of the long-termers were growing impatient. Time was, if someone became enough of a face round here and decided they wanted to leave, they'd find it wasn't as easy as just walking out. Emotional blackmail, literal blackmail, physical force; if you'd skipped through the grass with your hand in another's, good luck having them ever let go. But the virus of faith spread outwards, and without its center, the outer reaches had started to flag. I'd even heard some of those girls, chicks who'd been around as long as me, talking to each other about their growing impatience.

"I know he knows what he's doing, but fuck, I just wanna get out there and get the party started..."

My own frustration had begun to manifest too, particularly in my beating of a cocky jerk-off who was shit-talking about Charlie. I think I was more surprised than him when I tackled him to the floor and set about his face with my fists. I hit him so hard I cut my knuckles on his teeth, and by the time they pulled me off, he was a limp pile of rags I'd have tossed onto the bonfire without a second thought. Maybe I was stressed, or insulted that he'd come into the only home I had and started running his mouth. And sure, maybe Charlie was "a gay wizard," but maybe I felt like he hadn't earned the right to say so. I didn't think it was possible to hit somebody that hard, not even after the guy in Frisco, and after I was done I felt purged.

I never saw that guy or his friends again. But the ranks continued to bolster. Some kids had driven up in a black van and parked up at the side of the ranch, sleeping in it at night, and keeping to themselves during the day, like they'd found a place for a free vacation. Even the lure of the girls hadn't been enough to drag them from their private party, with the jangle of their 8-track wafting across when the winds were right. One day, I'd wandered over for a closer listen. The sound was jarring; forcefully different from the melodic layer of Beatles songs that poured from the dash of the Eden Ranch buggies.

"What is that?" I asked a kid with red streaks of dye rubbed into the ends of his long blond hair.

"New York Dolls," he replied, with a dismissive sneer.

"Yeah, well it sounds like shit," I said.

"Fuckin' A..."

I looked up to see Lowball, grinding on his teeth so hard you could'a thrown a rock in there and watched him spit out dust. He wheeled me away with an arm draped around my shoulder.

"We got a job coming up; something for Charlie. Ranch business. Me, Deezer, Johnny Dingo, we need one more. Gotta be a face they don't know, a regular guy. What'dya say?"

"Sure," I nodded, "whatever."

"Alright, cool. Go find Deezer sometime. He's busy right now gettin' his nob gobbled. Don't disturb that, he'll tear your ass open and ride his bike up there..."

Fucking Deezer. Anyone but him. Later, as I trudged slowly up the path towards the barn, my hole was twitching like a rabbit's nose as I spied his figure loitering by the bikes. I prayed he'd know what I wanted and we could keep the chat to a minimum. He didn't seem the type for small talk anyways. Lovely weather we've been having. Did you catch the big game last night? Say, is it easier shivving your way through to the internal organs of a child than it is the leathery skin of an older gentleman?

"Hey," I said, in a tone that was an octave or two below my usual speaking voice. My penis felt small and afraid, retreating turtle-like into the safety of my crotch. There was a barely perceptible raise of the head from Deezer, which was the closest you could ever hope to get for a greeting, but his face was stuck in that wind-just-changed snarl, which probably hung in place while he slept.

"We'll get you a piece," he said. Deezer walked off towards the house and I was glad to be away from him again. He turned back and yelled, "What the fuck you standing around for?" I hesitated for a moment, before hurriedly joining him over by the house.

My feet climbed those four steps for the first time, past the spot where the boy had been killed, and up onto the stoop. I glanced across at Manson's outbuilding-cum-shack where he'd sequester himself, maybe when the open skies got too big after all those years inside the comfort of a cell. Deezer pushed open the unlocked front door. I expected to be hit by all manner of sights, sounds and smells; of the perpetual Caligula's Woodstock we'd all imagined inside, but all was quiet. A shoulder-barge from behind shoved me over the threshold, and finally, I was in. The door banged closed behind us, and I suppose I could have been killed right there, but my first desire was to throw my hand over my mouth to stop from vomiting. The inside of the house smelt worse than the fuck barn with all the cum stains on the back of the door like a nest. The ceiling was yellow with nicotine and grass, and there were fist-sized holes in the walls. Deezer lead me down the hallway. I snuck a sideways glimpse into one of the rooms as I passed. A mattress lay on a bare floor, with a snowfall of crinkled old roaches.

The décor wasn't what I expected, looking like something from a visit to a spinster aunt. How did they say he got it? Left it by someone? Bought it? There was always a scam with him. Always something. The previous owners were probably at the bottom of the lake. That was what I'd been gazing up at for all that time; a sex-smelling, piss-pooled heap with metal shit-buckets and burn marks on the ceiling? Rotten and broken on the inside, but with a beautiful, aspirational exterior. Truly it was the king's own castle. Maybe the upstairs was spotless, all chandeliers and four poster beds; the red velvet chaise longue on which Charlie read the morning papers in his smoking jacket.

Deezer unlocked a door at the side of the hall and pushed me inside. My lungs froze as I stood in the darkness. A muscular arm reached inside and flicked on a light.

Guns. Lots and lots of guns. The walls of the room were lined with every kind of gun you could think of. Handguns, rifles, World War 2 shooters with rusty bayonets still attached, machine guns that looked like they belonged to Al Capone. On a table was another pile, stacked like pick up sticks, while the floor in one corner housed a haystack of bullets and shells.

"Holy fuck, you got a lot of guns..."

"This ain't shit. We got stashes all over this motherfucker. This is just the overflow. Here. Take this," he said, handing me a small pistol. "Ever use one?" I shook my head. "Don't matter. It's mostly for show. And a time comes when you have to use it, you'll know. You'll have to."

"Yeah, but..."

"It's a fuckin' gun." He said it with such derision that it almost lightened the mood. Like, how would someone not know how to use a gun? Jesus Christ almighty. You point and you pull. Don't you watch the cowboy shows, you little fruit? Even with a gun in my hand – a fucking gun, like a real heavy - nerves hung round my throat like an anaconda.

"We're gonna need some bodies with this one. This shit could go bad real quick."

"What about Jedro?" I babbled.

"Who? Say what?"

"Jedro Haze. He's cool, I can vouch..."

"Oh," he said, "you can vouch?" so sarcastically that you could hear what little paint was left flaking off the door. "Ain't no vouching to be done. Anyway, since that thing with the kid, Charlie's been real vigilant about *everyone*; we all have."

"Yeah, yeah," I said. "Totally."

"Naw, you don't know. He can be paranoid and all, but Charlie swears he can hear their thoughts; smell them. I can too."

"Smell who?"

"Whoever's here waiting to take him out." Deezer leaned a palm against the wall, blocking my exit and leaning in real close, eye to eye. "There's a rat in camp."

He flicked out the light.

15 FOURTEEN/EIGHTY-EIGHT

The morning of the big job. Lowball, Deezer, and the others would soon come down from the house, and together we'd go burn down a meth lab, or assassinate the governor, or whatever it was that scuzzy criminal types like myself did that separated us from the normal folks, out mowing their lawns and refraining from stabbing somebody in the neck for a whole working day. That's if there even was a job. Maybe the whole thing was a pretence for getting me out of the camp to make me easier to dispose of after I got plugged. Just bury me where I fall. I'll rot with the beetle husks while the world drowns.

As the years had gone on, a simple thought would increasingly snowball into daydreams that were so vivid and labyrinthine that shaking them off to re-enter the real world was like stumbling back through treacle. You could hose most of it off, but there'd still be pieces stuck to your ass, or in the crevices behind your ears, as you blundered around in reality. Maybe it was all the acid and peyote. I was picturing myself holding up a bank, shotgun cocked at the teller, Robin Hood and his Greasy Men, lost in thoughts of jewel-crammed security boxes and pretty hostages squealing "take me with you!" over the sirens, when, like the beep-beep-beep of an alarm clock that becomes a raygun, a voice cut through from one world to the next.

"He see everything."

The lone, looming presence with one foot permanently in both worlds. Larger than life and two feet away, was Charlie.

"Who does?" I replied, in a self-consciously frail wobble that made me clear my throat.

"Bird." He pointed towards a crow, a black shape silhouetted against the blueness of the sky like the player of an ancient Oriental shadow play; myths and fables and parables where animals spoke like men and Lady Irony dished out her just desserts. The boy who stuck his head in the lion's mouth. The boy who got in over his head and was stung by the queen bee. Charlie took a seat next to me on the ground.

"All the way up there, he sees everything, and it all looks so small. *He* ain't big, he ain't like a giant looking down. He could stand in the palm of my hand. But to the bird, everything else seems small, because he looks at the bigger picture. See?"

"Yeah," I said, with much-improved fake confidence. Charlie's gaze held firm, and he gently nodded at me as if I was to continue the thought, to show my workings on the bottom of the page.

"Uh... well, if you step back far enough, outside of the... outside of the world, and the people, and all their worries and plans, and schemes, you'll see that it's all small and petty, and you can..."

"...see exactly where they're all headed," he said, finishing the thought for me. Charlie smiled and slapped an arm around my shoulder. The test was passed, an A or at least a B-. Why did that feel so good? "When you talk about tomorrow, you always gotta think about today. Can't be a tomorrow without today. If you drop a rock into a pond, it's not all about that big splash as it hits the water; you gotta be watching out for those ripples, guy, and the ripples from the ripples. You see what I'm saying?"

"Sure."

"Think of today as the biggest rock you ever seen. I'm trusting you to carry it for me, Tom." Tom. That was the first time Charlie had used my name. To hear it gave me an embarrassing thrill; a skip of the heart, like the giddy flush that first time I saw him at the entrance. "Cuz there's something I've been thinking. A feeling I've got..." Charlie's grip around me tightened, and I suddenly felt trapped, rather than safe or loved; a father's embrace that could suffocate with the smallest squeeze. "You ever get a feeling?" Feeling? He allowed the end of the word to trail off from his mouth until it was almost smoke, a ghostly apparition that maybe neither of us had really heard. His fingers felt like insects under my skin. My spine was slightly bent towards his five-feet-two, my ear to his mouth.

"Feelings, man," he said, his voice soft and raspy, and the rough of his beard bristling my skin. "It's the funniest thing. Can't photograph it, can't tie a piece of string around a feeling and dangle it from your thumb, but every man knows when a feeling is true. Hell, most times they're truer than the things you *can* see."

I could feel his breath against my neck, hot and sickly;

an old well in a child's play park with a long forgotten corpse growing mouldy beneath the wishes. And he had a feeling. A feeling, and a grip around my neck. He knew. There was no fucking way he knew. I'd given nothing away. It was all in my head, every word, every notion of tearing down the church he'd built and paving it over with his bones. But there were stories. Everyone was so sure Charlie was more than man; that he could see inside you. The tales were plentiful, circulating back and forth throughout the days in Chinese whispers; stories about breathing animals back to life and seeing inside people's minds. Charlie can stop time. He can make the earth shake. And sometimes, he just has that look like he can see what's going on in your head, and he's watching it like a television. He always knew the right thing to say, the exact thing that somebody needed to hear. Maybe he *was* in there, crawling around in the sludge of my brain, sliding through my cortexes like a water park.

I tried to think of something else, anything else, to tune my head to a different channel, but when they tell you not to think about the blue horse or the pink elephant, that's all you can see. There were an army of red monkeys, in the form of gunshots, slashes, and my hands around Charles Manson's neck, his eyes bulging in surprise and terror, and finally, acceptance, as the lights went out. Anything but that; anything but murdered, gloriously dead Charles Manson, laying still at my feet. Puppies, flowers, a dolphin smoking a pipe, Charlie with his head sawn off... no. Fuck. And he was touching me. Why was he touching me? Did he need to touch someone to slide inside their souls? He was in me, I could tell; a human lie detector, and his next words would be "I know...."

"What goes down today," he said, "I need to be sure I made the right choice."

"I know," I replied. "I won't let you down." Charlie's

hand released itself from my shoulder and patted me on the back. Wordlessly, he slunk away, to sit with others and have them flutter and fuss. I looked across at Charlie, semi-circle of girls clucking for attention, revolver in my pocket, and thought, man, I should just do it right there. I should do it before he had a chance to look me in the eye and make me feel one of the many ways he could make you feel, all at once. I might not hit him in the head, but I'd probably be able to pop a couple in his chest. I knew I might never get another chance. My hand slipped inside my pocket and nestled the cold metal grip. Fuck being close, fuck being seen, just get to him before he gets to me. Even if he was more than man, he wasn't fast enough to duck a bullet. Two shots, that's all it would take – two squeezes of one little finger. One for him, one for me, so I wouldn't have to be around to watch his corpse carried aloft like the fallen Christ.

But no. More than the things he'd done and the things he was going to do, I remembered that night on tour, the night when his ideas and spirit had never seemed stronger. *If someone needs to have him silenced, what are they so afraid of? His ideas will live forever.* My fingers loosened, and I let go of the pistol.

...

"Naw, we ain't taking no bikes." That's what led to me and Lowball rattling around in the back of a covered truck with the cat named Johnny Dingo, and Deezer at the wheel. The darkness of the truck was penetrated by fingers of daylight peeping through small holes they'd bored out of the sides, supposedly so we could see where we were going, which coincidentally were also just the right size to poke a gun barrel out of. Not that you could look through them. The highways were smooth and fast, but every time we turned a corner or stopped at a light, we got hurled around like turds in a saucepan.

"Slow down you dumb fuck," yelled Lowball, banging against the cab wall, in a show of balls that was less impressive when you realised Deezer couldn't tell which one of us it was. Finally, the truck slowly wound its way up into the Hollywood Hills, and the speed at which we crawled past the opulent gated mansions immediately turned us into tourists.

"That's where Yul Brynner lives..."

"...the pool where Lana Turner farted in Sinatra's mouth..."

"...I hear they had pee-orgies, every famous name you can think of..."

"...drapes that close when he says 'Daddy's fuck time'..."

While waiting for a laundromat van to pass, we paused outside one particular house, giving us a good look at the palatial home sat at the bottom of a winding driveway.

"Hey," said Lowball, "that's Zsa Zsa Gabor's place."

"I fucked her," said Dingo, matter-of-factly.

"Bullshit you did."

"Fuck off. I fucked her. And she never had dick like it."

"Nobody had dick like it. Three inches long and shaped like a stop sign..." We started moving again, wending our way and glimpsing puzzle-piece fragments of the lives of the rich and the beautiful, like the dumpster diving wretches we were.

"Yeah, well you can suck on all of that three inches and you'll smile like it's your birthday. See that place?"

"Yeah," said Lowball, squinting across at the middle floor of a dirty-white 1920's Art Deco pile.

"Well, that's where you got butt-fucked by the Three Stooges." Johnny Dingo lightly poked me in the ribs, and regarded me with utter conviction. "He did."

"Hey," I said, "I don't doubt it." Suddenly, the truck came to a stop, sending the three of us clattering to the floor. "Fuck," I said, sandwiched inbetween the two bikers, "I guess we're here so they can finish you off."

The back doors slid open, bathing the man-pile in daylight.

"I can't leave you queers alone for two minutes without you fucking each other's asses. Get yourselves up here. We do the rest on foot. Well, you do." 'You' meant 'me'

"Your piece loaded?" said Deezer, as we skulked around the side of the truck.

"Sure," I replied, reaching back. Deezer slapped my hand clear of my pants.

"Not here. Fucking Christ. Stand outside a fucking two million dollar house waving a pistol around..."

"I'm sorry, man, I..."

"Shut the fuck up and listen." Shut the fuck up and listen I did. This time, I wouldn't be spectating. I was to gain access to the house of one Bedford Cutler, a not-so-public Neo-Nazi with an impressive private collection of Third Reich memorabilia that was of particular interest to Charlie. I had the cover story and code-words with which to dazzle him, and from there, my role was to keep him forcibly detained while my buddies got inside. And that was it. All on me. No real plan other than to get it done. Get it done, or get got. The Noose would follow behind in five or ten minutes, and if those gates weren't open and waiting, Deezer would probably cut a pussy into my face and fuck it right in the middle of the street.

I trudged past mansions on either side, with a vague curiosity for the oversized homes. I hadn't had a proper roof over my head for years. Sure, we'd shelter in the barns when the weather was bad, but that's nothing the cavemen and Red Indians hadn't done back in the day. On request, I was better dressed than usual, in a faintly less tatty pair of jeans and a t-shirt, and at a push maybe I could have passed for a young millionaire rockstar, out for a stroll in my neighborhood, rather than a free-loving shirker who couldn't pay the rent on one of their treehouses with a lifetime of his fuck-all salary.

Cutler's gates, solid black steel and hammered into thick bars like the door to Satan's prison cell, were marked by a Confederate flag flying high and proud. I pushed the buzzer on the intercom and waited. I felt exposed, suddenly super-conscious of the loaded pistol tucked into the back of my pants, hidden beneath the drape of my shirt. The street was quiet, with the only sound coming from the rippling flag that seemed alive, billowing over the top of the perimeter wall like a bird of prey, waiting to swoop.

"Who's that?" The crackly voice on the other end sounded old and cranky, and its sudden arrival made me flinch.

"Hey," I said, "I'm just passing through." No response.

"This is private property..."

"I've been spending some time down with Pastor Rothwell and the Tennessee chapter. I'm from Arkansas. West Ridge. Just making my way cross country. Learning, you know? Meeting folks." Silence. I'd lost him. Two sentences in, I'd already blown it. Short of clambering over a ten-foot razor-topped wall, my face was about to get a serious fucking.

A burst of static caused me to jump so hard, my hair almost flew off like a hat.

"Arkansas, huh? You're a long way from home, son. What's the scene like there?"

"The scene? Um... well, there's some black... people. Black people. Blacks. Probably too many, you ask me. I, I mean, *definitely* too many. Lot of us whites too, which is the good news, but..."

"And Rothwell told you about me, you say?" His voice was laced with a desperate delight that I'd come to recognise well, both in myself and others. Even in the Hollywood Hills, even among Holocaust deniers and noose-swinging cross burners, the power of celebrity never failed.

"Yes he did, sir. Said if I was ever in LA I was to come and pay you a visit. Gave me his personal recommendation." The speaker went quiet. With a haunted castle creak, the automated gates slowly opened, and I stepped out from the street and inside.

Bedford Cutler emerged from the front door to greet me. He was small and lined, like an uncle, with cropped grey hair and a paunch. Hell, he had to be sixty. I was a third his age and with a shiny bullet for each of his decades, my bravado didn't feel so fake anymore.

"What's with hair?" he said, no less raspy away from the buzz of the intercom. "You look like a fairy."

"Yeah. Been too busy to get it cut..." I rubbed my hands through it, "with all the travelling and..."

"So what'd the Pastor say?" Bedford eyed me excitedly; his head tilted like a dog's.

"Oh, he just said I had to come and see you, and that..." As I spoke, his hands found their way to a switch on the porch, and the gates began to swing closed behind me.

"Wait!" I said. My sudden desperation, coupled with Cutler's paranoia caused his face to change.

"Who the fuck are you?" said Cutler, his voice flipping from avuncular neighbor to enraged authoritarian, with all the fury of a man who'd probably lynched a hundred blackies without batting an eyelid. I pulled the gun from my waistband, fumble-fucking it towards Cutler with my finger poised against the trigger.

"Just keep them fuckin' gates open." Bedford Cutler didn't blink. There was no fear in his eyes, just anger.

"Son, you got no idea who you're fucking with." He was almost laughing. "No idea."

"Nor do you, so you'd best open those fuckin' gates."

With a cock of the hammer, his finger was back on the button, and the gates behind were ready for Deezer and the boys to slide on up. Cutler's eyes flitted back inside the house, and on the edge of my gaze, I caught movement inside the hallway. Suddenly, the doors flew open, and two young men burst onto the front step. Both were rocking tattooed necks and shaven heads, and armed with rusty-looking World War II bayonets, looking to spill some hippie blood.

"Aw, shit. Stay back." I motioned with the pistol for them to move aside, grabbing the old man as a human shield, gripping him close just like Charlie had with the kid. I pushed the barrel into the side of his neck, barking at the skinheads in my best pretend-psycho. "Back off, or I'll pop this old motherfucker." I'll pop him. Suddenly I was Clint Eastwood, and it was... it was fucking *awesome*. Despite the cover of a high wall and tall trees, I'd been told once about the stupidity of flashing a gun around, so I forced Bedford Cutler inside, with the skinheads following at short distance.

I pulled Cutler up the entranceway, with his feet dragging in squeaks across the polished floor, and into a large, open-plan living space. My eye was immediately drawn to a stone fireplace, above which hung an enormous swastika. Keeping the skins at bay, I took a moment to check out my surroundings. Instead of smiling grandchildren, picture frames on the walls and mantle were filled with sepia postcards of lynchings, and vintage racist adverts, where tire-lipped Negroes in straw hats hawked boot polish and laundry soap. A marble table in the center of the room had a domed glass display stand protecting a small leather book. At the back of the room, two large patio doors filled the house with sunlight, illuminating all the clean, white surfaces, and making the red and black of the wall-hanging all the more vivid. Above the doors, which opened out to the backyard, was a metal sign comprised of dark lettering pinched between two rails - *Arbeit Macht Frei.*

With still no sign of the bikers, I was getting edgy. Cutler was a squirmer, and I was almost holding him upright as his wrinkled hands sweated against my arm. I could smell the Prell in his hair. It felt like five minutes had long-passed, and suddenly the one-sided nature of the afternoon's activities struck me as more than just bad planning. What better way to get rid than lure me into a house filled with bayonets and Nazi houseboys? Maybe this was Lowball's way of whacking me without sticking me himself; a biker's kindness. The Noose must've had previous with Cutler; take out Charlie's snake and set Cutler up with the murder of a waster from Eden, in one easy hit. I took a mental step back to assess my position. The odds were not in my favor. But I was in control. I had the gun. The precious gun; fitting right inside my hand like the fingers of a soulmate, like it was made to be held by me; to be used. My gun; my friend, my guard, my lover. I was calmer when I felt the weight inside my hand, when I gently stroked my finger against the curve of the trigger, when I–

Then there was a bang. Instinctively, I released the old man, dropping him to the floor as I pawed at my face to wipe off a blood splatter that wasn't there. Cutler was alive, horizontal, and looking towards the entrance, where he'd heard the sound of a front door slamming shut. I pushed a boot down onto his face, pinning him against the floor, wheeled the gun around and pointed it towards the hallway.

"Holy shit, nice job," said Lowball.

Kicking the piss out of an elderly Nazi was the most morally upright thing I'd done in a while. After we laid the boots to his baldy boys and left them bound in the pantry, you could hear one of them weeping through the door.

We dragged Bedford Cutler out back, where even in the face of the Noose and one crazy longhair with a pistol, he didn't give an inch. Next to Deezer he looked like a crumpled toddler.

"Open the garage."

Cutler wore a measured mask of pretend cluelessness, but a look flashed across his face, just for a moment, a look that said 'busted.' Then, he cracked.

"You *fucking* cocksuckers."

Johnny Dingo flicked open a knife, but Cutler was more mad than afraid as he opened the three heavy padlocks on the garage and slid open the metal door. I don't know what I expected to see inside, but it wasn't that. A tank. Small enough to hide away, but a tank all the same. Four wheels, thick, steel armor-plating, a little view hole, and a big, suck-my-fatherfucking-cock swivelling gun turret. The old man was caught between pissed and proud.

"This still work?" said Deezer.

"Work? My baby purrs like a kitten, a tiger. A war machine of–"

"Shut your yap."

"Leichter Panzerspähwagen," said Lowball, "one of the few working models that survived the war."

"Look at the size of that fuckin' gun..." Johnny Dingo was almost salivating. Lowball continued, brushing past

257

Deezer and going inside.

"Fifteen mil thick," he said, clanging a fist against the side, "take something pretty fuckin' heavy duty to even make a dent. Pig couldn't get through it, no fuckin' way." He clambered onto the top of the tank, with his head pushed flush against the ceiling. "MG34 machine gun, three-sixty degree turret. You could bring down a chopper with this mu'fucka."

"Goddamn," said Dingo, "think of all the Jew blood that's washed over these tires. Gets my dick hard just thinking about it..."

"Yeah, well save your jerking off 'til we get back."

"What are you gonna do with her?" said Cutler, anxiously gripping the wheel arch like it was the wedding train of a runaway bride. "Don't you trash her. I swear to God, this is history you're messing with. Living, roaring history!" Deezer shoved him with one hand, so hard that he staggered backwards onto his butt.

"Watch the news; watch it real soon, then you'll see some fuckin' history. Alright, get the ramp down and get this in the back." The old man looked up at me, with wide, wet eyes.

"Did the Pastor really mention my name?" The next sound was the pop of Deezer pulling out his pistol and shooting Cutler in the knee.

"Now we've really gotta move," said Dingo, over the howls of Bedford Cutler, bleeding out over his immaculately mown lawn.

"You just gonna leave him there?" I said. "You blew his kneecap clean off."

"The fuck's he gonna do, call the pigs? With that wonderful souvenir collection he's got in there?"

As Deezer and Johnny Dingo set about getting the tank into the back of the truck, I pulled Lowball aside.

"Soon, then?"

"Put it this way, I wouldn't be making any plans. This is one of the final pieces. You know Charlie. He'll deny it, but he always wanna ride in style." The other two emerged from the back of the truck, with Dingo flexing out his arms, and gazing down at them as though he liked how jacked they looked when they'd been working.

"All packed up."

"'Bout fucking time," said Deezer. "I'm tired of all the talking. And the cocksuckers who think they're gonna stop this 'fore it starts. What do you think about that?"

"Me?" I said. That screeching noise was the world coming to a stop, and damn-near jolting me off of my feet to join Cutler crawling along the dirt on his belly.

"Yeah," Deezer replied, in a voice so loud it was like he was trying to attract attention, trying to make a point about how much of a fuck he didn't give if the neighbors heard. "Fucking snake on the inside, waiting to take out Charlie. One of his own men. Can you believe that? Fuckin' enemy wearing the costume of a brother. What would you do?" I mentally calculated the distance between me and the little tank, wondering if I could dive inside and take cover; if I could break out through the gates and make my bullet-proof getaway, Steve McQueen style.

"Whack him." I said, holding his eye. "There's no

place for that low shit, not anywhere."

"I knew this little fucker couldn't be as dumb as he looked." Deezer, pistol in hand, had the closest thing I'd seen to a smile tip-toeing underneath his moustache. Things can change so fast. Worlds destroyed in the click of a finger. I closed my eyes. I embraced it. I embraced death.

For the third time, I heard a bang. For the third time, somebody hit the floor. In the darkness and the oily stink of a freshly discharged pistol, I opened my eyes. Johnny Dingo lay in a heap. There was a small hole under his chin, and the top of his skull was blown open like a smashed up melon. Dark blood pooled outwards across the patio tiling.

"Look at this shit," said Lowball, "fuckin' mess. He ain't gonna clear this up." Deezer leant down and stripped the club jacket from Dingo's body, his limp arms flailing.

"He was looking to fuck Charlie on a drug deal," he said. "We knew he'd been skimming off the top, but he was gonna rip us off for two key. Snaky motherfucker."

I felt lighter. Not a weight off my shoulders, just, an emptiness. Dingo's eyes lay open, flatly fixed on some point in the far distance, like he now had a clear view of the horrible future awaiting the rest of us.

On the ride back to the ranch, I was left alone in back with the tank. Perched on the hood, I was unable to stop myself visualizing the slow, deliberate growl of the engine as it rolled through the city, people running in all directions, Charlie safe inside like the Pope, and one of his soldiers at the gatling gun, cutting them all down, washing it all clean.

Johnny Dingo's death hadn't helped me none. Though my snakiness hadn't been outed, it hadn't bought me any time, as The Wave was right around the corner. And Lowball had taken back my gun. At least I was safe until it all kicked off. Safe. A word that took on less meaning with each passing day.

I barely had time to wind down from the heist. As the sky was oranging into dusk, Freck made her way down from the house especially to talk to me. I never knew how to take Freck. With her red hair and stern, hard bone structure, she seemed like a grown-up in a land of children. A librarian or school marm; someone who could still tell you off and make you feel small. Sometimes you'd see her cutting loose, but never outside her own circle, and her devotion to Charlie was such, at times you wondered if she was the one really pulling the strings. Funny, but nobody ever talked about her in sexual terms. Everyone had fucked everyone else, or at least thought about it, but you couldn't imagine anything between her legs but the sexless sheen of a Barbie doll, or perhaps a scowling face with a rough, ginger beard.

"I hear you did good today," she said. She was actually pretty when she wasn't glaring. It was a good look.

"Thanks. I just do what I'm asked."

"Alright..." there was a little more business back in her voice, and she lightly touched my wrist, letting me know that I really had to listen. "Charlie wants to see you, tomorrow morning."

"Huh?"

"Sunrise," she said, pointing up at the shack beside the

house.

"That all he said? Just, he wants to see me?"

"Alone. Charlie said, be alone."

16 LAY ME DOWN TO SLEEP

I sat up all night; a night which, in all likelihood, would be my last on the planet. I'd taken myself off to be alone, to mentally prepare for what was coming, but I'd only gotten more agitated. I was a clockwork mouse whose taut metal innards were poised to come piercing through its skin; my belly a mess of sharp edges and hog-tied energy. Night hung over my head like an executioner's hood. Eden became Gethsemane.

One symptom of living on the ranch was that you didn't really get nervous. Anxiety, shyness, that sense of embarrassment regular people get when dancing or singing in public, or giving a speech; when you'd lived like we lived, nerves were a primitive concern, like Neolithic man cowering from the growls of the gods during a thunderstorm. These were the layers that he'd peeled away from us, to reveal the underlying, basic truth beneath; layers created by our parents; by society. He said that babies were born into a world ruled by fear, and it was the children who should be leading the parents. *We* were the children, and *our* world was one big game with no consequences, free to laugh and dance and play, to run naked and sing the songs in our hearts with no regard for what others may think. This freedom could only be attained when you became Brand New, stripped back to the level of the unborn. That was why, he said, we were the chosen people. We'd show them all how to be. We'd teach the world to sing. But a child with no fear will sometimes run into the freeway, or stick their head into the fire to see if the flames are as tasty as they look.

Charlie had broken down the barriers, but it left you as a husk. Most of the time, I felt like I was watching myself from so far back inside my own head that I couldn't stretch out my arms far enough to feel the inside of my fingertips. Shame and guilt were decaying bones we'd interred deep beneath the dirt of excess, occasionally growing flesh in the aftermath of a beating, or on the bloodied thighs of a young new groupie. Such memorials would briefly transport you back to a time when you gave a fuck, before quickly vanishing like smoke. Charlie's big thing was guilt as a creation of The Man, to keep us on reins like dancing bears. Burdened by these flaws will lead us to betray our true nature; that's what he said. A truly free man would only ever do things he felt were right, and as such, there were no wrong actions. No guilt, no shame.

I'd come to realize that this was part of his control. Yeah, I'd disposed of a corpse, hijacked a tank, lay in the middle of a twelve-person fuck-pile, and a thousand other things most people wouldn't dare imagine, and that I could barely remember now, but that shit wouldn't fly anywhere else. Go on, leave me and go back to that other life, and good luck holding down a job or keeping yourself out of jail or the nut-house.

In all that detachment, the man who'd taught us not to be afraid was the one thing we truly feared. Everyone loved Charlie; a love so deep it was the ground on which we stood, the air in our lungs. Our everything. But with love came the fear of disappointment; of rejection. Love is power, and Charlie welded his like a father's belt. A simple look of displeasure would crush, and we all knew that fear. But there was another reason to be afraid – Charlie was a dangerous man. And I still had fear. But I felt guilt too; was bursting with shame. But my fear was not of him, it was of failure; my guilt at visions of what that failure would bring if he wasn't stopped; my shame at having been part of the machine. That I was feeling these things; that I was feeling *anything;* meant that he hadn't won, not yet. He hadn't taken all of me.

One thing they had taken was my gun, leaving me to walk into the lion's den unarmed. I probably could've got a knife from somewhere, but Charlie was so dangerous that if you were gonna pull one, you'd better be sure to finish him real quick. There's no one-shot kill with a knife, and men like him were at home with violence; up-close and grubby. He'd bash in a man's head like other people would hug their mothers and think nothing of it. I'd have to use my bare hands. Kill him like a man. Not like the murders by those other animals, with guns and blades and the tools of the street.

The day broke, in the way that other things often do. Vases, mugs, hearts. Nobody else may have heard it, but when the sun came up over the horizon, I swear it was screaming, suddenly aware it was on fire. Like always, many around camp were still awake from the night before. Those who had slept, beneath the stars, lay on the grass under blankets or coats, or huddled together for warmth. Funny, but walking past the slew of sleeping bodies scattered across the lawn like fall leaves, I happened to see Melody, curled next to the fire with her knees pulled under her chin. I thought about waking her for a last goodbye, but instead, I kept on walking, without looking back.

Finally taking that path, at the behest of Charlie himself, I found there was no pride; no glory in any eyes that followed me up towards the house, where the king sat atop the throne of a filthy kingdom. In his absence, the ranch had fallen into disarray, strewn with loose-blowing garbage and shit-streaked underwear; the dumps of various animals; a girl casually sat between two guys, jerking them both off. We met eyes as I passed, and she slowed her whacking in some loose nod to abashment. One of the guys appeared to be unconscious. The rock on which Charlie had stood during the quake now wore the scribble of myriad graffiti sprays; the guest-book autographs of forgotten background characters. Soon, it was all behind me, and I was at the top of the hill, that once-promised land. It'd been a long time since I'd felt so fully within my own body. No distance. No numbness. Just the here. Just the now.

I stood outside the shack. I could feel him in there. As I raised my fist to knock, the door opened inward. Of course. Charlie wouldn't need a doorbell to know someone was calling. He ushered me in with a finger, closing the door behind us.

It was dark inside, and smelled worse than the house, with that fusty, lived-in stink, when someone's been sweating into their clothes and into the sheets and furniture, filling the cramped space with BO and farts, and every foul outward breath. A steel bucket sat in the far corner, but its contents had been emptied, perhaps for the benefit of a rare visitor. There was a single cot pushed against the far wall – a mattress on a bare wire bed-frame with two flat pillows – and one chair facing inward. There were no pictures or books, no stuff, just Charlie's guitar, propped up against a window which looked as though it had never been opened. The only lock on the door was a bolt on the inside, but in any other name, this was a cell.

"How d'ya sleep?" he asked.

"I didn't, really," I said, surprised at my own honesty. Maybe I'd just let it all out, and when he asked me what I'd been up to I'd tell him that I meant to kill him, and God willing, I wouldn't leave that place until I'd felt his heart fall still inside my own hands.

"Yeah, me neither. Hard to sleep around here." He scratched at his head in a way that was disconcerting, more like an animal than a man. From the state of the place, it wouldn't surprise me if he'd picked up a dose of the fleas. "Sit." The chair creaked as I perched down, emphasising the eerie quiet of the shack and the sleeping world outside.

"You look a little on edge," he said. "I get that, sometimes. I know you think I got it all together, but some days, the sky just seems a little too close, you know? Like you could touch it. Hard to breathe sometimes..." Charlie squatted on the edge of the bed, his bare feet an inch or two from the floor, the soles black with dirt.

"How long you been here?" he said.

"Me? Since day one."

"And why'd you come? What brought you here? You ain't from California, I can hear that."

"I don't know, man. I just..." It's not that I didn't want to answer, I just didn't know. I didn't know at the time, and still didn't know all those years later.

"You just ended up here, right? Heh, yeah. Nothing

happens by chance. Look at this planet, man. It's all too perfect to be random. The seeds land where the wind takes 'em, but you gotta think of that wind as more of a breath. Mother Nature, she blowin' exactly where she wants 'em to fall, you see what I'm saying?" Maybe he was right this time. Destiny. My destiny to be there at that moment and be the only one who's capable of stopping the wheel from turning. It all made perfect sense, and in that moment, I felt it. I knew exactly why things turned out as they had. From the bus to the fire to the chair, all just pin-marks on the map of our story.

"I was there when you gave that speech, about home being where the love is. I never heard anything like that before. I was there the day the protesters came and you made the earth shake. When they took you away, when you returned to us. I watched you walk back in, all busted up. I was there when they shot you! When they fuckin' took a pop while you were singing..."

"Yeah," he said, stretching back against the bed. It was a long word. *Yeeeeahhh*. More sigh than human speech – tired. I wasn't sure he was even listening. Charlie tugged at his beard. It was long enough to grasp inside a fist and striped with a slash of grey. His gaze was over toward the window, which was stained on the outside with countless layers of nose-prints from ranch dogs that had wandered over to peer inside. "It's a long road. You don't know when you start out, don't know how long. There ain't no signs. Salvation, 500 miles. Nuthin'. You wonder if you ever gonna get to the end, or if you do, some fella'll be there and he'll tell you to turn right around and go back the way you came." He gripped the beard tightly, pulling it out into a point and turning his head towards me. "What's at the end of your road, boy? How will you even know you got there when you git there?"

"How does anyone know? Same as anyone else I

guess."

"And how's that?" He was eyeballing me, probably
waiting on an excuse to backhand me and tell me I don't
know nothing.

"Well... you'll see that you're where you wanna be.
Ain't a one of us who wouldn't know that place when we
came to it. And you'll know if you took a wrong turn, 'cuz
you'll feel yourself falling over the edge."

"Mmh..."

After that, he just talked at me for a long while, about
this and that. At times, he repeated himself, either by going
over the same ground, or literally word for word, his
demeanor more erratic than I'd ever seen; the quiet, the
lucid, the manic, the theatrical; every face of Charles
Manson at play, those dual masks at the side of the stage.
At his most restless, the floor would pad and creak with
the footsteps of his pacing, and he wore a far-away look,
like his thoughts, which had always been so busy and alive
that they struggled to be contained, had finally gotten away
from him. Sometimes he'd snatch one out of the air and
carry on, but others would escape into the great beyond
and he'd trail off altogether into an uncharismatic mumble.
Occasional lightning flash smiles darted across his mouth.
He told me that "Jesus was a baby," and that "humans are
a disease," through their poisoning of our rivers and air.

As he alternated between standing, sitting on the bed,
or pacing the cabin as he spoke, I never once left the chair.
Usually this was a thing he did, to be clear about the
balance of power. He'd said something once, that if you
look up at him, you see a king, look down you'll see a fool,
but look straight at him and you'd see yourself. If this was

intentional, like things usually were, at least I knew where he wanted me. But it's hard to find the rhythm of a conversation when one half is playing off of twenty books of sheet music all at once. Eventually, we settled into a strange kind of equilibrium. Leave two guys alone for long enough, and the subject always comes around to one of two things; sports, or sex. And we weren't much for sports at Eden Ranch.

"You see that story floating around last week?" asked Charlie.

"What story's that?"

"Some rag called the *LA Word*, or *LA Talk*... LA Something. Cheap little tattle not worth the ink they shit onto the pages. Old booking photo of me where they'd colored in my eyes red, made me look all Satanic."

"Oh yeah, I saw that," I said. I remembered the piece exactly, although it had been about six months before, not a week. Magazine or newspaper features were always big excitement around camp. Over the years, they'd got more infrequent, but the press knew Charlie always shifted copy, so every now and then he'd be on a cover, alongside quotes from some schmuck who'd lived at Eden for a couple of days and knew shit about how everything worked. Usually the first we'd see of the magazines would be in the hands of a fly-by-nighter hoping for an autograph to take back home.

"Manson's Hippie Hate Cult. Pages one through three through seven through twelvety. 'Charlie hates the world!' It's a nonsense, man. A foolishness. How much hate you felt around here? I bet all the hate you had was in your old life." I nodded out a yes, but after years of sermons and talks, even words like hate had had their meanings diluted. "You came here and you found that love. And I bet you never had love like it."

"No," I said. "Never. Before I came here, I'd never even kissed a girl."

"Ah, see, you're talking about sex. I'm talking about love. But it is the same thing, at least in here, if you do it right. We know how to do it right." Charlie smiled, a cheeky, child-like grin, and I broke into a giggle as he cycled through his familiar repertoire of funny faces; naughty schoolboy, devil, little girl, eyebrows arched and shoulders up above his ears. "Everything's about love, if you're living right. If you're not, how can you have love? It ain't love, it's just a front. Ain't as much love in the rest of the world as we got here. Think your momma and daddy got much love in their yearly hump? Once a month and every birthday, just lay there and count the cracks in the ceiling..."

The mention of my parents was like an antique plate smashing through the window; a strange relic from a life that'd ceased to be mine.

"I bet you fell in love with a thousand different girls since you came through them gates," said Charlie.

"One or two." One. Just one.

"Yeah," he said, through a broad, teasing grin, "one or two. How come you never had no girls before that? You ain't no Frankenstein or nuthin'.."

"Scared I guess. A dork like me didn't fit in with all that. I never played football or rode a motorcycle..."

"And what you afraid of now? Nuthin'! I took those barriers and I pulled them down, brick by brick. You can be with the football players and cool cats and know you got as much right as anybody to stand where you stand,

271

and they'll *never* be as free as you! Man, those people out there. Ooh, I'm shy, don't look at me or I'll get so nervous, I'll hide here and shake like a little dog taking a shit..." Charlie danced around like a prissy little queer, his wrist cocked at a jaunty angle, "I'm afraid to do the things I know I should, so you just go ahead and dig my grave for me right now and I'll climb inside and wait..."

With the room suddenly filled by laughter, I chanced an interjection. You never know how he's gonna take it. Sometimes he'll pick up the ball and run, like a comedian riffing on audience members, others, he'll cut you down like a heckler; destroy you in front of everybody; just for daring to open your mouth.

"Ever wish you were back inside?"

"How do you mean?" He was curious, not angry, regarding me with an air that made me feel, for the first time, he was briefly regarding me as equal.

"It's just, like, this is *so* big, it's grown so much, and everybody wants a piece of you all the time. Half those motherfuckers that come through them gates ain't interested in being free, they just want a free piece of ass, or to tell their buddies 'Hey, I saw Charlie Manson!' That don't bother you?"

"Well," the beard was grasped again, Rodin's Thinker, strands of hair twisted between his fingers, "like I said, it's all destiny. If someone's meant to be here, they'll find their way. Don't matter what brings 'em to the dance, they'll all end up jiving to the right tune. As for being in jail, that's all just a state of mind. I met guys inside who only felt at home locked in an eight by ten. They'd do a ten stretch, shitting in a bucket and not seeing so much as a tree or a blade of grass, and first thing they'd do when they got out was hold up a liquor store or some petty little bullshit so they could get right back in. They couldn't take all that space, so they panicked. From nothing to everything, in the time it takes to step out a door. But others can't deal with being boxed in. They cry for their mommas all day long, or be talkin' to you about tunnelling out with a little plastic fork, losing their minds with the screaming at lights out. *Here* is where you make it, and you make your own jail cell no matter where you are. You can be wandering the deserts, but so locked up in loathing of what you are that you're trapped on your own death row. Man can never escape himself. I'm a gypsy. I'm a wanderer, man, but they wouldn't let me wander, so I found my place, this place, made my home, for the first time in my life that I stayed in one place for any length of time. Without being locked inside, anyways. A man needs to find a place, and whether that's inside or out, if it's locked in one room or on an open trail he never stops walking, both only got one way to be free. You have to make peace with yourself."

Charlie paced over to the window, shooting a twitchy look down towards camp.

"I been up all night. Need to get my head down for a while."

"Sure," I said, standing as if to leave, but pummelled by a thousand different thoughts of how I was going to do it. Been sat in there all morning, and it felt as though the task of killing Charlie had suddenly been sprung on me. It was now or never. Shut in a tiny shack, just the two of us. Destiny on a silver platter. I scanned the room for something; anything to help. A guitar to the head would probably do it, but the shack was cramped with a low ceiling. It'd have to be bare hands. I'd have to feel the life going out of him. My heart fluttered at the notion of what a windpipe would feel like as it popped beneath my thumbs, and a swell of faintness washed over me.

"Take this." Charlie shoved a gun into my hand. The wooziness was chased away by the comforting feeling of cold metal against my palm.

"What do you... what?" I said, reeling to a degree that surely would have set his alarm bells ringing if he'd had been paying any attention, but his back was already turned, facing towards the bed.

"Keep watch while I sleep. Don't let nobody in."

"What about..."

"*Nobody.*"

Without another word, Charlie lay on the mattress, on his side and facing the opposite wall. Was this a trick? A test? Maybe he was laying in wait like a lion in the tall grass, waiting to hear the imperceptible creak of the cylinder turning, the ignition of the powder, and the crack that sounded the march of the tiny lead assassin, and he'd spring off that bed to reveal a kevlar vest or to grin that wicked smile of his, with the slug safely resting between his teeth.

I watched the back of his head, and the rise and fall of his ribs. No. He was just a man. The seeds had fallen where they thought best. I raised the pistol, with one eye-closed, and looked at Charlie across the top of the barrel.

Not yet.

I spent a long time looking at the gun; holding it until it felt like an extension of all the things I felt about that man. It was different to the pistol, slimmer at the sides and without the tubby, round chamber. An automatic, a Mauser. German Army issue.

He slept with a stillness and peace that seemed inappropriate. A man like that should be racked with the twitches and grunts of night-terrors; creepily-lit flashback snippets of the things he could bury away while he was still awake, like Clark had pretended to suffer through on those first nights, when he must've known I was watching. Probably a sign. Maybe the man on the bed was faking sleep too; etching a row of cartoon Z's into the space above his head and blissfully aware of everything happening around him. Someone told me once that Charlie slept with his eyes open. He only needs fifteen minutes every two days, said someone else. Charlie can fly; he can breathe underwater; he can get a girl off just by fingering her with his mind. Regardless, whether he was asleep or awake, he wasn't moving, nor was he armed. I justified my inaction by thinking. More thinking.

I supposed I'd have to hide the body, to prevent Charlie being martyred like some magical saint. If they found his body, I swear you'd come back in two thousand years and see little plastic Charlies around people's necks; his songs piping out of glass-domed moon-churches every Sunday. "*We've got the love...*" they'd sing, those sweet old ladies, wearing flowery hats and elbow gloves flecked with the blood of the fuck-pigs they'd slayed to appease their God. Heaven help them all if Charles Manson's Ten Commandments found their way into the world. No, I'd have to get rid of the body. How hard could that be? Wrap him in a sheet, wait until the coast was clear and stash it in the back of a buggy. Job done. Skinny guy like that would sling over your shoulder no problem. And for sure, I could pick my moment, as they all knew better than to disturb him. This was my private audience. I'd have as much time as I needed. Hell, if I had to sneak out to get a knife and carry him out in twenty buckets to feed to the pigs, I would.

I sat watching and waiting, as though the final bolt of courage would appear with a knock at the door, straightening my clothes and pointing at its watch, giving me cause to rise from my seat and blow that fucker's wig clean off. I didn't know what this feeling would feel like, or if it would even show. Perhaps I'd be left, like a man waiting at a train platform as they turn out the lights.

In the distance, I could hear the sounds of camp, slowly coming to life. Laughing, yelling, the howl of a dog. The children of the night, that's what Charlie would say, in his best Vincent Price; "*What music they make!*" But that's all there was. No approaching presence, no voice to whisper in my ear and blow away the fog of indecision. Just me. Me and him. Tom and Charlie. Charlie and me.

I stood out of the chair and took three steps towards the bed, until the edge of the mattress was pushed against my thighs. He looked like a little kid, laying there. If you hadn't seen it yourself, you'd never believe the kind of things he could do. The sense of power was overwhelming. A life, in my hands. His life. Yet nobody who knew him would think it was a fair fight. A gun to the head of a sleeping man, and the odds were probably still tipped in his favor.

It takes a special kind of person to take the life of another. Not even a person – the opposite. It's inhuman; a crack in your soul that you'll never heal. Even though I'd been around death, I'd not been the one to cut the chord.

I didn't think about The Wave. I thought about Melody, and about Clark. The kid I'd dumped in the river. All the faces who'd arrived looking for a little love and acceptance. Even the ones who'd turned up because they'd seen Charlie on the news and thought he looked cool, or just wanted to take a vacation in hippie heaven. One by one, soul by soul, he'd fried their brains. Teenage girls he'd fucked while ordered to imagine their own fathers; kids who'd done so much acid you could see the spark of life in their eyes burning out like the wire in a light bulb. I thought about the funny dude I'd talked to for a cup of coffee, way back; bright guy from Colorado, I think, who introduced himself to me with a joke about a Rabbi trying to cut off Superman's foreskin. I don't remember the punchline, but at the time I thought it was a neat way to break the ice. When they drove him out to the desert to find himself, like many of us were, he'd returned with a skull full of mush. I heard him not long after, having a fit of screaming hysteria in the middle of the night. I never saw him after that. I thought about Mike and Linda, the married couple hoping for romantic adventure, and spiritual discovery. Such adventure saw them wrenched farther and farther apart by all of the 'freedoms' pushed between them. Linda was long-since AWOL, while Mike had played so hard at being the open-minded hippie kid he never got to be, he'd forgotten the way back; and all because I'd been so eager to show Charlie what a go-ahead guy I was. The girls who'd had to abandon their babies if they ever had a hope of getting out of Eden; babies that could have been fathered by any one of fifty different guys. Maybe him. Maybe me. The parents; mine included; who'd never have a chance to mourn the children that they'd lost. I had to do it for them, for all of them. I had to put an end to him, before his sickness infected the world outside.

I pulled back the hammer and pointed the gun at the back of Charlie's head. Two inches from his skull. He wouldn't even know it'd happened. It'd be a mercy, that's all. No pain, no torture or suffering; like snapping the neck of a wounded deer. His breathing; so calm and peaceful. Whether consciously or not, I couldn't say, but I found my own breaths had taken on the rhythm of his, our chests moving together in synchronised motion, father and son. In, out. Inhale. The piss-stinking air of life. Exhale. The waste, the used; purging the dead.

I took one more, long and deep – the final that we'd share – and held it. The next time I exhaled, Charles Manson would be dead. On the count of three.

One.

Two.

Three.

Three.

Three...

I exhaled, deep and hard.

"It's alright, kid," said Charlie.

17 JAMES DEAN, NORMA JEANE, THE SPACE BETWEEN

"Not everyone's got it in them to pull that trigger. Don't make you any less of anything. If it was survival, you could'a done it." Charlie rose up, swivelling his legs across so he was sat on the edge of the mattress, meeting me eye to eye. I kept the gun pointed towards him; a limp cock at an orgy. "If I came at you, you'd find it in you to pull that trigger. You'd have to."

He stood with his palms up like claws, as if ready to pounce, but there was a calmness to his tone that betrayed the words, castrated their threat – almost.

"We're animals, don't you see? We drive our cars and write our books, and we can fly up to space in a rocket and walk on the moon, but the one thing that never leaves is the will to survive – the will to evolve. I've dined from silver platters with kings and eaten out of garbage bags with hobos, and you know what? Them, and every man-woman inbetween, would fight for their life if it came to it. You find a man who put his head inside a noose, ready to jump, but you start pushing him off that stool, man, he'll be kicking and fighting for the right to make that decision himself. It's instinct, guy; that can't be learned or unlearned."

Now that we stood on an even keel, I felt ashamed, like he'd caught me doing something I shouldn't. I raised the gun higher, so I couldn't see his face behind my fist, but he kept on talking, as though I carried all the threat of a baby wielding a feather. His voice became a soft whisper, where you had to really listen to catch what he was saying. The balance of power felt all wrong. *My* finger, resting on the trigger; my head, craned towards the sleepy little unarmed man; my bones, cold with vulnerability.

"I mean you're standing there, pointing that thing at me, but you still ain't shootin'. I'm wondering what it would take. If I went for your throat, maybe. Like a wolf, just *rawr-rawr-rawr*, sunk my teeth in, gnawed on you like a hunk of meat. What do you think? How far would I have to go before you took that decision? Mm?" Charlie tilted his head from the barrel, fixing me with a glare, his face stone-hard, challenging me, *daring* me to make a move; to defy him. His eyes became the center of the universe. I knew I couldn't be the first to break, to expose myself as so utterly weak, that even armed, I wasn't man enough to hold his gaze. I reflected the look, as hard as he gave, thinking of 'fuck you, Charlie,' and not listening to the timid rattle of the pistol shaking in my hand. I'd seen that look before, in a rattlesnake I damn-near stepped on one day out in the desert. All I heard was "don't move!" and there it was, two jet-black pinprick eyes, and its body arched in warning. Lowball blew it to soup with a shotgun just as it was about to strike. Charlie was always coiled, even at his most relaxed, and he could pounce in a heartbeat if he smelt blood. Fuck you, Charlie. I stared so hard that it stopped being a face; just random Picasso shapes sliding around a grimy canvas. Then, Charlie broke and looked away, taking the tension with it.

But I felt no victory. He always had a way of making you feel like you'd been kicking up a fuss about nothing, so relaxed it was insulting, idly rubbing the nap out of his face.

Maybe it was the bravery of a loaded gun, but I suddenly found myself yelling full-bore, in that way you sometimes see people do; insane people with red faces and spittle-dripping mouths who've been tipped over the precipice. They get rear-ended, or someone pushes in line, and now suddenly they're an animal.

"Is this all a fucking game to you?!"

You never know what kind of angry you're gonna be until it happens. Worse, I was one of those eloquent ones; more syllables than just the fucks, cunts, and go-suck-an-unwashed-cocks from the people who screamed themselves into an aneurysm when the dam broke. "Yeah, I can see it in you, it's in the way you carry yourself. You know exactly what's going on. That's why you're holed up in this shack like a leper. The crumbliest cocksucker on the whole colony. Even from up here, you see your empire falling into ruin. Have you been out there lately? There ain't no revolution. It's a ghetto, man, a giant, open-air crack house. I'm always hearing from you about the beauty and the love, and how this is the only place to find it. Right this morning, as dawn broke, I watched a guy pooping into a hat and throwing it over the fence. Is that the dream? We X-ed ourselves out of society so we'd have the freedom to walk around with warts on our dicks, eating garbage and smelling like shit? You've created your own Third World nation, congratulations! Bunch of brainwashed burnouts who'll never belong anywhere but this cum-stinking fuck-hole. Some of us ain't felt hot water on our bodies for years – how long can someone live like this?"

"Pretty long," he replied, without missing a beat, the tips of his moustache twirling between his fingertips; eyebrows dancing like the psychotic lost Marx Brother.

"Shut the fuck up! Don't try and charm me. I can see through your shit. All the clowning and the posturing, acting like you're the Godfather of the San Fernando Valley. Those hands of yours never get dirty. Fuckin' Noose doing all the work, so long as you keep the pussy and the pills coming. That's the length of your reach; petty drug deals, grubby little violences. Seducing schoolgirls who buy into the Man of the World schtick. It's all a schtick; all a front. Big man when you've got a biker buddy with a knife to go slashing up a kid for you. If a real criminal came up in here you'd probably break both your legs in the rush to find someone to hide behind..."

Charlie laughed; hard, thumping ha-ha-ha's from the pit of his stomach.

"Yeah, hilarious, right? It is a joke though, all of it. You're the biggest joke of all. They might not be able to see it out there, but I can. You sure as hell ain't no fucking guru..."

"When you heard me say that?" Manson snapped bolt upright, back in that punch-counterpunch-jab-jab of the exchange that he so dearly loved. "Tell me one time I gave myself any label. Guru..." he scoffed at the notion, "Jesus, Buddha, King of the Mountain, Belle of the Ball," he bowed deeply, twirling his hand like a medieval jester. "People hear what they wanna hear, always have. S'like the news, they keep saying Charlie's a hippie, ol' Charlie

Manson and his hippie cult. I ain't no hippie, man, I was born in the thirties, raised in the hills of Kentucky, raised by women. We didn't *have* no fathers, our fathers were all fighting and dying for those fat cats in D.C., just like how their fathers out there, your fathers, all died in Korea or Vietnam, or came back after stickin' a bayonet in a baby's head and didn't know how to rock one in their arms and love it like they should. We're the lost children; we got no parents but the system; the corrupt, murderous system; out for no-one but itself. And they gonna be all shocked when we rise up and show them all the ways we were taught to be? I'm telling ya, when it happens they'll all say the same thing, you listen. 'Look at what Charlie Manson made those kids do!' *You* raised these children! If I'm guilty of anything it's of caring too much. I'm just trying to undo the mess *you* made!"

Manson's voice had transformed, and he with it. Huge and booming, the voice of God, it filled the walls of that shack, which seemed to creak and buckle under the strain.

"You hear what the kids are talking about these days? Punk rock. You hear that shit? Sounds like a deaf guy tryin' to fuck his way out of an oil drum. Punk rock? Now I'm two generations behind. I was in the fifties before the hippies came along. That lasted a little bit, and I threw my bindle on the freight and rode for a while. And then there weren't no hippies 'cuz I broke that party up, know what I'm saying? Suddenly, I walk out, and they want to lay that on my doorstep like I betrayed my people. *Who are my people*? I'm my people; me. 'Hey man, you ruined it for everyone. Why'd you go do that? We was having the Summer of Love and you cut it all into little bitty bitty bits and now we can't have fun no more...' Well that ain't my fault, and if it was, maybe I just did something you, uh... something you..." He trailed off, his posture sinking, and pausing for a couple of beats before continuing.

"Don't you see? It's all... all roads are leading here, all paths and ladders, and that other nonsense with the chutes, that's just the... the piggy..." Charlie broke off again, rubbing his hands across his face and through his hair. "If you're gonna shoot me, *just fuckin' shoot me!*" The rage of his plea fell away as quickly as it appeared, with another of those scuttling smiles splintering his face for a blink and dispersing the solid black wrath of Charlie's anger into a misty fog that wafted a thin veil over the whole room.

What had appeared to be skittishness now seemed like a man lacking the nimbleness of thought that'd previously talked the birds down from the trees. At the height of his powers, he never slipped; never. Never stumbled or stuttered, or meandered into a verbal cul-de-sac, even at his most chest-pounding and violently incensed. He still had it, no doubt, but you could see hints of what lay close around the corner; small, dark clouds and the smoky smell of burning synapses that were cooking like ants under a microscope; the ache in the arm before your heart gives way; an elderly widower standing in the rain while he fumbles a banana towards the keyhole. Fuck, maybe he was just tired. A life like that can't leave a lot in the tank. Every day he probably did enough drugs to kill an elephant. And then, with words so guttural they were almost a bark, he went right back into it, picking up the trail halfway down a whole other map.

"Fuckin' punk rock. You see those kids in here singing that shit? Howling? '*1-2-3-4, let's go!*' Yeah, you can go. Go drink from the toilet like the beast that you are, the hog rolling in the filth. What can you say to a cat like that? They they don't want love or peace, they want anarchy. You tell some little East Coast fag to love his brother and he don't dig on that."

"And you can't put reins on anarchy, right?" I said, still gripping my piece, still wary of the rattler's strike. "Anarchist don't wanna follow anyone."

"Two generations out. Generations aren't a birthright; they're a movement," he replied. I don't even think he was listening, just caught in the mad flow of his thoughts. "Ain't about when you were born, it's about the scene you're born into. We're the lost generation, us, this ranch. But sometimes they can't see what they got, and someone has to come along and learn' em what they know deep down, but are too afraid to feel." Charlie was at the window, looking down at his people. "Billions of human beings have walked this Earth, and you could count on the fingers of one hand the people who even *started* to get it. Crowley, Blavatsky, Timothy Leary, Baba Ram Dass..."

"Charles Manson? Come on, look at yourself. What are you, forty? How can you talk to these kids? You're old enough to be their father. You're old, broken, tired. You're a relic, man. The sixties ended a long time ago. You wanna know what I think? I think you want me to shoot you so you don't have to be around to watch it all fall. The leash is getting looser. We're all getting older. Think the kids who're coming through the gates are gonna listen to you? Fresh meat who look at the flower power and Woodstock thing as some square jive their older brothers and sisters talk about, from back in the day?" Finally, I'd got his attention. Charlie turned from the window, with the corners of his mouth curling at the sides, yet still impossible to read. I pushed on.

"If you go out now, at the end of a pistol, you don't have to have the world see that happen, you get to stay as Charlie the rockstar, Charlie the icon. You won't ever become those assholes in San Francisco, talking about the good old days to any sorry fucker that's only listening 'cuz you've got a floor or a roach, and when you're not looking, they're laughing. You get popped right now, that don't happen, and you know that. Fuckin' Peter Pan, you'll never grow old..."

"Marilyn, she'll always be beautiful. Got it all figured out, huh?"

"You bet I do."

"Yeah. Well then, that's fine. You nailed me. Why don't you take a walk. Go tell everyone how smart you are and leave old Charlie here to wither."

"Naw, that ain't enough. I know what you've been planning, your 'Wave.' You see them lot out there getting further away every minute that passes, and you gotta act soon, right? Much longer, and you'll never get them out into those streets, laying down their lives. Charlie, man, you gotta go. You gotta go, and I've gotta do it. I can't let you get away with this."

"Boy..." Charlie broke into a huge, mocking grin which set me so far on edge, it was alls I could do to stay on my feet, "I already did."

"What?"

"I knew you were the one. I saw it in you." He took a step toward me, advancing like a beast of prey, until I felt the tickle of his hair against my skin.

"What?

"Why do you think you're in here?"

"You *wanted* me to kill you?" I said.

"Kill me? If I wanted you to kill me, I'd already be dead!" Charlie's voice was now at its loudest and most theatrical. "I just had to see you was the right one. I had to see it with my own eyes. Why'd you think you're in here? Why'd you think you got hold of that gun and pushed it to my head? Why'd you think you couldn't go through with it, after all those weeks picturing yourself shovelling the dirt on my face? Yeah, I saw it in you. You can't hide those things from me, I see into your soul. I'm in there, and that's where I'm gonna be. All this, where we're at right now, I made it happen. Everything! Don't you see how I make things happen? It's all up here, guy," he tapped his temple, "I've said it a thousand times, you might be stokin' your fires and chugging along, but I'm the one laying down the track. Don't a raindrop fall or a bullet get fired or a baby get born from here to Ungo-Bungo Land without Charlie knowing about it. There ain't a breath you or anyone else takes that ain't passed through my lungs. I got you on that bus, boy, got you through those gates, did whatever it took to keep you here all these years. Every step you took was on the end of my strings. The universe. All. Up. Here." With one finger twisting into the center of his forehead, he snatched the gun out of my hand. All I could do was stand gawking. A sound came out of my mouth, but nothing that could be considered speech. Charlie was headed down his own track, the train going so fast it was a dark blur screeching past so loud I just wanted to put my hands over my ears and throw myself to the floor.

"But even books got endings. There are new questions; questions there ain't answers for; answers only I can find; questions that ain't even been asked yet." Charlie's manner softened once more, the tropical storm of his ever-changing mood quietening to a gentle breeze. Or the eye. "Things gone as far as they can go. I have to do what needs to be done before they slip away. Man..." he said, almost laughing

"What?"

"You were right. See, you can always learn a little something from everyone you meet."

"Right about what?" A pause, and then –

"I don't feel myself falling."

In that moment, we exchanged a look. It was a look that, in all my years at camp, I'd never seen in him before. Not with me, not with anybody. There was love there – real, genuine love – but something else. A strange, but undeniable sense of – was it pride? This brief moment between us was broken by the sound of his voice.

"Guess what?" No answer came. I was frozen. "You're Brand New."

In one swift motion that took all of a half-second, but felt like the pass of a moonlight eclipse, with a beaming smile on his face, and looking right at me, Charlie lifted the gun to his temple and shot himself in the head.

Bang.

The sudden shock brought on a near-out-of-body experience. On the smoky crack of the impact, I felt myself come untethered, and watched the scene play out from above. I saw Charlie slumped against the wall, beneath a wet, red sunset, and the top of my own head, as I stood numb a few feet away. It lasted but a couple of seconds, before I shot back down into my own consciousness so fast and hard it was like waking from those dreams where you're thrown off a cliff.

In the silence that followed, I waited for Charlie to pop back up. "The resurrection," he'd say, "three days early," while urging me to poke my fingers into the wound and feel for myself. Or, it was just a joke to help pass the time, and Melody and all the rest would come bursting through the door, pointing finger pistols at their own heads and embracing me in laughter. I prodded his bare foot with mine, but he did not lurch awake; did not flip me a wink. All those months, I'd played the moment of his death over in my head almost infinitely. Dreams, daydreams, trips, idle fantasies while shitting; mental pictures of his disfigured corpse to help hold back the dick-tickle of a cum when I was fucking; I'd seen him die a thousand times, and each at my own hand. Little fucker had robbed me of that too. Everything on his terms. And now there he was, dead as Kennedy. He'd done what I couldn't. No mind, I couldn't get precious about it. I hadn't set out to be a hero, it was just a job that had to get done. One good thing he'd taught us was to have no ego. What's done is done. What's dead is dead. No more Charlie, no more Wave.

A leg was tucked underneath his body, with one arm sat in his lap and the other limply hanging by his side, finger still grazing the trigger. Half of his head was missing, exposing the damaged brain-matter inside. I wondered which specific parts of Charlie's brain were among the pink and black purée splattering the inside of the shack; the evil parts, the bits that'd been gentle and sweet and kind to animals, the tiny little pieces that held memories of innocent times from before he wanted to burn them all. For a second I had an overwhelming urge to dip my finger in the detritus and taste it, like I could finally get some perception of the man himself, imbibing a sense or a memory, or some great secret truth, and learn what nobody else ever had – what goes on inside the head of Charles Manson. I didn't; I'm not crazy. There were fragments of bone embedded into the wood of the walls, and one eye had fallen inside the shattered cavern of his head. The other lay wide open and rolled skyward, as if regarding his maker, or taking a hopeful gaze toward the one place he musta knew he'd never be allowed into.

The nearby bark of a dog snapped me out of the tiny world of me and him back out into a world filled with other people; people who loved and worshiped the dead man; who'd have done anything to keep him safe, and would bring fiery retribution down on anyone who brought him harm. Gun in his hand or not, everyone was so paranoid, you'd get the blame just for seeing that shit. And if he knew it would be me, then others might have known too.

My mind began to race. I could feel the cold, rising embrace of a panic attack, slithering around my chest; around my lungs; sweeping up and over my head like a plastic sack. Everything in my body; air, blood, every thought and feeling and organ, seemed to whoosh into my head, pushing at the inside of my skull to make a break for it. Clasping handfuls of hair between my fingers, somehow, I caught my breath. The boiling, seething lake inside dulled to a simmering pot, and then, stillness. A degree of subjective rationality crept back into the room.

I was in a building with a dead body. The body needed disposing of.

As nobody would dare interrupt his business, time was the one thing on my side. I'd hunker down for a couple of hours, mop up the blood, and be ready for when the opportunity came to bolt. And opportunity could come. For all its randomness and illusions of spontaneity, Eden was a multi-headed creature of habit. Come dusk, everyone's down at the fire, and a guy could maybe, *maybe*, sneak along the back way and out under the fence without being seen. Or, the house was pretty close; if I could grab a quiet moment, I could make my way around the rear, body slung over my shoulder if I had to, and hop in one of the old cars that sat around with the keys in the ignition. Worst came to the worst, I'd just hightail it out of camp and be far enough away before anyone realised or cared that I'd gone.

I took a sneaky glance out of the window, just to get a feel for the life out there. A small, lone figure stood looking towards the shack. Freck. She'd probably heard the gunshot. If she came over to check, to find him dead, they would tear me to pieces. I had no choice, I had to get away; out of the camp and as far away as possible, just run and don't look back. Fuck Charlie's body. Maybe a few hundred hardcore believers would see it as the silencing of a man with truths too dangerous to hear, but without their glorious leader to march them through the gates, The Wave would never happen. Look how we fell apart when they took him away. No. He'd gotten the dirty death; the grubby, sordid out, and there'd be no televised blaze of glory, no Hollywood martyrdom.

With mad desperation, I hunted for something I could use, anything that might be of value. I prised the gun out of his hand. Charlie's fingers were small and girlish, still warm, and the clip was empty. Goddamn, even as a rotting stiff, he was still five steps ahead. I tipped the bed over on its side, sending the mattress and frame clattered loudly on the floor. Nothing. Then I saw something – a scattering of LSD tabs. He must have hidden them under the pillow. I knew from watching him closely that he never took as much as anyone else. He'd make out like he did, but he'd short himself on his dose to retain just enough control.

"Ain't that right?" I said, placing them into my jeans pocket. He didn't answer. I chanced another look outside. To see the house, you had to push your face right up against the window.

"You really fucked me this time," I said, squashing my cheek into the cold glass. Freck was standing on the stoop, and she wasn't alone. A small gathering of a half-dozen were milling around, in discussion and looking towards us – towards me. In the midst was Deezer. Like Mickey Mouse, you could pick that silhouette out of a line-up of thousands.

That was it. No time to think, no time to take out the trash. I had to move. Just move. Run. Run or die. Run or find my limbs lashed between two motorcycles and ripped asunder. My skin flushed hot, heart pounding so hard that every thump wreathed my body in undulations that rippled my flesh. I stood on rubber bones by the window, pushing in for one more look. The group gathered by the porch still had their gaze cast towards the shack, and towards the two figures who'd broken off and were on their way over. This time, would be no counting to three. I filled the cabin with a sound unlike anything I'd heard from myself before; some kind of animal shriek, or madman's war cry. And then–

I was out of the door and on my way; not running, but that queer waddling this-ain't-suspicious walk that makes it look like you've gambled on a fart and lost. I headed away and out, following the curve of the distant perimeter fence. They'd see me, but maybe I could lose myself. A hundred, hundred-fifty yards and there'd be enough bodies to get lost in the mix. I tugged my shirt off over my head and tossed it. A fool's disguise. The Lot in me felt the self-destructive compulsion to throw back a look towards the shack, to catch sight of Freck's head disappearing through the door, while Deezer stood in wait, shotgun in hand. Feet pounding the ground, I passed a couple making out against one of the outbuildings. It was going to be okay, it really was, I could get out of there, and–

"*There he is!*"

Freck and Deezer; giving chase, rapidly closing in on the hill behind me. I broke into a sprint across the grass; long, wild strides, my knees straining on the incline, mind afire. A beautiful girl with her hair in pigtails came lurching toward me, arms outstretched like a defensive tackle. I shoved her hard and she tumbled backwards. Suddenly, there seemed to be people everywhere; faces, bodies, grouped as though they'd been waiting. I pushed my way through the sea, the footsteps of Deezer shaking the earth in my wake. A hand clutched my wrist; another my belt. I yanked and shoved and twisted myself clear, pushing onward down the hill to freedom.

"Stop him!"

Everywhere were arms and hands, reaching, grabbing; and voices. A swarming cacophony of rage and accusations, each knowing, somehow, what I'd done, they bayed and smothered, circling on all sides with shrill screeches and hard syllables of hate. I fought like the dying man I was, shunting and clawing with a primal desperation. This, I thought, this is what people talk about when they speak of fighting for your life – what *he* talked about – when the spirit discovers what it's capable of only in its final moments. Charlie's survival instinct. But even the most desperate will yield to numbers. Someone rode my back, their arms around my shoulders; feet to the backs of my knees took my legs from underneath me, and I was wrestled to the floor.

Then, they would rip me apart, shredding my body with their bare hands to scatter over hills like spring dandelions. Flat on my back, I couldn't see the sky through the poppy field of faces, lost beneath their mass, with infinite hands clamping my limbs; wrist, forearm, ankle; hands that were small and big, and warm, all wanting one thing. A scream absconded from my mouth.

I think I was still screaming when I realized I was flying.

I landed, gently in their arms as though a child, before hurling skyward once more. And again. Only once I came back down for the final time, dizzy and flushed with fear, did I realize their cries were not of anger, but ecstasy; of mad religious fervor. The hands that grabbed at my flesh weren't looking to harm, but to caress; to hold. I sat atop their outstretched arms, as they moved below me like ants, carrying me aloft across the camp. From my position, I could see others further down the ranch, running towards us. I thought back to the day of the earthquake. Weeping and cheering, they surfed me across to a small outbuilding on the edge of camp that was always locked. A tool shed, perhaps. We got within ten yards, and as one, they lowered me gently back onto my feet, before surrounding me from behind. Freck was waiting by the open door of the building. She took a long, close look, scanning her green eyes up and down me like a watchman's flashlight.

"You don't remember yet," she said. I didn't know if it was a statement or a question.

"I..." *I.* The sense of self. It's all I had. No more words.

"You're the shell," she said. "It's the greatest gift he could have given, and he chose *you*..." Her hands cupped the sides of my face, tears streaming, as though I was the most beautiful creature she'd ever seen. With her arm around me, she pulled me close, whispering into my ear.

"See you soon..."

If I'd found the words in that moment, it wouldn't have mattered. Before I could react, Freck shoved me through the door, closing it behind me. On the other side, I heard two sounds.

A heavy padlock clacking shut.

The cheers of jubilation.

18 "I"

I pounded on the inside of the door, my fists beating out the words that were stuck in the knotted rasp of my throat.

"Open up!" I yelled, finally. "What the fuck?" With an ear to the door, all I could hear outside were sounds of merriment like I hadn't heard around camp for years, not since the early days. "Freck, don't be insane, open the door!"

"Calm down," she said, almost laughing. I could feel her on the other side, I could practically hear the crack of her smile – a rare flower that fully bloomed once every few years. "You might as well rest up, 'cuz we're not letting you out just yet..." It was strange; unsettling; to hear a playful, almost kindly tone to her voice. Shouldn't a captor be angry? Aggressive? It somehow seemed apt in a place where everything was done out of love, even when you were beating someone unconscious.

"Freck?" I rapped the wood with my knuckle. "Can't we just talk?" I listened hard, waiting for a response. Nearby, an open chord was strummed on a guitar, and like

I'd heard a thousand times before, under a thousand starry skies, only not, came the eruption into song. Off-kilter, with little regard for tune, but joyous and vibrant with passion, everyone united. It was one of Charlie's numbers, what else? The girl with no heart and the city that cried. I turned from the door and faced the tiny room in which I was locked. It was lit by a single lamp, and all around me were faces; hundreds of tiny little faces, all staring at me. Male, female, blond, brunette, old, not so old, happy, or just plain indifferent.

Anyone who entered those gates had to hand over everything they had, and merely coming inside was a tacit agreement to become Brand New, which meant relinquishing everything of your old life. This included wallets, purses, and whatever money, photographs, or means of identification were contained within. The green went straight to Charlie, but all the driving licences, student IDs, passports, and family photos; they'd been dumped in that little shed. They were pinned to all four walls, and across a ceiling that was so low I could reach up and touch it with my palms. There was a huge open trunk on the floor, with hundreds more piled inside, maybe even thousands. Everyone who'd ever passed through Eden Ranch with something to give up had given it up, and it had landed here. The pictures were papered so thick that you couldn't see anything of the wall behind. Besides the door, in any direction you looked, seemingly endless pairs of eyes stared back hard. It was like being inside the head of Eden Ranch herself. Hundreds of individuals operating with a single mind, and me, the subject of their unyielding attention, stood alone in the center.

"This," I thought, "must be what he felt, every day." If I'd had to live with that, I'd have shot my fucking head off too. I tried to push away the furore by rooting around in the trunk. Anything, so I wouldn't have to think about what Freck had said. Even by entertaining a thought like that, God... I think it was Charlie himself who said once that it's all well and good to have an open mind, but if you leave it open too wide, you never know who might waltz on in and make themselves at home.

"*The city ain't so pretty,*" they sang, "*she pull you in and she bite down hard.*"

There were whole past lives there; innocent faces who beamed out at the world with no idea what their futures would hold, or who glared at me accusingly, like I was somehow to blame for how things turned out. International student identity card. Raijko Hanssel. Finland. How the hell did Finland know about Eden Ranch? Driver's licence. Sharon McPeters. Boston. Pretty girl. I'd probably fucked her. Face after face, life after dead, forgotten life. Then I caught sight of a name that jolted me like that first finger up the ass. Tom. It wasn't me, at least I was pretty sure. I had to inspect the ID closely to be certain. I could barely remember my surname anymore, and after a while you start to lose that image of what you look like on the other side of your own eyes. I scrutinized the tiny photograph, feeling the contours of my nose and cheeks with a quivering hand. No, not me. Just *a* Tom. But mine would be there, somewhere, and maybe if I could find it, it would help me get back to that place; to regain even a little of my old self, and maybe that'd help me find a way out. If not, then at least I'd die a little more whole, knowing he hadn't managed to take it all.

I began frantically rooting them out of the trunk like a dog digging for a bone, tossing them behind me. I couldn't even remember if I'd had anything on me when I'd arrived. And how could I be sure, if I did come across a family portrait? Would I recognize my own parents? Infrequently I'd dream of my old family, but only as brief images that were wiped blurry upon waking.

"...sunshine man, does what he can..."

Now in a frenzy, I scooped them out of the trunk, one by one, barely looking as I flung them over my shoulder, with this intense perception that I'd just know, from touch alone. Then I caught sight of a familiar face, with an unfamiliar name.

"...cloud been comin' and he oughta ran..."

I held it up to my face, so close the plastic cover was fogged by my breath. Judy Trushkie. *Judy.* Judy the B student, Judy the daughter, Judy the ghost. Until that moment, I'd forgotten she came here with a different name. There she was, the girl I'd fallen for, so hard and so long ago that the memories whirred in my head like a silent movie, our eyes ringed with theatrical make-up, thoughts etched on faded caption cards, back in those days when we still felt. She looked so young. You don't notice aging when it's happening in front of you. Before she'd been ruined by that place; by Charlie; by me. There was something in her eyes that was no longer there. Even in a photograph, lit by a lamp in the darkness and mottled from the dank of the shed, they were more alive than when you saw her walking around out there. What would bring a girl like that to a hole like this? Who could push her from their arms and into his? My lips were wet with the salt of muted tears streaking my cheeks. Then I remembered the acid that was in my pocket and slipped a single blotter in my mouth. I'd built up such a tolerance over the years that I knew it wouldn't knock me completely fucky, but I just needed something to take the edge off, just to throw a little space between me and my life.

Charlie was dead; it should have all been over. His feet

going out from under him should have toppled the house of cards, the hypnotist's fingers snapping everyone out of their daze, but still they sang, harder, louder, more devoted than ever. But devoted to what? Despite his insinuations otherwise, he was not going to rise in three days. They had to have believed, *truly* believed, that I'd be released from that place with Charlie's spirit alive in my body. I was a human being, not one of the Sabbath shirts from the clothing barn.

"*...night time come and he run away...*"

As the dose started to kick in, I thought back to that movie some of us had seen at the midnight theatre a while back. Maybe all the singing and dancing was prelude to torching me inside a giant wicker Charlie, with just enough room inside the dick for a man to stand and burn. Unfortunately for me, the actual truth was far crazier. Sometimes the wackiest idea turns out to be the plan all along. Helter Skelter.

They were so happy – ecstatic – you could hear it in their voices. I could almost feel it, seeping through the cracks in the wood like gas; bright yellow clouds that rolled across the floor in plumes, right up to my waist. I pictured them out there, arms around each other, swaying, embracing. A few; those who hadn't been around for long; would be thinking how insane it was, but were going with it anyway, because it was fun and felt good. That's how it starts. Become the lie.

Charlie and his fucking plans. He talked so many times about the moment of his death; about communing with the gods, and speaking the language of the angels, so's he could return to walk among us in a new vessel, truly omniscient. He'd been setting it up all along. One enormous, chucklicious gag, with me as the punchline. He probably didn't even believe it himself, but this way, he could get the fuck out of Dodge and pass on his debts as he vacated the premises. Here; *this* is what I have to put up with, now see how *you* like it. I wondered how long the others had known and who was in on it. But no, it was all bullshit; crazy hippie bullshit, and I wouldn't think about it. Couldn't let it in. All anyone did around there was become the lie. I had to keep those thoughts far away.

The skin on my hands was starting to feel loose, like wearing gloves three sizes too big. I had enough awareness to know it was the trip taking hold. Weird, but that was the one recurring theme whenever I dropped hallucinogens; baggy hands. Sometimes I'd look down and see the tips of my fingers dripping like candles. Charlie said once that—

No. Not him. Stop it. Step around the blue horse in the room. Distract yourself. Anything to not think about that. About him. I'd masturbate. That usually took me out of myself. I'd had bad experiences jacking off while tripping before. Once, I thought my cock was breathing fire, and ran, bow-legged and sneezing gobs of milk from my bell, to put myself out in a laundry tub.

I pushed my hand down inside my pants, but it was like trying to catch a bluebottle, my fickle prick bobbing and weaving and recoiling from my grasp. A thousand pairs of eyes watched this pathetic display. I dropped to my knees and began fumbling around in the pile of pictures for Melody's ID. The cards scattered and scuttled like cockroaches, moving in a phalanx towards the darkest corner, before breaking into groups that encircled me. The rippling pictures clattered against each other like playing cards on a bicycle, meeting in the middle from all four corners and climbing into a tower as tall as my head before collapsing in on itself. Then, in the center, presenting itself to me, was Melody's ID. A rose by any other name. I took a rough fistful of reluctant penis, holding the image close to my face and closing one eye. Melody glared back, Mona Lisa look of is-she, isn't-she offering up a resounding No. No, she's not. You fucking creep.

I fell back hard against the outer wall of the shed, chin-to-knee, tossing her picture back into the pile and closing my eyes so I wouldn't see where it landed. I could feel the wall vibrating against the back of my head from the sounds beyond. And that's where I stay, for hours, maybe. It was hard to tell. Time didn't exist at Eden Ranch, much less in a world that span wild and free with the death of its god. I sat weeping, snivelling like an infant. Tears fell from my jaw like hot rain, sizzling when they hit the floor and pooling at my feet.

Try as I did not to let him in, my train of thought was barrelling down tracks already laid. I felt condemned to never leave, locked forever inside a facsimile of Charlie's head. Maybe it'd been me who'd died, and this was my spiritual punishment, to find myself within these walls, even if it took ten thousand lifetimes to come to terms with the things I'd seen; done; allowed to be done, discovering the ancient truths within before landing into *his* body. Then, I'd show them. I'd show them all, guy, and the whole world would see exactly what could be done with such power.

As I sat, at times I found myself caught by the beauty of the music and thinking that yes, truly this is paradise. The singing became louder as more voices joined, becoming layered with chants and howls of jubilation that passed into and through me; through the spaces in my atoms; *filling* the spaces. For a moment, the room became surrounded on all sides, above and below, by a choir of angels. Had Charlie's death torn down the walls of Heaven? Had he charmed St. Peter and snuck through the gates to start a revolution? But then, the intent behind the voices turned dark; a smile becoming a smirk; as malevolent storm clouds of something awful peeled over the horizon and enveloped the shack. An uprising *down there*, in the other place didn't seem so hard to imagine.

Eventually, the trailed swirls of color that swished about my vision began to fade. Life, again, started edging up a little too close. The faces on the wall eyed me from the other side of the room. To a man, they worshiped him – but who would remember me? Was it better to be loved and remembered, though your life was full of wicked deeds, than to be good, but forgotten and alone?

I heaved myself to my feet. I was dripping with perspiration, with dark, circular patches on the thighs of my jeans. I slid the remaining tabs out of my pocket. A little damp, but down the hatch.

I paced the cramped space between the stale, sweat-lodge walls, with my striding feet occasionally catching the slippery plastic of a driver's licence, whipping my legs from under me, and forcing me to brace against the wall. If a thought can stay with you while you're being battered back and forth then it must be worth thinking, and thoughts were what I had.

Everyone knows that when you die, your body returns to the earth, and your soul goes to heaven. Unless you've been bad. But what if your soul dies – or loses a piece of itself – when you're still alive? Then where does it go? Each face in that room represented a piece of a life that'd been lost; the soul-echoes of empty hosts. Perhaps lost souls haunted the scene of their demise, like the spectres of English country houses; tormented wailing lovers who walked through the hedges of a garden maze; pregnant maids who'd hurled themselves off the Earl's highest balcony. If you looked closely enough, I bet you could see them, weaving their way around camp, hopelessly looking for a way back to their keeper.

I focussed on the atmosphere; the dull, yellow light bleeding from the lamp, and everything became clear. Like answers to the most important questions usually are, they were there all along. The lost souls of Eden. You just had to know what you were looking for. They moved snakily, as hazy puffs of translucent light that slid above the ground, in a rather desperate sort of motion, like a lost child searching for its mother. They passed through the wood of the walls, mostly an anaemic white but with occasional dashes of color. Somehow, I could tell their identities just from looking; a small fragment from a girl who'd been used by so many guys, her white-wedding glimmer of romance had gone forever; San Francisco Mike, almost fully sized, having lost virtually all of himself to that Brand New; and that one, the big one – that was mine. A whole soul, handed over to the Devil himself, red and crackling as though racked by electrical storms. I reached down to reclaim it, but it slid through the bones of my hand. It didn't even recognise me. The souls swarmed about my ankles, weaving into, between and through each other, forever doomed to their futile search.

All these souls; all this death, everywhere you looked, and who out there had stopped it? Who'd come here to put an end to what was going on? He'd been right about one thing; the outside world was corrupt, and it was selfish. They didn't care about outsiders, or anyone who didn't fit exactly into the little shapes. For all their talk of what he was and what he'd done, they'd been happy to let us all rot. Herd them off into their concentration camp and let them destroy each other. The pigs hadn't done anything.

To think what Eden could have achieved with the

right leader, with someone who wasn't fucking psychotic. I remember Clark said to me once, "*Just imagine what you could do with an army that size.*" I wanted to know what it felt like, to have that control, that power. I had to know it. I had to know it immediately. Like a rabid desert coyote, I tore into the IDs, ripping off the little faces and stuffing them into my mouth. I had to know what Charlie felt when he devoured people's souls; when he chewed up everything they were and shat out something new, shaped into his own image. The faces were dry and tough, and I had difficulty forcing them down past my throat. I didn't even have to look, I knew who they were. Clark, Melody, Jedro, little Mary, the Japanese girl, the kid Shank, Scat, the Cat in the Hat and the rat-a-tat-tat, and Johnny Dingo and Blonny Blingo –

A strange laugh came out of my face that I barely recognized as my own. It was loud and scornful and I cowered from it, pulling myself tightly into a corner and wrapping my arms around my head. I stayed that way for a while, until I realized that the singing had stopped. The world was silent, and I felt terribly, achingly alone. I wanted to hear those voices again, to feel the roof warm with their love, or to quake with their fury and threat. Anything, but to be alone.

I was so hot, I could feel the walls dripping. I peeled off the rest of my clothes, shedding them like an old skin. I stood naked, arms outstretched, and breathing as if for the first time. Brand New. Brand Brand New.

I crouched on the floor next to the door, squatting like an animal, and listened. All was quiet. Inside. Outside. Same thing. It's all in your head, that's what I always said. Here is just here, don't matter where you are. Ha, yeah.

Things started getting closer again. It's funny how quickly it all just slides away sometimes. I could feel the pokey, proddy fingers of feeling and truth sliding near. Shafts of orange sunlight streaked through the gaps in the beams, falling on the faces left on the wall. I had a thought – something important, but I forget. Everything was so still. For a moment I have a flash of going home. It lasts no more than a couple of seconds, but it's the most intense flashback I've ever had. In it, I'm in the back seat of my dad's car. He and my mom are in the front. They turn and face me, smiling warmly, and in that instant, I see my parent's faces perfectly.

The door to my left creaked open, flooding the room with daylight.

I staggered, naked, into the early morning sun, wondering what would greet me. Be it death, love, or a '62 Imperial with the engine running.

It was the entire camp. The whole Family, waiting. Waiting for me.

There they were, five, six hundred strong, maybe more, and standing in a big row, four or five people deep. And they were armed to the motherfucking teeth. The crisp morning air chilling against the sweat on my body. I stared at them, and they stared back. A cheer erupted. Whoops, hollars, fists in the air and expectant eyes.

An army, just like they'd said. My vision stung with sleepless acid-blur, but I couldn't see anyone who wasn't carrying. A gun for every home. Everybody ready to roll; cocked, locked and waiting on their orders. I could barely pick out individuals, just a congealed mass. Conjoined bodies, but with what mind? But in all those figures, of all the people to see, who should be seen but Melody, beautiful Melody, her sweet little hands that'd fit so perfectly inside mine, now wrapped around the grip of an AK-47. Her face was hope, even... veneration, with pregnant tear-drops hanging on her eyelids. Front and center was Cutler's little tank – a Popemobile with a 360 degree death-turret. Freck, with a string of grenades across her chest like a beauty queen's sash, stared me down with a look of savage intensity.

With a single gaze, I looked into the eyes of hundreds, each with that look of devotion. The second skin of Thomas No-One lay empty on the floor behind. We stood in a silence so swollen, it was as though the world had ceased turning, stopping taut, and crooking her head just to hear the words that would be spoken next.

"It's okay," I said, "I remember..."

ACKNOWLEDGMENTS

Thanks to Flix Gillett (mockingbirdcomic.com), Gary Fenn (bigspud.co.uk), and my mum (who does not have a website, but without whom I could not have written this book, or indeed existed at all).

26436040R00185

Printed in Great Britain
by Amazon